To Florence
Best
[signature]

MW01059066

THE SECRET OF
THE JUST

JEFF BRAUN

THE SECRET OF
THE JUST

Austria

Vienna

Italy

Milan

Gorizia
Monfalcone
Trieste

Possagno
Treviso

Yugoslavia

Brčko

Novi Sad

Tuzla

Sabac

Adriatic
Sea

Ancona

Split

Rome

The Journey of Ernst Mann

Copyright © 2011 Jeffrey S. Braun

All rights reserved

The Secret of the Just is a work of fiction that was inspired by actual events. Although some character portrayals are true, most are the creation of the author and any resemblance to real people or events is purely fictional.

ISBN-13: 978-1461058113

ISBN-10: 1461058112

Library of Congress Cataloging-in-Publication Data

Braun, Jeffrey S.

The Secret of the Just, registered under the title: *The Story of Santo Spirito*

Registration Number: TX 6-884-702, September 1, 2008

This book is dedicated to my wife Cindy and to Alexandra, David, Emily, Harrison and Michael. As well as, to Yanko, Judi and Jonathan and to the loving memory of my mother, Hertha and my father Ernest...who helped sustain my faith in the legend of the Just.

ACKNOWLEDGEMENTS

I have a number of people to thank for helping me with the writing of this book.

Gale Abrams, for her editing assistance.

Dawn Devoter, for being my loyal sounding board.

Neal Carpenter, who stood by me, through thick and thin.

Boris Bjelos, who helped me to understand the traits of the Serbian people.

And finally, my father, Ernest- whose spirit inspired me to write The Secret of the Just.

O my God, let me escape from the might of the lawless,
from the hand of the enslaver and of him who (would) cloud
happiness

Psalm LXXI

To save one person is to save the world

Talmud Sanhedrin

AUTHOR'S NOTE

"An ancient Hebraic legend states that the world is prevented from being submerged in folly and wickedness by the presence in each generation of thirty six "Just Men" who, through their conduct and good deeds, ensure the safety and survival of humankind. These individuals operate inconspicuously, scarcely recognized by others or even themselves.

It is believed that the Thirty Six are always present. They were given the name *Lamed Vav* after the numerals in the Hebrew counting system: *Lamed*, the twelfth letter in the alphabet which has a numerical value of thirty, and *Vav*, which has the numerical value of six. The *Lamed Vav* embody the suffering for all of humankind, thus assuring the stability of the universe." *(Reference 1)*

Through two of the story's main characters, Ernst Mann and Bishop Lorenzo Giraldi, the worlds of Christianity and Judaism converge. As sages from opposing worlds, they are independently driven to perform extraordinary acts of salvation and saving grace and, in doing so, come to the same realization- succeeding in saving a single soul in one's attempt to save many is tantamount to saving the entire world.

Jeff Braun

FOREWORD

This is a story that took place at a time when God was napping and the devil ran wild. The world was at war. Battle lines were drawn. It was a fight to the finish, no holds barred, no referees. The place was Europe in the late 1930's. The Nazi virus was spreading through Europe like wildfire. For those who caught this virus, the emotional and physical manifestations were similar - a murderous frenzy of rapturous delight.

During the ten thousand odd years since man has occupied the earth, wars have been the norm. In fact, looking back at history, times of peace have been nothing less than brief respites between vicious brawls. Humans like to believe that they're superior to the other beasts that roam the earth. After all, man's creative juices flow, translating into prose and poetry, engineering and science. Animals kill in order to survive, while humans murder for fun, lust, revenge, or simply to fulfill their morbid curiosity. Mozart's sonatas played while the innocents were gassed. Like an orchestra conductor twirling his baton, the diabolical Dr. Mengele wielded a riding crop, directing his victims in one of two directions - labor camp or the ovens.

The story you're about to hear begins in Vienna, Austria in 1938. It is my father's story. His name was Ernst Mann. His adventure was told to me in bits and pieces over several years. While other fathers took their children to baseball games, my father took me on long walks to cafés and restaurants. I was like the brother he never had. We spoke of life, politics, and the arts. There was a topic, though, that came up time and time again—his story. Over time, his stories took on a fictional quality that transcended space and time. These weren't tales of dragons or white knights, astronauts or sports heroes, but of storm troopers, assassins, turncoats, and demons. I became his foil, his sounding board.

There is a force in the universe that sees the big picture. It has a master plan that spans generations. This force may handpick certain individuals for survival. These individuals are protected, averting disaster for some higher purpose. One possibility for this is to assure the birth of an Isaac Newton, Gandhi, or Churchill, generations later. We like to label such phenomena as chance, potluck, or destiny.

Looking back, it seems that my father had told me his stories for a specific purpose. On his deathbed, Ernst Mann told me that "the truth lies within the story." What he meant by that, I'm not exactly sure. What I do know is that there is something, some force that has compelled me to write his story.

It was November, 1965 and a cold day in New York City. I was thirteen years old. My father asked me to accompany him to the hospital to visit his friend, Rabbi Michael Ber Weissmandl, who was dying.

Weissmandl had been the dean of the Nitra Yeshiva in Slovakia. This Jewish theological seminary was the preeminent institution of the day. My father had graduated from Nitra just before the Germans destroyed it in 1939. As one of only a handful to survive the fires of the holocaust, Weissmandl emigrated to the United States after the war.

Jewish persecution was rampant in Slovakia. The Nitra Yeshiva was liquidated on September 5, 1944. By September 17, the Nazis had murdered or deported every remaining Jew in Nitra.

Weissmandl his wife, along with six hundred poor Jewish souls, were rounded up and packed into cattle cars, destination - Auschwitz. There was no room to sit and hardly enough air to breathe. With his bare hands, Weissmandl managed to pry off two wooden planks from the wall of the car after hours of painstaking, grueling labor, tearing most of his fingernails to shreds in the process. He managed to make an opening that was just large enough to squeeze through. In the darkness and chaos of the cattle car, Weissmandl hollered to his wife to grab onto his hand. As the train slowed down to make a turn, he yelled, "Now, now." Holding her hand fast, Weissmandl, finally succeeded in squeezing himself and his wife through the narrow opening. The cold, hard snowbank didn't make for an easy landing.

In the darkness, he was able to make out the silhouette of his wife. With his heart pounding out of his chest, he ran to her and lifted her to her feet in a tight embrace, only to realize that it wasn't Rachel, but some other woman. He put her down and stared helplessly as the train rolled on into the dark night.

From his hospital bed, Weissmandl looked over to my father and said in a quiet voice, "What saddens me now more than anything is that, in your lifetime, Ernst, there will be people of stature and repute who will declare, unequivocally, that what took place was all just a mere exaggeration, that it never really happened. They will say that it was just some fantasy created by the Jews to gain sympathy for one of their selfish causes. Ernst, you, for one, *do* know the truth, for I know that you, too, suffered terribly. Nonetheless, I know that there are times that you also believe that it was all just a horrible dream."

With that, we left. My father and I didn't exchange one word until we were outside. "What was that all about?" I asked.

My father didn't answer until we crossed Fifth Avenue and entered the Park. "It's time that you knew. It's time that you knew the entire story. Weissmandl was right. There are times that I think that it was all a terrible dream. You need to know the truth before it fades, before it is lost forever in the deep recesses of oblivion."

So began, on that cold November day in New York, the recounting of my father's odyssey. The story was told to me over the years in various settings and venues. I'd be doing my homework in the living room, and my father, while sitting in a lounge chair reading the paper, would catch my eye. He'd smile and begin telling me of one of his adventures. He would transport us back in time to a boulevard in Vienna, a forest in Serbia, a library in Milan, or Vatican City and the inner sanctum of the Pope himself.

Percolating beneath the surface of most of the tales was a hint of the supernatural. There seemed to have been a guiding light directing the activities. It was as though Ernst was singled out to survive, saved for some greater purpose that would reveal itself years or decades down the road.

Once, while walking on a street in New York City, we saw birds gathered high on a telephone wire. They were perched in groups. My father stared up at them, mesmerized, deep in thought.

He turned to me and said, "Those birds won't be harmed by the high voltage running through the wire. God saw to that thousands of years ago. He had anticipated that, one day, man would succeed in harnessing electricity. He knew that as a result, high-tension wires would be strung up the world over. He knew that birds would use the wires as natural resting places. Logic dictates that the mere touching of a high-voltage wire would result in electrocution. If that had been the case, all birds by now would be extinct.

To protect those members of His creation, God established the scientific law of 'grounding' and of 'potential difference.' This allowed the birds of his kingdom to safely perch on telephone wires, saving them from extinction. There now is the proof of God's existence."

Looking up at those birds, chatting with one another, oblivious to the outside world, I noticed one bird, sitting alone, segregated from the group. I saw my father as that lone bird on the wire.

PROLOGUE

Vatican City, 1943

Young Bishop Lorenzo Giraldi walked rapidly through the Vatican's labyrinthine corridors, passing the numerous Swiss Guards who were stationed at their designated posts. It took him more than ten minutes to arrive at the papal wing. Two Swiss Guards were standing at attention at the entrance to the Pope's study. As Giraldi neared, one of the guards knocked twice on the door then opened it widely.

Expecting to find a grandiose chamber commensurate with the Pope's stature, what Giraldi saw was a modest yet highly elegant sanctum sanctorum. The room's octagonal, birch-lined walls were draped in rich, flowing fabrics. The scalloped ceiling displayed breathtaking frescoes, designed by Michelangelo himself. To one side was a large fireplace whose dancing flames filled the room with comforting warmth and soft light. Seated at a large mahogany desk, leaning forward, his hand on his brow, intently reading a document, was the Pope. Cardinal Luigi Maglioni, secretary of state to the Vatican, stood at his side.

"Ah, Father Giraldi, please sit down," the Pope said, waving his hand toward a divan that was situated in front of his desk. "May I introduce, Cardinal Maglione," he said, briefly looking at his Secretary of State. "It is my understanding that you have something of importance to discuss." The Pope then folded his hands on the table, awaiting Giraldi's response. Giraldi could feel the sweat forming on his brow. "Yes, Your Holiness, it is a most delicate matter," he said hesitatingly, his voice, cracking.

"Go on," said the Pope, nodding.

Taking a deep breath, Giraldi said, "I have strong reason to believe that I have in my midst, one of the Thirty Six."

Startled by the remark, the Pope looked at Giraldi and with piercing eyes asked, "What is that you say? One of the Just?"

Hardly able to meet the Pope's glance, Giraldi nodded in the affirmative.

"Are you certain of this? Is he safe?"

"I am most certain," answered Giraldi. "His name is Ernst Mann. He escaped from Vienna at the outbreak of the war. He is in safekeeping in a residence in Rome."

"Of what do you speak?" Cardinal Maglione asked with a look of bewilderment.

The Pope, gazing across the room, as if in a trance, said, "There is an ancient Hebraic legend that states that on this earth, at all times, are thirty six just men. They are called the *Lamed Vav*. They are thought to embody the pain and suffering of this earth, and as a result, they assure the delicate, moral balance for all of mankind. Each of the Thirty Six inherits his position from his father and, in turn, passes it on to one of his male progeny. They themselves may go through life unaware, oblivious of their station. These 'Just Men,' as they are called, cross all social lines. They could be anyone- farmer, teacher, or even beggar. It still remains unclear how it is determined that one is of the Thirty Six; one of the Just. One school of thought maintains that a Just Man can only be recognized by another, by one who himself embodies saintliness." The Pope shot a quick, brief glance over to Giraldi then continued. "For whatever reason, a Just man, or a *Lamed Vav*, who perishes before his time could throw the universe into chaos. A Jesuit school of thought considers that our own Savior, Jesus Christ, may well have been a *Lamed Vav*- one of the Just."

The Pope looked up at Giraldi and said, "Tell me more of this person, Ernst Mann.

"Mann was a student of Jewish theology. At the outbreak of the war, he left his home in Vienna, made his way through Yugoslavia, and finally settled in Italy. Somehow he always managed to keep one step ahead of the Germans. His parents were captured and delivered to Auschwitz. Ernst is their only male offspring. There is, however, one surviving male in his line, his six year-old nephew, Yankl, the son of his sister, Nelly, and her husband, Romy Schreiber. They had been in hiding in the Yugoslavian town of Sabac until it was overrun by the Nazis. Before being captured, Nelly delivered young Yankl to a neighbor for safekeeping. It is my hope that nothing has befallen this child, as our very survival might well depend on it."

The Pope, after a long and silent deliberation, responded, "Indeed, the Holy See must save this child. This is a sensitive and most delicate matter. Even if there is only the slightest possibility that this man, Ernst Mann, descends from the Just, he and his nephew *must* be protected at all costs. The future of the Church itself may hang in the balance." Holding Giraldi's glance, the Pope said, "Mind you, my dear Lorenzo, it goes without saying that we proceed with the utmost secrecy. No one outside of this room must know of what is unfolding, not even your friend, Ernst Mann."

CHAPTER ONE

Vienna, 1937

My name is Ernst Mann. I was born at the onset of World War I. The times were serious, ergo, my appellation—Ernst, *the serious one.* I grew up in Vienna the youngest of four children. I, the only boy, was sheltered and very spoiled. At thirteen, my father, realizing that I needed further cultivating, sent me off to the renowned Nitra Yeshiva in Slovakia, where I completed a grueling five-year course of Talmudic study. After graduation, I returned to Vienna and was promptly hired by the prestigious architectural firm Lansmann and Sons as their primary correspondent. How I, a simple *yeshiva bocher,* managed to ever get that position is still a mystery. I found the job to be mundane and uninspiring; nevertheless, I worked hard and responsibly. By the end of my second year, believing that I had a higher calling, I resigned and returned to my family home, to the welcoming arms of my loving parents. I was itching for something new, something challenging. What that something was I wasn't quite sure; although I knew that, in time and with patience, my destiny would surely be realized.

It was early one afternoon on a perfect day in May. Sitting by myself in Vienna's University Park, my legs stretched out with the soft blades of grass tickling my toes, I could only watch from a distance as the graduating students poured out from the auditorium and onto the rolling lawn. They were laughing and joking, all with the security of knowing that their futures were bright. *Why couldn't I have studied here? Why did I waste my time at the Yeshiva? What could a man like me do with a Jewish theology degree in Hitler's Europe?*

My cheeks began to tremble. Squinting and clenching my jaw was all I could do to fight back the tears. I could hear my mother's words: *Smile, Ernst. You're too hard on yourself. Look at you; only a child and you have more worry marks than your father.*

My loving mother was the pillar of our house, the glue that held our family together. But, oh, how she worried. As it turned out, her instincts were valid. Seeing the political events unfolding, she intuitively recognized the events of recent years as the foreshadowing of the present.

It had been one month since my return to Vienna after graduating with honors from Nitra, the theological seminary in Slovakia.

The Nitra Yeshiva was the preeminent Jewish academy of the day. Students, ranging in age from ten to over seventy, came from all corners of Europe for the grueling five-year course of study. Classes were held each day, except for the Sabbath. The academy closed for two weeks during the summer.

Each new arrival would be assigned a second-year student who served as roommate as well as tutor. Students

would rise at four o'clock in the morning and study until nine in preparation for the headmaster's ten-o'clock
lecture.

*Six years down the drain. In that same period I could have
obtained my medical degree right here in my own backyard. I, too,
would be running down the lawn in a cap and gown, waving
my diploma proudly for all to see.* I couldn't take my eyes off
those students, each one merrier than the next. *Oh, how I
envied them.* My brow furrowed; I clenched my fists. *What
will become of me?*

What I didn't realize at the time was that I would soon
be tested. Little did I know that my years of Talmudic study
armed me with the very tools that I would need to survive.

CHAPTER TWO

The Jews of Vienna were in limbo. They couldn't work. It was mandatory that they wear the yellow Star of David on their coat sleeves. They were under a curfew. Any Jew caught outside after six o'clock at night risked arrest or much worse.

An event was being held one afternoon at the municipality honoring Austria's fallen soldiers. My friend, Martin, and I thought it would be fun to watch the festivities. I grabbed my jacket, gave my mother a peck on the cheek, and rushed out the door. The streets around the municipality were teeming with people. It seemed as though half of Vienna had turned up for the event. Politicians gave exuberant speeches, dignitaries proudly pranced about among the entertainers (who included the Vienna Youth Choir and many popular song artists), tables were set up offering free refreshments, and people broke into impromptu dance. All in all, it was a very merry scene.

Then I noticed the time—five thirty. Curfew was nearing. Even if I were to leave immediately, I'd still be cutting it close. From across the room I saw Martin dancing with several other young people. He appeared to be having the time of his life.

When I told him that it was time to leave, Martin shooed me off with a wave of his hand, wanting to hear nothing of it. "I'm staying right here," he said. "You go on without me."

"It's almost curfew. If we're caught—"

Raising his hand, Martin cut me off mid-sentence. "You go, Ernst. I'm staying right here. This is great...."

As I rushed off, I noticed a group of young men entering the square. I readily recognized the leader, Jerold, one of the neighborhood ruffians. I knew Jerold all too well. In school, he was the class bully, looking for any excuse to bloody the nose of anyone who crossed his path. Jerold was now a member of the Nazi paramilitary group, the Brown Shirts. These thugs were given carte blanche to taunt, harass, and beat up anyone crossing their paths— gypsies, homosexuals, and especially the Jews. They were even known to turn in their parents for just the slightest off-color, antigovernment remark.

If the Brown Shirts were to find Martin, especially now that it was past curfew, his life wouldn't be worth two cents. I needed to go back, find Martin, and get him out of there. Scanning the area, I saw Martin dancing among the group of his newfound friends.

"Hey, Ernst," Martin said, seeing me approach, "get over here. You're missing all the fun." Martin was rhapsodizing and dancing wildly, his reddened face dripping with sweat. When I tried once more to warn him of the danger lurking, Martin spun around and said, "Didn't you hear me the first time? I'm staying right here!"

As I reluctantly turned to leave, I saw Jerold glaring back at me. In a flash, Jerold and his thugs pounced. A fist caught me squarely in the jaw. As I hit the floor, out of the corner of my eye I saw Martin lying in a bloody heap being kicked over and over again by Jerold and his rabid gang. Luckily for me, the police broke up the brawl. The last thing I remember before passing out was being dragged across the floor.

CHAPTER THREE

The Place: Vienna's Central Jail
The Accused: Ernst Mann
The Date: June 5, 1937
The Crime: A Jew caught in the street past curfew
The Sentence: One-year incarceration

That was the extent of my hearing and sentencing. The bailiff called out my name; the judge slammed down his gavel. The arraignment and trial took less than a minute. I wasn't allowed to say a word. I had no rights, no attorney, and no phone call.

I was transferred to a larger cell that already contained two other prisoners, both university professors who had been convicted of similar "crimes." Professor Edelstein headed the Department of Economics at the University of Vienna. The other, Professor Zeiskind, was chairman of medicine.

Through Zeiskind, who was on fairly good terms with one of the guards, I found out what had become of my poor friend, Martin. By the time the police arrived to break up the riot at city center, it was already too late.

Martin was no longer breathing. He was pronounced dead on the spot and carted off to the morgue.

Save for bumps, bruises, cracked ribs, and a mild concussion, I was still in one piece. Under their guidance and watchful eye, the two professors delicately and lovingly nursed me back to health over the ensuing days.

Time seemed to grind to a dead halt. The three of us remained confined to the cell twenty-four hours a day—no walks in the yard, no fresh air.

The cell was located on the fifth floor of the prison. In it were three wooden stools. Beds were in the form of wooden slabs that protruded from the walls. There was one pot of water and a toilet. High up on the wall, a narrow window overlooked the street below. I would pass the time by standing on tiptoes and peering out the window, only able to see but a sliver of the world outside. From that vantage point, the only things I could make out were a street corner, a few trees, and a lamppost. I would let my mind drift off, recalling life as it once was. My mind became a safe harbor, a refuge to where I could turn, at will, whenever I chose. No physical retreat could have been more comforting. Standing before my little window, I would, at times, be overcome by a strange force, a magnetism that gave me the power to delve into my own soul and attain a perfect tranquility.

One evening, on one of those occasions when I was staring dreamily out onto the street below, I saw a man standing in the misty light of a streetlamp. He was of middle age, wearing a hat and long overcoat, casually reading a newspaper. Every so often, the man would stare up at the prison then return to his paper. He remained there for about twenty minutes and then casually folded his paper and slowly walked away. There was something familiar about the person, but I wasn't quite sure what it was.

Could it possibly be my father? In the hazy mist, it was hard to tell. From my vantage point, I couldn't make out the man's face. The man returned again the following evening.

This apparition appeared night after night at the same time. I counted the minutes until his arrival. Although we could never communicate directly, I felt a mysterious, deep connection, like the comforting embrace of a mother assuring her infant that he was safe and not alone.

The days, weeks, and months passed ever so slowly. The professors and I found several ways of passing the time. We played chess from pieces cut from cardboard and paper. I reaped the benefit of the professors' wisdom, as they would deliver dissertations in their respective fields— economics and medicine. The discussions could last for hours. Given my deep and extensive knowledge of the Talmud, I comfortably fell in step, contributing equally to the ersatz lecture series. My first talk dealt with rabbinical law, the subject closest to my heart.

The cell became a veritable university, a pure, unadulterated house of learning. Subjects would be analyzed and hair-split to the minutest detail. At any time of day, an impromptu lecture could begin and last for hours. The audience of two would give the speaker their undivided attention, expecting full well that they would each get

the same respect when they took to the stage. Had the
sessions been transcribed, there is little doubt that they
would have translated into a host of very respectable doc-
toral theses.

Despite the confined space, we did what we could to
respect one another's dignity. We communicated in the
formal *thou*, paying careful attention never to cross social
lines, never to become too familiar.

In the course of any given day, there were enough
distractions to keep me occupied. It was the nights—the
long, dark, silent nights—that were insufferable. Jolted
awake by wild and disturbing dreams often within mere
minutes of drifting off to sleep, I could do nothing but
reflect on how life once was and on what could have been,
this in the backdrop of darkness and the soft sounds of
my cellmates' rhythmic breathing. Wallowing in this way,
I had no way of knowing how radically the world outside
was changing, never to be the same again.

Vienna in the mid-1930s was the cultural center of Europe.
Its citizens were very proud of their heritage. Hailing from
that great city were the likes of Goethe, Strauss, Mahler,
and Freud, just to name a few. Cafés would spring to life at
the end of each day. The opera houses and theaters would
open their doors each evening to the elegant habitués,
who would sooner go without dinner than miss a debut.

Vienna had a prominent Jewish population that played
an active role in the city's business and cultural activities.
There were those who considered themselves Jewish by
name only, holding their Austrian citizenship high above
their ethnic heritage. The pain was that much more acute

when their fellow countrymen welcomed the government-sanctioned scourge of anti-Semitism that was seeping like spilled oil into each crevice of the nation's socioeconomic fabric.

In the days following Ernst's arrest, the Gestapo launched a campaign against the Jewish population of Austria. Synagogues throughout the land were desecrated and burned to the ground. The main synagogue of Vienna became a torture chamber. All Jewish property and businesses were seized, including that of my cherished uncle Bernard.

Bernard was the embodiment of elegance—the quintessential bon vivant. He was a partner in a successful investment-banking firm. As an active patron of the arts, he could be spotted any evening at the opera house or theater, more often than not with a beautiful woman on his arm. His watch was set on Wall Street time, as his workday began at three in the afternoon (nine in the morning New York time) for the opening of the stock exchange.

When the Nazis launched their horrific campaign, Bernard was one of their first victims. His business and property were confiscated. He was ruined. Luckily for Bernard, he wasn't in the office when the Nazis first stormed in. They grabbed his partner from behind his desk, beat him mercilessly, and threw him out into the street. A short time later, his body was found near the railway station in a mangled heap on the railway tracks.

A dark, diabolical cloud descended steadily and methodically on the Jews. Before the rampage was in full swing, some individuals succeeded in reaching safe havens elsewhere in Europe as well as Asia and America. This was, in part, due to the good offices of certain people of influence. Bernard's sister, Jenny, was one of those individuals.

Jenny was a prominent gynecologist in a large practice whose clientele included many Nazi socialites. Through her political connections, Jenny was able to secure exit visas for select individuals, including one for her brother, Bernard. Within a week, with passport and Visa in hand, Bernard arrived in New York.

Once through the gates of Ellis Island, Bernard found himself in the melting pot that, for decades, had been harboring refugees from the world over. Bernard was quick to find the cafés that captured the mood of pre-war Vienna. Throwbacks from days gone by, these coffeehouses were where the Continental refugees would meet friends, have a meal, or just sit and pass the time. Waiters, wearing starched, white jackets and black bow ties, glided about the floor like tango dancers. Whether serving a party of ten or an elderly gentleman nursing his one glass of tea the whole night, it made little difference—the waiters fussed over their patrons as if they were royalty. At any given time, one would find an old university professor at a table by himself, myopically perusing a book review or meticulously jotting notes in his agenda. At another table, a buxom woman dressed in a fine woolen suit fashioned from another time could be seen sitting with her anorectic, mink-wrapped counterpart, holding her coffee cup daintily, with little finger extended.

These émigrés were somehow still loyal to their mother country, the land that had robbed them of everything. They viewed themselves as Jewish Viennese rather than Viennese Jews. Many had been rooted in Austria for centuries. Like the abused child curiously longing to return one day to the home of his youth, these refugees were in a similar state of denial. They retained their national habits and dignity in the hope of one day returning to the homeland that they had known in better times.

Although he was free, Bernard was doomed. A Viennese through and through, Bernard felt like a fish out of water in the New World. Hitler slaughtered millions of innocent people. What, then, became of the countless, nameless souls who managed to survive his wrath? What became of the broken, dispirited, and forlorn in desperate search of a place to call home?

Some refugees succeeded in mastering a new language and culture. Most of them were young, with enough reserve to crawl out of their emotional abyss.

What became of the old and infirm? What became of the lone souls, the brokenhearted whose children, parents, husbands, and wives had perished? From where did they find the will, the drive, and the vision to carry on? And, so, what finally became of the likes of Bernard?

It didn't take long for Bernard to reestablish himself in New York. The financial community welcomed him with open arms. Although he succeeded in resurrecting his financial losses, his spirit was dead. He was consumed by loneliness and by the guilt of having survived.

In Vienna, Jenny's reprieve eventually came to an end. One by one, her patient's were "reassigned" to the "Aryan" doctors of the practice. Within months, the borders were sealed shut. Jenny was on the run. There was no way out. Bernard and Jenny's parents were driven from their homes in the middle of the night and, along with thousands of other Jews, were beaten and crammed into cattle cars—destination Auschwitz.

With her medical practice confiscated and her parents shipped off to certain death, Jenny lost all reason to be.

Defiance, cowardice, desperation, and heroism are actions that are defined by circumstance. That which is viewed as cowardice by one could be seen as heroism to another. Knowing that her parents were being tortured in Hitler's death camps was too much for Jenny to bear. In a last defiant act, Jenny purchased a train ticket to her final destination—to a place where there would be no possibility of return. Late in the afternoon on a cold November day, Jenny stepped off the train and walked through the gates of hell. With only a small satchel in her hand, she entered the gates of Auschwitz, where she was welcomed with open arms.

Before boarding the train, Jenny poured her heart out in one last letter to Bernard. She wrote of the unspeakable horrors that were unfolding in Europe and of their parent's deportation to a concentration camp. She wished him well and thanked God each day that he had made it to safety and could now start a new life in a new land.

Little did Jenny know, but that letter, written with the best of intentions, tipped the scales that would seal Bernard's fate.

Bernard's heart would skip a beat whenever he received a letter from his sister, Jenny. He enjoyed reading her letters in the park on Riverside Drive overlooking the Hudson River. One afternoon, he made his way to the park with one of her letters. Bernard found his favorite bench, sat down, and began to read. Typically, Jenny's letters were up beat and optimistic. This time it was different. She wrote of the cloud that had descended on Vienna, the daily roundups, and the humiliations. Worst of all, she wrote of the probable death of their parents.

For Bernard, this was the final blow. He had lost all hope, all reason, and the will to go on. He walked aimlessly through the streets until he came upon a pawnshop. He felt the precious Schaffhausen watch in his pocket and remembered when his father had given it to him twenty-five years before on the day of his Bar Mitzvah. Bernard pawned his pocket watch for a pistol. He slowly walked back to his bench in the park. His body was found later that same night after he took his own life.

Seven months had passed since my arrest. Confined twenty-four/seven to the tiny cell, segregated and incommunicado with the outside world, I hadn't the faintest idea of what that world had actually become. For all I knew, the political turmoil that first landed me in prison had blown over, and it was just a matter of time until my release and my safe return home.

Early one morning, I awoke to footsteps outside the cell door. Expecting my ration of soup, I sat up ready to grab the pot that was normally shoved under the door. There was the sound of keys in the lock. The guard who entered wasn't there to deliver a meal but, rather, to deliver the statement, "Edelstein, collect your things; you're about to be released." The guard then left, slamming the door behind him.

We couldn't believe our ears. Professor Zeiskind and I grabbed Edelstein and held him in tight embrace as we cheered his good fortune. We were giddy at the realization that there *was* a light at the end of the tunnel and the glimmer of hope that we wouldn't rot away in that cell forever. It then occurred to me that I could now get a message to my family; moreover, I could put Edelstein in touch with my Aunt Jenny, who could surely use her connections to help us all. (At the time, I had no way of knowing what had become of Bernard and Jenny—that it was already too late.)

I quickly scribbled my home address and that of my Aunt Jenny on a small piece of paper and gave it to Professor Edelstein. Moments later, the guards came and took Edelstein away.

In Edelstein's absence, the cell felt enormous. Professor Zeiskind and I each leaned back on opposite walls of the cell, exchanging thoughts on what we hoped would be our own impending release.

Not two hours had passed when the cell door suddenly flung open. In came two guards and a police official. He was the same individual who interrogated me on the evening of my arrest almost one year before.

"So you thought that you could get away with this?" the officer said slyly as he waved my note in the air. He turned to the guards and snapped, "Take him!"

I was kicked, beaten, and then dragged out of the cell and down a long corridor. They stopped in front of a room with a heavy steel door. They stripped me naked then shoved me inside.

"After three days in this hole you'll think twice before trying to pull off such a stunt again. Let this be a lesson to you!" the guard barked before slamming door.

The cell was four meters square. More a tomb then a cell, it was cold, dark as pitch, and as silent as a vacuum. Feeling my way around on my hands and knees, I found the cell empty, save for a small metal basin containing a little bit of liquid.

Settling down against a wall, I discovered that I could attain the most warmth and comfort by curling myself up in the fetal position. Lying in this way in that dark, cold, silent space, I soon lost all concept of time. What felt like an hour may well have been only a minute. I tried marking time by counting to sixty over and over again. After several rounds, for what felt to be an eternity, I lost count altogether. I began again from the beginning, but it was no use. My frustration swelled. I began to scream, louder and louder until my throat was raw. When I finally stopped, there was silence. I strained to hear something, anything, but there was nothing. At one point, I thought I heard a hissing noise. It steadily increased in volume. The pitch rose higher and higher. Realizing that the noise was arising out of my skull, I covered my ears, but it didn't help. I pulled at my hair and tore at my skin. Exhausted, I stopped and sat perfectly still, curled up with my hands over my ears trying to muffle the raging noise that was mounting from within. Eyes open, eyes closed—it didn't make a difference. "It's cold, I'm cold, I'm shivering," I cried. I wailed and wept, tasting my salty tears as they fell to my lips. In a violent rage and mad frenzy, I groped on the floor. Finding the metal pot, I picked it up with both hands and poured its contents on my head. The water chilled me to the core. Stunned from the cold, I lay shivering on the wet cement floor until I was startled awake. *Had I been asleep? Sleep, yes, precious sleep—that's the answer.* No luck. It wasn't to be. Hunger gnawed at my insides. My mouth was parched. I sat with my back to the wall, knees up against my chest, so numb I could no longer weep.

I see myself in my cell standing on the stool and staring out the window, waiting anxiously for my friend, my apparition. I know he'll be here; he always comes. Maybe he forgot. Please, you must come, you must…. Then, from out of the mist, I see him standing quietly beneath the streetlamp. The man stares upward as though looking for something or someone. "Look, I'm here! Please, look this way," I cried. Then, for the first time, our eyes met. My heart pounded so hard I thought it would jump out from my chest. The specter looked at me knowingly. He nodded slightly, assuring me that he was there and that I need not fear.

My three days of solitary confinement seemed like an eternity. The cell door swung open. A sudden flash of light cut into my eyes like a knife. Covering my face with both hands was all I could do while the guards dragged me out of the cell and into a nearby room. I heard voices, some talking, others laughing. I gasped as I was pummeled, head to foot, with cold water. I was then given dry clothes and brought back to my original cell. The room was vacant. I was all alone. Not daring to ask what had become of Professors

Zeiskind and Edelstein, I slowly made my way over to the wooden slab—my original bed.

My limbs felt as though they were made of dough. It took all of my strength to make my way across the room. On the floor was a bowl of tepid potato soup and a piece of bread. Compared to the horrific conditions of the previous three days, this was paradise. I felt as though I had come home.

In the professors' absence, alone without distractions, I lapsed into a state of catatonia. As though a mental switch had shut off, I found it difficult to formulate the simplest thoughts.

I opened my eyes to see faces staring down at me. I felt a strong, vice-like grip on both my arms as two guards pulled me up. They walked me rapidly out of the cell and down several flights of stairs and out into the street. Without a word, the guards turned and walked back inside the building, leaving me on the street—alone.

CHAPTER FOUR

The surroundings were unfamiliar. Dazed and disoriented, I walked across the street to a small park and sat on a bench. I became aware of a man sitting beside me.

"Good morning," he said.

Startled, I looked up to see a middle-aged man smiling back at me. He was wearing the Roman collar of a priest.

"Is everything all right?" he asked. His expression changed to one of concern.

I was dumbstruck, unable to utter a sound. Then out of nowhere came the sobs—uncontrollable, sudden sobs. It was as if I had been punched in the stomach. I trembled and wept; there was no controlling myself. The priest put his arm around me and held my head to his shoulder. After several minutes I calmed.

"There, there, my son. It's all right." He placed his hand on mine.

I looked into the priest's eyes wanting desperately to pour my heart out.

Reading my thoughts, he nodded to me encouragingly and said, "Yes, yes, go on. Tell me everything."

For the next hour, I told him of all that I had been through—everything, starting from the evening of my arrest one year before. I must have gone on for over an hour. When I was done, I felt exhausted, yet purged, as if a heavy weight had been lifted. It then occurred to me where I was.

My parents—I must get to them right away! I jumped to my feet and was nearly overcome by dizziness. The priest reached out, catching me as I stumbled.

"Easy now. There, that's better," he said, easing me back to the bench. "Wait right here." The priest returned moments later and patted my brow with his handkerchief, moistened from a nearby garden hose.

My head started to clear. "Thank you so much," I said, attempting once again to stand. "Now I must go home." I realized then that I didn't have a clue as to how to get there.

Recognizing my perturbed state, the priest smiled, took me by the arm, and said, "Come, you're in no state to go it alone. Tell me your address. I'll accompany you."

We walked out of the park and through the inner city, passing the magnificent St. Stephens Cathedral and the huge complex of buildings that was once the residence—known as the Hofburg—of the imperial family along the way. The city was majestic. I was awestruck by its beauty. It was as if I had been seeing Vienna for the first time. We walked past the broad tree-lined Ringstrasse and toward Mariahilfer Strasse, known for its vast array of unique and eclectic shops that could satisfy the delights of any-one, from housewife to the discerning dilettante. As we walked, there came a distinct shift in mood, a pall, as if a dark cloud had descended upon us. The streets that I remembered as being abuzz with activity were desolate. Many shops were in ruins, with their doors smashed in and windows shattered. The word *JUDE* was painted sloppily on many storefronts. The sidewalks were strewn with filth and shards of broken glass.

"Let's get a move on," the priest said, holding my arm firmer as we quickened our step. Reading my mind, he said, "It all happened in a matter of days. At first the Jews were segregated from the general public, then the massive arrests. Overnight, Jewish property and businesses were destroyed."

We entered the Second District and on to Schiffgasse. I knew then that my apartment building was not too far off. Turning a corner, I glared in shock at the spot where our synagogue had once stood. What was once a stately, elegant structure was now nothing but a mass of rubble. Dark-gray smoke spewed amidst charred embers and broken pieces of bricks.

"It was mass frenzy," the priest whispered in a quivering monotone, his words barely audible. "Jewish-owned stores were shattered and looted. Jews were humiliated; many were beaten to death. The ones that survived were carted away."

Overcome with a sudden fear for my parents' well-being, I began to run. The priest trailed close behind. *Dear God, please let them be safe.*

As we neared the courtyard of my apartment complex, the priest held me back. He was breathing quite heavily, trying to regain his breath. "Appearing unannounced at your parents' door might pose a terrible shock. Let me go up ahead of you. Don't worry. I won't be long. I pray that your parents are safe and well."

I wanted to protest, but after a moment's reflection, I realized the priest was right. It was decided. He would tell my parents he had knowledge that my release from jail was imminent and that I should be returning home at any moment. He squeezed my arm and gave me a look of assurance. I watched nervously as he went up ahead of me. The few minutes the priest was gone felt like an eternity.

Upon his return, he smiled and said, "You need not worry; your parents are expecting you." We embraced, and then, with teary eyes, he looked at me and said, "Go to them now, and may God bless you."

We stood at the threshold staring at each other in disbelief. Without a word, I fell into my parents' open arms. They were so frail. I shuddered as I felt hard ribs through their clothing. *Oh, how they aged.* My father's hair, once dark and wavy, was now thin, wispy, and gray. My mother's eyes were sunken and surrounded by dark shadows.

We walked into the kitchen. My father and I sat together at the table as my mother made her finishing touches at the stove. After tasting the stew from a wooden ladle, she filled up a bowl and placed it before me. She took her place at the table and, along with my father, watched intently as I ate.

My father, forcing a smile said, "Ever since Dr. Vogel told me to limit my salt intake, Mama's famous dishes have become a bit bland. Ernst doesn't deserve this. Here, sprinkle in some of this." He passed me the saltshaker. Despite my shaking it vigorously, no salt came out; it was clumpy.

My mother took another saltshaker from the shelf. "Here, use this one," she said, handing it to me. "It contains some kernels of rice in order to keep out the moisture."

I wolfed down two full bowls of stew and topped it off with a large piece of her famous apple strudel. Feeling as if I were going to burst, I pushed back from the table and loosened by belt.

"Mama, you haven't lost your touch—you're still the best cook on the continent."

She gave me a weak, half smile and then looked away. I saw the tears form in her eyes.

My father, always elegant and proud, was dressed in a vest and necktie. His shirt cuffs were frayed. Although worn and cracked, his shoes were polished to a high sheen.

The year had certainly taken its toll. Except for the couch, table, and a few chairs, all the furniture was gone. My father looked around and then back at me with an expression of resignation and surrender.

The authorities had confiscated his business. I wanted to come up with some assuring words, but I realized that it was futile. There was nothing left to say. We walked to the living room, where we quietly sat staring at one another over the rims of our tea glasses as we sipped the hot, soothing brew. It was the ringing of the telephone that broke the silence. My father twisted quickly in his seat and stared at the telephone. His face hardened in anger. No one moved. I was suddenly overcome with an ominous sense of doom. My father finally walked across the room and picked up the hand piece. His face became ashen.

Then, in a strong and steady voice, he spoke into the receiver. "My son? I haven't seen my son in months.

I thought he was with you." After listening for another moment, my father quietly hung up the telephone and stared off in a trance. "The police are looking for you." His words were barely audible. "They will be arriving shortly. You must leave right away." He then picked up the telephone and made a call.

Through the efforts of my Aunt Jenny, an escape plan was already in place. I was to be smuggled across the border to Yugoslavia masquerading as a member of a skiing party. The necessary paraphernalia was packed and ready, including skis, boots, lederhosen, a jacket, a hat, and gloves as well as an ID card, tickets, a passport, and currency. A car would be arriving within minutes to transport me across the border to the town of Brcko in northern Yugoslavia.

It took no time. My father left the room and returned moments later with a rucksack. With my parents on either side of me, we walked to the front door. I wrapped my arms around both of them and somehow knew that it would be for the last time.

My mother cried as my father placed his hands on my head and recited a prayer: "May the Lord bless you and guard you. May the Lord show you favor and be gracious to you. May the Lord show you kindness and grant you peace." My father then looked at me with piercing eyes and said, "You are about to leave, and I will never see you again. You will suffer, but you *will* survive. For should you not, then everything that I have ever believed to be true would have been a lie, and *that* is an impossibility."

Moments later, I left the apartment, never to see my parents again.

CHAPTER FIVE

It was no sooner than the car arrived that we were off. The driver, a portly man of around forty, was all business. He drove skillfully while keeping below speed limit, so as not to attract attention. He asked if I was hungry and offered me half of his sandwich. Aside from that, we hardly spoke at all. The drive took about four hours. I nodded off to sleep several times, only to be jolted awake by bumps and quick turns in the road.

I rummaged through the items in my backpack and studied my new passport, in which was transcribed my altered name, Ernst Von Mann. There were envelopes containing both German and Yugoslavian currency. There was also a letter written in my mother's hand:

My darling Ernst,

Seeing you today had been my dream come true. I had almost given up hope. Although we were together for but a few minutes, my faith was rekindled. You look marvelous! God willing, you will find peace and safety in Yugoslavia. Your sister, Nelly, along with her loving husband Romy and little Yankl have settled in the town of Sabac. We received word that they are well. Go to them as soon as you are able. Your father and I will pray for you. Hopefully we will soon be reunited.

My strong embrace, with all my love,
Mama

I folded the letter and tucked it safely away and settled back in my seat. A myriad of thoughts and feelings played havoc in my mind. Being with my parents for so brief a time was almost worse than not having been with them at all. My father, once so stately and proud, had been reduced to a mere shadow of himself. He was like a reflection of a biblical sage of old—gaunt and aged, yet with eyes that burned with a timeless fire.

Closing my eyes, I thought of my poor parents and heard my father's parting words: *I will never see you again. You will suffer, but you* will *survive. For should you not, then everything that I have ever believed to be true would have been a lie, and that is an impossibility.*

I lapsed into a trancelike state, into a zone that was somewhere between meditation and a dream:

There was my father, standing among cedars and olive trees, on a high, dusty hill. His head was covered in a rabbinical robe. His countenance was peaceful and loving. He looked directly at me, and in soothing, loving tones that bathed my soul in peace, he said the following: "You, my son, are in the direct line of the Lamed Vav, *one of the Thirty-Six Just souls that roam this earth and assure the moral balance of mankind. As one link in that chain, you embody the "hearts of the world multiplied." (Reference 2)*

In you is the grief of the world contained. With the male ancestral chain intact, the balance will be forever sustained. As my father to me, I am to you, and from you to yours.... This is your calling; this is your station."

I awoke with a start. For a moment I had no idea where I was. My face was covered with sweat, and my heart was pounding. Whatever it was that I had dreamt had already dissipated into thin air. I took a deep breath and managed to contain myself. I looked over at the driver. His eyes were fixed on the road. His hands seemed to dance through the gears as if they had a mind of their own. He seemed oblivious to my inner turmoil. I realized that I was at the mercy of the gods and chose to surrender and let them do their bidding. Only then was I able to relax as I watched the city flash by as we raced through the dark, damp Vienna night.

CHAPTER SIX

We had no trouble at the border crossing. The guard glanced lazily at our documents and waved us through. It was close to midnight when we arrived at the Hotel Central in Brcko. From his seat, the driver pointed to the hotel entrance. Hardly giving me time to alight, he gunned the engine and sped off.

The hotel clerk welcomed me by name and confirmed my reservation—three nights, prepaid. He handed me the key to room 212 and directed me to the stairwell across the lobby. No sooner did I enter the room than I dropped into bed, fully clothed, and fell asleep.

When I awoke late the following day, the sun was streaming through the room. I opened the window wide and breathed in the fresh air. It was hard to believe that a mere twenty-four hours before I was being held captive and now I was free as a bird. I felt reborn, without a care, and excited to begin this new adventure.

I dressed and set out to explore the town. It was late morning, and the sun was shining. The town center was already bustling with activity. The cafés were full. People of all ages pranced, unhurried, dressed proudly in their Sunday best.

Among them were young mothers pushing prams and lovers strolling arm in arm, oblivious to the envious onlookers.
Soldiers, off on furlough, strolled among giggling children
playing hopscotch. Vienna seemed a lifetime away.

I managed to find a front-row table in a café and ordered
a cup of dark, sweet coffee. It was hard to believe that, just
a few hours away, the world as we once knew it was coming
to an end. *Is it possible that Yugoslavia could be immune to the
Nazi scourge? Could I possibly remain here and make a new life for
myself? What would become of my parents? Could there be a place
for them here? Surely Jenny could help them as well.*

With these thoughts swirling about in my mind, I
tossed back my last drop of coffee, sat up erect, and with
a rush of enthusiasm, took out my pen and on a napkin
began jotting down my plan of action. Get word to my parents that I was safe, make certain that Jenny gets them to
safekeeping and contact the local Jewish community for a
more permanent lodging.

Sitting in that lovely café on that beautiful, sunny day
intently scribbling my to-do list, I had no clue that it would
all be for naught. I had no idea that my cozy little bubble
was soon about to burst.

The marketplace was located at the south end of the
square. On Tuesdays, from six in the morning until noon,
was the farmers' market. The area bustled with activity as
the local farmers gathered to sell their fresh produce. On
Sundays, the stalls were moved off to the side in order to
make room for soccer games. That day's match was par-
ticularly well attended, as it was the play-off game between
the two most popular teams of the area.

That day's game was a nail-biter to the very last minute, ending with a penalty kick. As the fans dispersed, one could hear the loud, rumbling sound of an engine in the distance. All heads turned as a motorcycle with sidecar came speeding into the plaza. Before skidding to a sudden halt, it spun around in a circle, generating a large cloud of dust. The motorcycle then remained in place with the engine idling. The driver and sidecar occupant were German soldiers. No one said a word. The soldier in the sidecar removed his goggles. He stood up and peered at the crowd of onlookers. No one moved. People watched, dumbstruck. The soldier then raised his machine gun and began firing. He rotated in place, firing methodically and indiscriminately, covering a full 360 degrees.

There was a mad rush for cover. I sheltered myself behind a building column. Bullets ricocheted off the walls. Windows shattered. Men, women, children, soldiers, and infants lay wounded and dying in pools of blood. People scattered every which way in a mad frenzy. It lasted for less than a minute. Throughout it all, the motorcycle driver remained in his seat, staring forward, not moving. The shooter then calmly returned to his seat, put the machine gun back at his side, and revved the engine twice before speeding away.

Among the slaughtered were several soldiers who were stunned to the point that their rifles never left their backs. The scene was pure carnage.

That was the prelude to the German occupation of Brcko. Within hours, convoys of German soldiers entered the city. Prior to occupying a town, they sent agents in advance to make the necessary preparations: securing maps that detailed the location of each street and alleyway as well as all official buildings, including city hall, police headquarters, and departments of utility. The mayor, in return for his safety, was "urged" to produce detailed lists of the town's prominent businessmen and politicians. Of paramount interest were the names and addresses of all Jewish residents. The German officials kept the mayor and his staff in place to run the day-to-day municipal operations while using their offices to carry out the will of the Reich.

I hurried back to my hotel room and locked the door behind me. Sitting on my bed, I tried to come to my senses. I had to think. I needed a plan. It was all too unbelievable. Having been released from jail just the day before, I again risked imprisonment, or quite possibly, death. Alone, without contacts or friends, I had nowhere to turn. I was worse off than any fugitive of justice. A criminal at least has rights; I had none. As I sat on the side of my bed, head in hands, a peculiar calm descended on me. Despite the present horrific events, I began to feel unburdened, independent, and free. *I can do this*, I thought. *Alone was good.* I would reshape my misery into a renewed dedication to succeed.

With these thoughts in mind, I then lay down, closed my eyes, and fell into a deep, deep sleep.

It was late afternoon on a balmy day in August. The waves were splashing off the bow of the schooner as I lay basking on the warm, wet, salty deck. The boat rocked steadily in the rhythm of the sea as we made our way westward on the dark-blue Mediterranean. Sitting in a comfortable deck chair was my father with an open book on his lap. He looked up. Our eyes met, and he smiled, nod-

ding briefly and knowingly. Gulls squawked as they soared above the mast, swooping and gliding in free, heavenly, timeless bliss. Then the sky darkened. The wind started to howl as icy rain began to slash at the sails. The boat heaved. I looked up and saw my father trying to stand. The sea was rough. As I tried to reach him, the boat rocked violently. Falling sideways, I smashed the side of my face against a support rail. I watched helplessly as my father disappeared in the raging sea.

I awoke with a jolt. My jaw throbbed. I had an agonizing pain in my tooth. The mere closing of my mouth sent a thunderbolt shooting through my head. The side of my face was swollen. I was burning up with fever and covered with sweat. I dressed and went down to the lobby. Holding the side of my face with my hand, I approached the concierge. Taking one look at me, he picked up the telephone and called his dentist, who agreed to see me right away.

A few minutes later, I was lying back in a dental chair. An abscess had formed beneath a molar. The tooth had to come out. As the dentist manipulated and groped, I dug my fingers into the arms of the chair. The pain was excruciating. Then, all of a sudden, with one violent yank, the tooth was out. I collapsed in the chair and let out a moan. The dentist was grinning from ear to ear, proudly displaying my tooth within his steel pliers. He then took a bottle of cognac from the cabinet and filled two glasses. Handing one to me, he clinked my glass and hoisted it in one gulp. I tried doing the same and, in the process, spilled most of the contents of the glass down my shirt. The dentist laughed and toasted *zivoli*. I forced a clumsy smile and toasted *prost*.

As he was filling our glasses for another round, the door flung open. Two German soldiers were standing in the doorway. They were huge. Both had the same dull and vacant expression. On their helmets was the death-squad insignia of a skull and cross bones. With machine guns poised at me, they pushed past the dentist and pulled me from the chair.

"Rouss!" One of them yelled, as he shoved me out the door.

A few minutes later, we arrived at police headquarters. The soldiers marched me up the stairs to an office on the second floor then left, slamming the door behind them. A man entered through a door on the opposite side of the room. Dressed in a wrinkled dark-gray suit and short necktie, he appeared to be in his forties. He offered me a cigarette and asked me to sit down. The man identified him as the chief of police. In German, he asked me my name.

"Ernst Von Mann," I answered quietly.

He let out a laugh. "Von Mann? It's unbelievable how our town is crawling with spies." He pointed a finger in my face and said angrily, "You are nothing but a rotten Russian spy!"

I didn't know what to think. *Was he insane?*

He then said, "You know what happens to spies, don't you?" In a threatening gesture, he swept his thumb across his neck. He walked around me as I sat nervously in the chair. I decided that my only recourse was to tell the truth.

"I am not a spy," I yelled. "I am a Jew!" *How absurd! Me, a desperate fugitive in this city occupied by Nazis, and I'm trying to convince this maniac that I am, in fact, a Jew in hiding.*

The police chief walked to the window. He let out a loud laugh and muttered, "Come over here." In the court-yard was a man leaning against a wall. He was blindfolded with his hands tied behind his back. "That is exactly what *he* said. He, too, is a Russian spy who claimed to be a Jew!" There were half a dozen soldiers with rifles pointing at the poor fellow.

We watched as an officer raised his arm and gave the command, "Ready...fire!" They shot in unison. The man fell to the ground in a bloody heap.

Aghast and sickened by the sight, I stumbled back into the chair. The police chief pranced about the room like Benito Mussolini delivering one of his long-winded disser-tations. He ranted, first about corruption, then about the indecency of today's youth. He then cursed the lazy oafs who were working under him.

I never saw it coming. All I can recall is the brief flash of the shiny blade and then the pain. It came out of nowhere. From behind, he thrust a knife over my shoul-der, directly into my chest. Everything went black.

I don't know how much time had passed. When I awoke, I was lying on the floor. My clothes were wet and sticky with my own blood. I was alone. Evidently, I had been left for dead.

When I tried to get to my feet I was overcome by light-headedness and nausea. The slightest movement and breath triggered a sharp pain in my chest. The morning sun was beaming through the window. It then occurred to me that before long the building would be teaming with people. I had to get out of there. Utilizing every ounce of strength, I managed to get to my feet. The door was ajar and the hallway empty. I made my way down the stairs and stumbled into the street. I needed to find a doctor. I walked and walked, stopping every few feet in order to regain some strength. I came upon a house that had the medical insignia of a spear and serpent on its front gate. Beneath it was the name Doktor Stefan Baric.

Utilizing every ounce of my strength, I leaned on the doorpost and pounded on the door. After what felt like an eternity, the door finally opened. Standing before me was an elderly hunchback woman with smiling eyes. She took one look at me and helped me inside, easing me into a chair. She left the room and returned moments later accompanied by a man, no doubt her son, as he, too, was hunchbacked and had similar facial features. Together, they helped me into the next room and onto an examination table. The old woman helped me out of my bloody clothes and gently washed my wound. The man introduced himself as Dr. Baric.

As I began to speak, the doctor put a finger to his lips and said in slow and precise German, "The less I know the better. I don't want to know who you are or what you are doing in Brcko. I will mend your wound, but then you must be on your way."

With his sleeves rolled up and eyeglasses balanced at the tip of his nose, the doctor bent over me. He performed his task slowly and methodically. All the while, the old woman hovered beside him, periodically wiping my brow with a cool, wet cloth. I drifted off to sleep.

When I awoke, I saw the old woman's face before me. She gestured for me to relax and then left the room. She soon returned with some bread, butter, and hot coffee. She watched quietly as I ate.

While I was on my third piece of buttered bread, the doctor entered. He re-taped a portion of gauze that had come loose then stepped back to assess his handiwork. With a look of satisfaction, he said, "There, this looks fine." He sat down beside me and gave what was his final summation. "Aside from losing a fair amount of blood, your injury wasn't all that serious. By some miracle, the knife missed all vital organs. In a few days, you should be as good as new."

He gave me some gauze pads and a small bottle of disinfectant and instructed me on how to clean and dress my wound. He put his hand on my shoulder and said, "Now you must leave. My clinic patients will be arriving any moment. I don't want to be accused of harboring a fugitive. Please, finish your meal and go." Before I could say a word, he shook my hand and left the room.

The old woman brought me my shirt, now mended and cleaned, and helped me dress. We sat for a while, neither of us saying a word. Her expression was that of a concerned mother. She then walked me to the door and handed me a cloth bag containing some bread and a few pieces of fruit. I bent to kiss her cheek then left.

What was I to do? I needed to get out of Brcko right away. Despite the danger, I knew that I first had to risk returning to the Hotel Central in order to retrieve my backpack. I had no choice. Without it I was lost. There was no longer any doubt that it was the hotel clerk who had betrayed me. How else could the soldiers have known to find me at the dentist's office?

Trying not to draw attention to myself, I slowly made my way back to the hotel. I peeked through the lobby window before entering. I spied a woman standing at the front desk conversing with the clerk. I circled the block. This time as I glanced through the window I saw there was no one there. I had my opportunity. Entering surreptitiously, I walked directly to the front desk, leaned over and snatched my room key off its hook, and quickly rushed up to my room. To my delight, my backpack was under the bed just where I had left it. After checking it to assure that nothing was missing, I fastened it tight and hurried back out through the lobby and into the street. I walked in the direction of the train station and never looked back.

CHAPTER SEVEN

There was a throng of people at the station, which made it easy for me to blend in. I nonchalantly sauntered up to the ticket window, looked the attendant squarely in the eye, and with a smile, said, "Sabac."

The clerk wrote out my ticket and then, pointing in the direction of my train, said, "Sabac...go, go!" I dropped some money on the counter, grabbed the ticket, and boarded the train just as the doors were closing.

I only hoped and prayed that my sister and her family were safe and secure. The little that I knew of Sabac was that it was a small agricultural town located forty miles south of Brcko. It was where my sister, Nelly; her husband, Romy; and their little boy, Yankl, had been living since being smuggled out of Vienna several months before.

The train was packed. I made my way to the end of the car and found a small space between two elderly men. The seats were wooden and very uncomfortable. I crossed my arms in front of my chest, using them as a cushion to dampen the pain caused by the train's frequent jolts.

As I watched the magnificent Bosnian countryside drift by, I pondered the fate of my sister's son, my sweet, little

nephew, Yankl. This was certainly no experience for such
a little tot—or anyone, for that matter. *Why couldn't this all
be just an awful nightmare? Why couldn't I, as had happened
so many times before, wake up with a gasp, pause, collect myself,
and realize that it was all nothing more than just a bad dream?* I
rested my head against the seat, and with the steady clack,
clack, clack of the train's steel wheels on the tracks, I was
soon fast asleep.

Oh, what a truly perfect day, *I thought as I walked in step
with my parents. It seemed as though all of Vienna was out strolling
in the park. The wide, stately paths were lined with benches.
Finding a free one was a premium, an impossibility, but not for
me. I had my ways....*

*My mother, looking over at me with a challenging smile, said,
"Ernst, let's see if you can work your magic and find us a place
to sit."*

*I gave her a knowing grin and ran ahead. Not twenty meters
away, I saw the perfect spot—a half-empty bench with a clear view
of the duck pond. On it sat a middle-aged couple. There appeared
to be just enough room on the bench for one more person. As I
motioned to take the seat, the couple politely slid to one side to give
me more room. After a couple of minutes, I took out my handkerchief, covered my mouth, and coughed.*

"Oh my," I said, staring into the cloth, "blood again."

*The couple looked at me with fright, and like scared rabbits,
they quickly scurried off.*

*Seeing my parents approaching, I stood up, and with a magnanimous bow and wave of my hand, I gestured for them to take
their seats. My father sat down willingly. He removed his hat and
patted the beads of sweat from his brow with his handkerchief. My*

mother, with a playful curtsy, took her place between us. She asked how I managed to find such a perfect spot.

I smiled and said, "I have my ways."

The train jerked abruptly, awaking me with a start. As my dream dissipated, I realized, with sadness, that the individuals seated beside me were not my parents. The man on my left was leaning against me, using my shoulder as a pillow. He was sleeping so deeply I didn't have the heart to wake him. All I could do was, once again, contemplate my lot. My sense of security had been shattered by the German occupation of Brcko. From the ease with which the Germans occupied that town, there was little doubt that they had similar designs for all of Yugoslavia. No place was safe. I reminded myself that I could never let down my guard. My first priority now was to find my sister and her family. Beyond that, divining any future events would be but an exercise in futility.

An hour later, we arrived in Sabac. I alighted from the train, and among several other people, I headed to the town center. The atmosphere was calm. I was happy to see that there didn't appear to be any Germans in the area, but after my Brcko experience, I recognized that that, too, could change from one moment to the next. I was prepared for anything.

Within a few minutes, I came upon the marketplace. The stall-keepers were beginning to close up for the night. One of the merchants was wearing a black skullcap. His stall was replete with dried fruits, nuts, and a variety of delicacies.

"*Shalom Aleichem,*" I said in the usual Yiddish greeting.

"*Aleichem shalom*," he replied sotto voce and with suspicion. I told him that I had come to Sabac in hope of finding my sister, Nelly. At the mention of her name, the man's face lit up.

"Such a zeiskeit. She is a darling, always with a smile. Nelly was here just this morning with her little Yankl. Seeing them is like a breath of fresh air."

I couldn't contain my excitement. My heart pounded so hard I thought it would jump out of my chest. I became light-headed. Seeing the change in me, the man took me to a nearby chair and gave me some water. Within a moment I was feeling better.

"Relax, you needn't worry," he said. "They're fine. They live in a farming commune less than a mile from town."

Anxious to get going, I jumped to my feet and was hit by a wave of dizziness and nearly fell to the ground.

"Sit right down. You're not going anywhere just yet." The man went behind the stall and returned with a bottle and two glasses. He put some dried fruit on a piece of wax paper and pulled up a stool and sat beside me. He introduced himself as Mendl and poured two little glasses of schnapps. "This is my own brew," he said proudly. Raising his glass, he said, "*Lachaim!*" and washed it down in a single gulp.

I followed suit. The drink was very strong and went right to my head.

As he was about to pour me another, I put my palm over the glass, thanked him, and declined. I had to move on.

Mendl locked up his stall, walked me out of the marketplace, and pointed to a road in the distance that led directly to Nelly's house. He shook my hand heartily and walked back toward the market.

I had no trouble finding my sister's house. It was more a shack than a proper house, the tiniest among several others that was situated on a wide, grassy cul-de-sac. There were two windows on either side of the front door and a small garden off to the side. When I appeared at the door, you would have thought that the Messiah had arrived. Nelly let out a scream, and little Yankl, startled by my sister's reaction, began to cry. Romy jumped out of his chair and gave me a bear hug that was so strong it nearly reopened my chest wound.

We settled down in the living room, which, in essence, was the only room in the little house. By strategically situating little knickknacks, flowers, and batiks throughout the room, Nelly succeeded in turning the crude hut into a cozy little home.

"Thank God you're alive," Romy said as he bounced Yankl on his knee.

Nelly sat down on a little stool opposite me. She was so close that our knees touched. "Tell us everything," she said excitedly. "Don't leave out a thing. How are Mommy and Daddy? You look tired. Are you well? When did you leave Vienna? Wait right there. Let me prepare some tea and a bite to eat. Don't say a thing until I'm back."

Nelly came back a few minutes later with tea, honey, and a plate of biscuits.

"Forget about me; I'm just fine. I want to know how this little rascal is doing," I said as I reached over and pinched Yankl in the belly.

"Yankl is in kindergarten and loves it, don't you, Yankl?" Nelly watched lovingly as little Yankl sat giggling on Romy's lap.

"Yeah, I'm a finger-painter," Yankl said proudly.

"And what an artist he is," Nelly said, handing me several pages of Yankl's artwork. "Here, have a look."

While leafing through the pictures, I looked up momentarily and saw Nelly looking off into oblivion. In a brief second, her expression revealed an underlying resignation and sadness, an expression of someone who has overcome despair, who has accepted his or her lot.

"And you, Nelly, what have you been up to?"

Hearing her name, Nelly snapped out her trance, smiled, and said. "I work part-time at the medical clinic."

"I don't know what they would do without her," Romy chimed in. "Nelly is a natural."

Nelly blushed, waving off Romy. "I bandaged his finger, and he calls me a surgeon."

"I nearly sliced the whole thing off while repairing a neighbor's carriage. Nelly sewed it back on as good as new." Romy stood up, caressed her, and facetiously said, "If not for my lovely wife, I'd be a cripple." Romy sat back in his chair. "We have found our own little utopia. Nelly and I make enough to scrape by; little Yankl has made friends. Until the storm passes, we'll be fine right here."

I knew otherwise. I told them of the recent events that took place in Brcko. I told them of the dramatic way in which the two German soldiers on motorcycle "introduced" themselves in the Brcko plaza.

"The Germans have arrived, and they're here to stay. There is no doubt in my mind they have their sights set on all of Yugoslavia. Sabac is next. They could be at your door within hours. I will be leaving tomorrow, and you must come with me. There is no time to lose."

"That's insanity," Romy said with an incredulous smirk. "We don't have anything to worry about. Sabac is perfectly safe. Come on, Ernst, you're being quite irrational."

"You must understand," I pleaded, "it was the very same in Brcko until all hell broke loose. We should all be on the next train to Belgrade. From there, with the help of the 'underground,' we will make our way to Palestine!"

Either they couldn't understand or they refused to do so. Nelly and Romy both looked at me as though I were insane.

Nelly was defiant. "This community accepted us with open arms. They look out for us. Yankl has made friends at school; he already speaks the language. We will take our chances right here."

No amount of begging could change their minds. I was about to try one more stratagem when Nelly shot me a glance, imploring me to back off.

I began to understand what Nelly was trying to say. She was too proud, too dignified, to traipse through the countryside with her husband and child in tow. Had she been alone, I am certain she would have left with me. The subject was now closed. I held up my cup for more tea. Nelly filled it to the brim and gave me a sad and appreciative smile.

I slept that night in the small alcove at the side of the room. I played with little Yankl and then told him an adventure story. As his eyes became heavy, I gently picked him up and put him to bed.

Nelly took me aside and, with teary eyes, said, "Dear Ernst, I know you understand why you must go alone and why we can't leave." She then kissed my cheek and said goodnight.

Romy and I stepped outside. We sat down on a long, narrow bench in the garden and lit up cigarettes. The warm night air was filled with the rich, pungent perfume of a plum tree that was in full bloom. The stars in the cloudless, black sky seemed close enough to snatch with one's hand. The combination of the sweet garden scents and the harsh, acrid smell of tobacco was dizzying.

As I tried once more to reason with Romy, he raised his hand and said, "You will take the six a.m. train to Novi Sad. You will go to city hall. There, you will tell the clerk that you wish to speak with a certain Max Deutsch. He will help you to find temporary lodging." Romy flicked away his cigarette and opened the door to the house. Before entering, he turned and faced me. His eyes were red and misty. He took my face in his hands and whispered in my ear, "Please pray for us." He looked closely in my eyes without saying another word and went inside.

Yankl's quiet, rhythmic breathing interrupted the stillness of the little room. I lay wide-awake, nestled on my soft mattress under an open window. A moonlit, star-studded sky illuminated Nelly's little cottage in a blanket of soft light.

What role, if any, did these nocturnal orbs play in this drama that was unfolding? Were they merely dispassionate bystanders or inanimate objects placed on the set by an invisible director to function as backdrops for His macabre drama? What was my role? Was I even written into the script, or was I mere floor dust being scattered under the shuffling soles of the actors? This was no time to wax philosophic. There would be ample time for that if, with God's help, I should ever extricate myself from this nightmare. I needed to snap out of it and focus on the trials that lay before me.

It was a little before dawn when I awoke from a sound, dreamless sleep. Careful not to awaken anyone, I quickly dressed, collected my few belongings, and tiptoed out of the house. Before leaving for the train station, I sat in the garden and composed the following note:

My Dearest Nelly, Romy, and Yankl,

It was marvelous seeing all of you. I was especially thrilled to be with my favorite nephew, Yankl. Your finger-paintings are beautiful. I'm sure that you will be a great artist one day. I only wish that we could have spent more time together. As you know, I will be on the early train to Novi Sad. I may have spoken in haste when I asked you to leave your beautiful home in Sabac and come along with me, but I spoke from my heart and from deep-seeded concerns. I'm sure that there is still more time if you choose to reconsider. I will communicate with you in a few days.

With all my love,
Ernst

CHAPTER EIGHT

The sun was just rising as I neared the train station. I purchased a ticket for Novi Sad and stepped onto the platform and waited for the train that was due in twenty minutes. While standing there, I contemplated my lot: Brcko, Sabac, and now Novi Sad. It had only been a few days since my arrival in Yugoslavia, and it felt like an eternity. The events were changing so rapidly it became clear to me that I couldn't let my guard down for even a second.

The train ride to Novi Sad was uneventful. I tried fitting in among the other passengers by assuming a bored and casual air. I felt like a chameleon who, without batting an eye, could alter its characteristics from one instant to the next. I had to suppress any thought that could cause me to deviate from my new path. My instincts were becoming a sharp and finely tuned engine; I was running on all cylinders. To survive, I had to resign myself to the fact that this mad adventure was not about to end anytime soon. I was rechanneling all my energy in order to formulate the new, more resilient "Ernst Von Mann."

The Jewish community of Belgrade had organized safe havens for refugees in a handful of towns in Yugoslavia.

Although there were signed agreements between those municipalities and their Jewish representatives, the destiny of the refugees remained at the whim of the local authorities who, more often than not, were Nazi collaborators. The town of Novi Sad was one such "safe haven." Its chief of police, Anatole Rakovic, received a monthly stipend from the Jewish community of Belgrade to assure the safety of the one hundred Jewish refugees who were residing in his town as "guests."

As soon as I got off the train in Novi Sad, I went directly to city hall to arrange for my "safe haven" status. The building, situated in the main square, had the look of a typical bureaucratic office—a large, nondescript room with a counter that ran along one wall. I introduced myself to the woman seated behind the counter. Barely looking up and without uttering a word, she handed me some forms and directed me to a desk.

While seated, engrossed in my task, a man's voice caught me by surprise: "Welcome to Novi Sad."

I looked up to see a portly man with a thin mustache and steel-rimmed spectacles.

"Allow me to introduce myself," he said, extending his hand to me, "Max Deutsch, representative of the Jewish community of Belgrade."

The man behaved as though he had been expecting me. He said he was in town that day to discuss refugee issues with the mayor. We chatted for a while, and as it turned out, Deutsch knew my father's cousin, Miksha, from Belgrade. He and Deutsch were members of the same synagogue and served together on the brotherhood committee. This fact thrilled Deutsch to no end. He had only good things to say about cousin Miksha.

Deutsch then grabbed the forms that I had only started to fill out and said, "You've written enough. Leave the rest to me." He then went to the clerk and, within a few minutes, returned with my registration papers, all signed and in proper order. "Come," he said, "let's get something to eat. You must be starved."

We walked to a nearby café. Over lunch, Deutsch told me that most of his time was spent traveling from town to town to assist the displaced Jewish refugees. "I'm so busy," he said, "I hardly have time to see my family." He raised his hands skyward and said, "God knows, there is still much that has to be done. Thank goodness it won't last long. I have friends in high places who assure me this all will blow over in a few short months. At least I have a city to which I can return. If not for Belgrade, I'd really be lost."

I had no idea what Deutsch was talking about. *How could he consider* any *place as being safe?* From what I gathered, the Germans planned to overrun and occupy all of Europe. At the rate they were going, it would be just a matter of weeks until Yugoslavia would be completely occupied.

I looked at him squarely in the eye and asked, "How can you possibly believe the Nazis have no interest in Belgrade?"

Deutsch chuckled and said, "Germany would never occupy Belgrade. The city and its Jewish inhabitants have a long and prosperous history together that goes back centuries. My family is, and has always been, an integral part of the national fabric. I have friends in high places," he quickly reminded me. "Just last month, we spent the weekend as guests of Prince Adelbert at his seaside villa. We are very safe, indeed. There is nothing that could happen to us in Belgrade."

I was dumbfounded. *Did he not get what was happening? How blind could this man be?*

"The Jewish community of Europe is doomed," I said, raising my voice an octave. "The Jews of Vienna fell into the same trap. They were lulled into complacency. By the time they realized what was really happening, it was too late!"

"The German government is only making an example of some of the locals in order to keep everyone in line until this all blows over," he said confidently. "I'm here for the displaced people like yourself. Our benevolent brothers in Belgrade are offering their financial support and have chosen me to represent them. Of course, there is some danger. For the next few months, there will be ethnic reorganization. That, too, will pass. It is only temporary. I know the Germans well. It is their nature to behave like strict taskmasters. It's in their blood—the Teutonic influence. Once they blow off a little steam, all will return to normal."

I then told Max of my plight, of what I had experienced since fleeing Vienna. I expressed my conviction that it was just a matter of time until all of Europe would be overrun by the Germans. Deutsch's expression remained unchanged. He looked at me as a father looks upon his dim-witted child, with both love and sympathy. At that moment, it became clear to me that I was on my own. Deutsch didn't recognize that the world we once knew was falling apart, crumbling before our very eyes. I had to be prepared for anything. I would have to follow my instincts. Each move I made would be determined by circumstance. There was no possibility for long-term plans. I would live hour by hour, day by day in the hope of an exit strategy. *How absurd*, I thought, for I knew deep down that there was no exit.

Like oil on oak wood, the German venom seeped smoothly into every nook, cranny, and crevice of Europe. Like lava, it consumed everything in its path. I needed to keep one step ahead of the flow.

Deutsch slapped his hand on the desk and said, "I have a wonderful idea. I believe there is a way we could help one another. You are alone, without the constraints of family. Why don't you become my representative here in Novi Sad? You would act as the go-between on behalf of our little refugee population. Most of them are old and keep to themselves. You would deal with whatever rare day-to-day problems that might arise. This would allow me more time to spend with my family. You would be in regular contact with Police Chief Rakovic. He, in turn, would refer anything of major importance to the mayor. I pay them both well for their efforts. Naturally, I could set aside a modest sum for you as well—to cover your expenses and the like. Rakovic will arrange for your ID papers and travel documents."

What did I have to lose? I was on the run without a plan, with nowhere to go. After a moment's reflection, I decided to take Deutsch up on his offer. Deutsch was delighted. He stood up, and we walked arm in arm out of the restaurant.

"I will introduce you to Rakovic and his people," Deutsch said as we made our way back toward the town center. "We'll inform him of our arrangement. You, too, will get along with him just fine. But, first, I will show you to your living quarters. With any luck, I'll be able to make the last train to Belgrade."

A few minutes later, we arrived at the entrance of a modest, little house. We were received by an old woman wearing a long, black dress. She gave Deutsch a wide, toothless smile and beckoned us to enter. In the middle of the room was an elderly man sitting in a wheelchair, fast asleep. After Deutsch exchanged a few words with the woman, she took me by the hand and walked me to my room. The room contained a bed and a dresser. There was a little window that overlooked a plot of grass. On the dresser was a washbasin. There was another door that connected to the outside. The woman asked us to stay for tea, but Deutsch gracefully declined. She gave me my room key. Deutsch and I left right away to find Chief Rakovic.

The police station was a two-story building located in the main square. At the mere sight of the building before me, I was stopped in my tracks by a sense of trepidation. I had a flashback to that night, one year ago, when I was beaten by the mob at the city hall in Vienna. I could feel the vice-like grip of the police as they dragged me to the jailhouse. I remembered seeing poor Martin's lifeless body on the ground.

"Mann, are you all right?" Deutsch's voice sounded distant and hollow as if he were talking inside a tunnel.

My head began to clear. "Yes, I'm fine," I said, wiping my face with a handkerchief. "I'm fine."

We walked up the several steps leading to the building entrance. Deutsch pushed open the door and walked in as if he owned the place. Two policemen were speaking with the sergeant behind a high counter.

"Hey, Deutsch," the sergeant said, looking our way, "what brings you here this time of day?"

"I was hoping to find Rakovic. Is he in?" At that moment, a man entered the room. It was Rakovic. He was a stout fellow, almost as wide as he was tall. He brandished a mustache that made him resemble a walrus.

"Who is talking about me?" he said with a wide grin as he walked toward Deutsch. With arms opened wide, they exchanged kisses on both cheeks. "Thanks for the cognac," Rakovic said. "It was the best! It was good of you to finally show up, you bastard. I've been waiting all day. Who's your friend?" he asked, glancing in my direction.

Deutsch put his arm on my shoulder and said, "This is my friend, Ernst Mann. Our families go back a long time. Ernst will be my representative in Novi Sad while I'm away. You two should get along just fine."

Rakovic slapped me on the arm and, with a toothy smile, said, "Any friend of Deutsch is a friend of mine. Let's drink."

The three of us sat around a low table in Rakovic's office. We watched in amazement as the chief gulped down three glasses of brandy in quick succession.

Rakovic looked over to me and said, "So, you are going to assist Mr. Deutsch?" He then gave me a wink and said, "You should have no problem; Max Deutsch is an easy act to follow." He laughed heartily at his own comment and reached over to squeeze Deutsch's cheek. By now, Rakovic was quite tipsy. Then, recognizing his own behavior, he feigned a serious air in a futile attempt to contain himself. He cleared his throat and said, "You needn't worry. So far, you Jews have behaved quite well." He then took a folder from his desk and handed it to me. "Here is an updated list. In total, there are about ninety of you. I will get the word out to them that you will now be their new contact person. Not to worry, should any true problem arise, you can always turn to me. My door's always open." Then, looking into his glass, he waved his hand in the air and said, "Frankly, I'd like to be left alone. You can do as you wish."

Rakovic poured himself another drink, leaned back in his chair, and staring off glassy-eyed, said, "Your Jewish brothers seem to be overly concerned with Germany and the Nazi issue. They really haven't anything to fear in Yugoslavia. I believe Germany would actually prefer to steer clear of our local politics. We have our own unique internal issues that date back centuries. Rather than overrun us, the Germans realize that they can save manpower by letting us destroy ourselves." Rakovic belched loudly and continued. "Take our town of Novi Sad, it is a microcosm of Yugoslavia. We are made up of mostly Croats and Serbs. There are a minority of Muslims and a handful of Albanians. The one thing they have in common, of course, is their hatred of Jews, but that is neither here nor there. The Croats and Serbs have been at each other's throats since the beginning of time. When I was just a little boy, I watched as my father and uncle were both strung up by the Croats. As far as I'm concerned, the only good Croat is a dead Croat. That's all there is to it!" Rakovic then stretched out his legs. Moments later, he fell asleep, snoring loudly.

"Don't worry, Mann," Deutsch said as we left the building, "you have nothing to fear. Rakovic is just a harmless bag of wind. For now, relax, get acquainted with the town, and put some meat back on your bones. I'll be leaving for Belgrade tonight. The Jewish Agency is trying to organize a transport to Palestine. We have managed to get some funding from the American Jewish community. As long as the money holds out, Rakovic will help us with the first leg of the journey. If all goes according to plan, you and the rest will soon be safely settled in the land of our forefathers. We should be ready in two to three weeks." Looking at his watch, Deutsch said, "I almost forgot—I have a train to catch."

Walking with Deutsch to the station, he looked at me and said, "It was good that we met." Then, as an afterthought, he reached into his breast pocket and took out a folded piece of paper. "Here, Mann, take this." It was a list of the Jewish refugees under his care. "It won't be too bad. Save for one or two loud mouths, they tend to keep to themselves. You won't have much to do. Check in with Rakovic every couple of days to remind him who you are. I should be back soon. Good luck."

With that, we parted ways—Deutsch to his train and me to my little room.

CHAPTER NINE

Possagno di Grappa, Province of Treviso, Italy, 1911

Sister Angelina Giraldi couldn't take her eyes off of young Lorenzo. *How independent he is,* she thought. Each morning he would rise on his own, prepare a pot of coffee, and set the breakfast table for two. Angelina would sit opposite him and watch lovingly as Lorenzo would dip his biscotto into the steaming coffee and then swallow it down in two bites.

Lorenzo was more delicate than the other boys in the monastery. His anemic appearance always made Angelina fear for his health. This was especially true in winter, when the howling, cold winds would sweep the countryside, all too often leaving plague and death in its wake. Lorenzo's countenance, however, was deceptive since his physical constitution matched that of his mind—hearty and robust. In fact, Angelina could not recall ever seeing Lorenzo suffer even the slightest sniffle. She was of the fervent belief that he had a special guardian angel who was looking out for his well-being.

Lorenzo's teachers marveled at his analytical skills. In debates, no matter what the topic, Lorenzo had the knack, or rather, the gift, of gathering, dissecting, and reducing every facet of information to its lowest common denominator and then formulating the perfect argument. His mind was like a magnifying glass that captured and converged the sun's rays to a high-energy focal point. Years after studying a topic, he could draw upon it and recite it verbatim. His fellow students admired his talents as well as his humility. As final exams drew near, Lorenzo could frequently be seen conducting impromptu review sessions. The other students listened intently as Lorenzo would explain complex problems in terms that even a child could understand.

Angelina's mind wandered as she looked upon Lorenzo. *It feels like only yesterday when I happened upon this little* fanciullo *in the forest. How quickly the years have passed. He looks so much younger than his nineteen years. With such delicate features, he could pass for a schoolboy.*

Angelina's thoughts drifted back to when she had been adopted by the Monastery of Sacro Cuore at the tender age of nine. She shuddered as she recalled the masked men pulling her from her mother's lifeless body. She remembered the wooden carriage that transported her to the monastery, together with several other children. Angelina could still smell the musty, cold room where she sat all alone for days. At the time, she believed that she was being punished. She later learned that the men had their faces covered to stave off the putrid humors of the infected, necrotizing corpses. Her isolation, she also would later learn, was the quarantine that assured her safety as well as that of the villagers.

Early one morning, two sisters entered her room and tenderly took her to the bathhouse. After being stripped of her clothing, Angelina was examined from head to toe. Aside from her chafed skin, the sisters could identify neither pox nor bubo. They washed her with warm, wet cloths then patted her dry with soft fleece. Her skin was then stroked and kneaded with aromatic balms.

For weeks, Angelina didn't utter a word. She walked through the convent grounds, her hands dangling at her side and her head drooped. Sister Rachel was forever with her, lending support and coaxing her on. When anyone tried to engage Angelina in conversation, she would only return a blank and vacant stare.

Sister Rachel was given temporary dispensation by the Mother Superior to make Angelina her ward. It had become Rachel's mission to see Angelina through her mental trauma. She recited verses from the Psalms and read stories of the saints and apostles. All the while, Angelina would listen without uttering a word. Still, Sister Rachel remained patient. She knew that, with love, patience, and time, Angelina's trauma would one day fade to the remote recesses of her memory.

Early one morning in late spring, Angelina's troubled cloud finally lifted. Rachel watched quietly as Angelina slept. Her breathing was calm and untroubled. There was a slight upturning of the corners of her mouth that gave her an angelic appearance. This was the first time that Rachel could recall that Angelina's sleep was uninterrupted by nightmares.

"Sleep, my little cherub," Rachel whispered. Then she kissed her cheek and left for the chapel.

A short time later, Rachel returned to find Angelina sitting at her desk, charcoal in hand, drawing feverishly. Pieces of crumpled paper were scattered on the floor. Rachel watched quietly as Angelina drew her designs with broad and confident strokes. Angelina was so focused on her task that she didn't notice Rachel standing beside her. Angelina's drawing captivated Rachel. It depicted a young girl genuflected in prayer and surrounded by three individuals who were gazing up to the heavens, their hands extended with their palms angled upward. Two angels were hovering in the heavens above. The scene was cast in a graceful light. Angelina managed to capture a saintly mood as well as distinct facial expressions, utilizing nothing more than a charcoal pencil. Angelina then looked up to see Sister Rachel standing before her.

"I made this for you," Angelina smiled broadly as she proudly held up the picture. Overcome with a sudden burst of emotion, Rachel's tears spewed forth as she took Angelina in her arms and held her closely to her breast.

From that day forward, Angelina dedicated her each and every spare moment to drawing. In time, her prolific artwork made the drab walls of the convent come to life. Church attendance, once meager, blossomed as people came from near and far to view Angelina's designs.

Although still emotionally frail, Angelina's artistic outlet helped distract her and mollify her recent trauma. She moved into the convent's student wing and was embraced by her fellow parochial students. Sister Rachel still kept a close and watchful eye on her. In time, their relationship grew. Rachel evolved from a mother figure to becoming Angelina's close friend and confidant.

As the years passed, Angelina found it more and more difficult to balance her religious activities with her art. While her religious convictions continued to grow, her artistic abilities stagnated. She eventually reached a void. Angelina needed further schooling and nurturing in the arts—the kind that couldn't be obtained in the little town of Possagno. It was Angelina's dream to study at the renowned Accademia Dell'Arte di Trieste, one of the foremost art institutions in all of Europe. The academy attracted students from all over. For the student of means, admission was difficult; for a poor convent orphan, it was a veritable impossibility.

Like a replay of when she was first adopted by the convent, Angelina's black cloud had returned. She became mute, distant, and reclusive. At any hour of day or night, she could be seen walking alone in the gardens of the convent. Concerned over Angelina's troubled state, Rachel sought the advice of the convent's spiritual director, Sister Agnes.

Seated opposite her in the rectory, Rachel started to tell Sister Agnes of Angelina's precarious state. "I implore you," Rachel said emphatically. "We must do something!"

"Calm yourself. It can't be all that bad. Maybe it's just a passing phase—"

"Forgive me," Rachel said, raising her voice. "I beseech you. Angelina is suffering. When she first came to us, she was sad and mute. Through art, she eventually found her voice, both physically and religiously. The beautiful images displayed on the convent walls are a testimony to Angelina's gift. Her God-given talent requires further feeding, nurturing. Without it, her delicate soul will wither and die. I fear this process has already begun."

Sister Agnes listened intently. "I understand. Please go now. Go to Angelina; stay with her. Don't let her out of your sight. Something will be done, I promise."

Alone in her office, Sister Agnes let her thoughts drift back to her own troubled and tormented childhood. She remembered how the church had opened its arms in her time of need.

Raised by servants following her mother's death in childbirth, Agnes's youth, like that of Angelina, was one of isolation and loneliness. Her father, Count Achille Bartolomeo, was more interested in hunting game than in raising a daughter. The two were nothing more than strangers under the same roof. Lonely and alone, Agnes spent her days perusing the religious texts in her father's vast library. It was there that she discovered her true calling. Inspired by His word, Agnes definitively decided to enter the convent and dedicate the rest of her life to God.

Poor Agnes's only obstacle in that pursuit was her father. A Christian by name alone, Count Bartolomeo felt nothing but disdain for the church and what it stood for. Agnes recalled how her father had once slammed the door in the face of a clergyman seeking alms for the poor.

What if he doesn't let me go? After all, he hates the church and everything it stands for, and he has never shown anything but disdain for me.

When Agnes finally built up the courage to confront her father, to her surprise, not only didn't he resist, but no sooner did she tell him of her desire to leave than he instructed his driver to prepare the carriage. The following day, with nothing more than a wave of the hand, the count bid his only daughter a final farewell, and Agnes was off to the Convent of Sacro Cuore, never to hear from her father again.

In the convent, Agnes found peace and tranquility. She rose through the ranks, reaching the position of Mother Superior by the age of twenty-five. When not involved in the administrative responsibilities of the Church, Sister Agnes divided her time between parochial teaching and prayer, trying all the while to keep a finger on the pulse of the community. Her mission was to make Sacro Cuore a sanctuary for the homeless and the needy.

Like most other churches, Sacro Cuore was forever in need of funds. It barely managed to sustain itself through its vineyard, which annually yielded a modest one hundred barrels of wine. Other funds came through personal donations and a paltry stipend from Vatican City.

Sister Agnes contemplated Angelina's plight in silence. She acknowledged that, through her art, Angelina had breathed fresh life into the vacant corridors of Sacro Cuore. The sanctuary pews were now full, thanks more to the congregants coming to view Angelina's stunning artwork than to prayer. Sister Agnes had to act—and soon. Angelina was spiraling into an emotional abyss. She required the kind of help and guidance that the convent could not offer. Sister Agnes now understood that the one place that could give Angelina what she needed was the Accademia Dell'Arte di Trieste. *How can this be accomplished? Sacro Cuore has barely the means to sustain itself, let*

alone fund private study. Attending such an institution would
cost a fortune.

Sister Agnese would do anything in her power to help young Angelina. She thought long and hard, and then it dawned on her. Although estranged from her father, her surname, Bartolomeo, still carried some weight. Agnes Bartolomeo, the daughter of a count, of nobility, had access to the higher orders of Italian society. She would now act on it.

Sister Agnes made a personal appeal to the Bishop of Trieste, Monsignor Francesco Franchetti, to sponsor Angelina at the academy. Several weeks later came his response. Agnes's request was granted. Bishop Franchetti had awarded Sister Angelina Giraldi a full scholarship to the Accademia Dell'Arte di Trieste, beginning immediately.

CHAPTER TEN

As I made my way back to my residence, I pondered the day's events. I wasn't quite sure what to make of Max Deutsch. He was probably on the up-and-up, but I couldn't be sure. And Police Chief Rakovic-some character he was. I shuddered just thinking of my recent "chief of police" experience in Brcko. Each breath I took reminded me of the blade lunging into my chest, splitting my ribs. By the same token, each breath I took reminded me to be at the ready, to be prepared to flee at a moment's notice should my inner sonar signal me to do so. I couldn't think beyond the moment.

Sitting on the side of my bed, I perused the list of refugees under Deutsch's care. Names and addresses were organized in columns. These desperate Jewish souls were housed among the Jewish families of Novi Sad. I thought of the five thousand–year history of the Jewish people. I thought of their impact on civilization as a whole. Never representing more than 2 percent of a population, their contributions far outweighed their number. Moral law, justice, family values, and the sciences were the pillars and foundation of any civilized society. *How, then, could it be that such a small number could elicit so much discomfort, confusion, and hatred?* Living up to the tenets of the Ten Commandments is the obligation of the Jewish people and, thus, is the living reminder to all others to act in kind.

Just as Moses instilled fear and awe among his people as he held the stone tablets before them, the gentile reacts in kind in the presence of the orthodox Jew.

As God's emissaries on earth, Jews are obligated to live up to His higher standards. Through them, He watches from the heavens as irreverent acts are committed the world over. Moral law is the sine qua non for a society to maintain its ethical balance. The origins of Judeo-Christian doctrine hale from the stone tablets, on which these tenets are chiseled. Much like the unruly child who reacts in anger to his father's discipline, so, too, the gentile may react with hate toward the ever-present Jew who bears witness to his straying from the moral path.

We are all well aware of our imperfections. Flaws are part and parcel of human existence. When such flaws are forever reflected back at us through the mirror held before us, generation after generation by one of the "chosen," by the Jew, it generates feelings of repulsion.

Thou shalt not do this; thou shalt not do that.... But why not? After all, it does feel good. I want to covet; I want to lust. But, no, we're not allowed since, at every turn, there is the Jew, the living conscience, policing, watching, and taking note of our misdeeds, our irreverent behavior. *So, what is to be done? Why not just get rid of them?* Of course, yes, let's just kill those Jews once and for all.

The Jew answers to no one but God himself. There is no intermediary. So, by annihilating the Jews, we get rid of all witnesses. God will never know.

Reading through the list that Deutsch gave me, I came upon one Lucien Adler. *Could it be? Could this be the same Lucien, my classmate from the Yeshiva?*

I remembered Lucien as being an easygoing, light-hearted, and not very serious student. He dedicated most of his time to creative writing and chasing girls. He was a rogue who, through his charm, could get away with almost anything. It would be great to see a familiar face. I would seek out Lucien Adler first thing in the morning. It was no sooner than my head touched the pillow that I was fast asleep.

Hours later, I awoke to the warm sensation of sunbeams that were streaming in through the window. I dressed and entered the main area of the house. In the center of the room sat the old man, asleep in his wheelchair. The old woman was standing at the sink in the kitchen area peeling potatoes. Hearing me enter, she wiped her hands and showed me to a small table, where she served me breakfast. We communicated through gestures, as neither of us could speak the other's language. I showed the woman the piece of paper with Lucien's address. She took me by the hand and, from the front door, pointed me in the right direction.

A short time later, I stood in front of a hardware store whose address matched the one on the paper. A bell sounded as I opened the door. Behind the counter was a man on a stepladder organizing items on the shelf. He looked up, smiled, and mumbled something in Serbian

as he climbed down. I said in German that I was looking for Lucien Adler. He looked me up and down and, in
Yiddish, introduced himself as Mayer Levy, the store proprietor. As I began to introduce myself, a man walked in.
I recognized Lucien immediately. He was exactly as I had
remembered him from school—lean, good looking, and
with baby blue eyes.

He squinted at me and said in German, "Ernst Mann?
Is that you?"

"In the flesh," I said.

Lucien then rushed over and gave me a big bear hug.
"It's good to see you. How are you doing? When did you
get here?" Turning to Mr. Levy, Lucien said, "This is my
good buddy from the old country."

I gave him a knowing smirk.

"Let's go for a walk," Lucien said. "I want you to fill
me in on everything." Then, turning to Mr. Levy, he said,
"We'll be back in a bit." Lucien wrapped his arm in mine
as we walked out of the shop.

Lucien described how he had made his way to Novi
Sad from Saltzburg, Austria, where he had been living
since leaving Vienna six years prior. He had studied at the
School of Music and Art and joined the school faculty after
his graduation. Seeing the writing on the wall, his family left Vienna for England in 1938. Believing it was safe,
Lucien remained in Salzburg. Six months later, he nar-
rowly escaped with his life when the Germans overran the
city. He remained in hiding, and finally, through family
contacts, he made his way to Novi Sad as part of Deutsch's
group. Lucien spoke excitedly about the planned exodus

to Palestine. He was thrilled to hear that I might be taking part.

Lucien spoke very highly of his hosts, the Levys. Mayer Levy and his wife, Hanna, had a daughter, Mia, who was in her last year of high school. The Levys enjoyed having Lucien as their houseguest. They treated him like the son they never had. Mia saw Lucien as the brother she always wanted. Their Croatian housekeeper, Goustie, came to Novi Sad seeking a job for the summer. She was hired by the Levys and remained with them ever since. That was ten years before. The rest was history.

Compared to the living standards of her village in Croatia, Goustie lived in the lap of luxury in the Levy household. She grew up sharing one bed with her younger sisters, while she now had her own cozy little room near the kitchen. With her domestic responsibilities fulfilled, Goustie sang in the local glee club and spent her evenings doing needlepoint. Now, at the age of thirty, Goustie accepted the fact that her home was with the Levys. Despite one or two brief affairs, Goustie was most content remaining single, enjoying her place in the Levy "family."

Novi Sad was certainly a lovely town. As Lucien and I walked through the streets, everyone we passed either gave us a nod or friendly salutation. It wasn't long until we had come full circle and found ourselves, once again, at the Levys' store.

Entering, we heard the booming sound of Mr. Levy's voice, "So, Lucien, now that you have your friend, you no longer have time for family?" Levy said jokingly. "I have a good idea—why don't you finish helping me unpack

these supplies, and then you and Ernst can continue talking about old times tonight over dinner. Six o'clock sound
good?" Levy shot me a smile.

"It would be my pleasure. Six o'clock it is," I said as I
took my leave.

Walking back to my residence, I felt happiness for the
first time in I didn't know how long. Seeing Lucien's smiling face helped alleviate a deep loneliness that had been
consuming me ever since my flight from Vienna. The
emotional weight that I had been carrying was starting to
lift. My heart was light, my step buoyant and gay. I envi-
sioned how Lucien and I could continue on together—
whether in a convoy to Palestine or to wherever the winds
of fortune might take us. Having a good companion is far
better then going it alone.

Upon entering the front door of my residence, I found
the old man as before, snoozing quietly in his wheelchair.
The elderly woman blushed as I handed her the bunch of
flowers that I had picked from the side of the road. She
put them in a water-filled vase and positioned it carefully
on a doily in the center of the kitchen table. She gestured
for me to sit. After serving me some tea, she took me to
the next room and drew me a bath. A little while later,
I was submerged to my neck in hot, fragrant water. The
feeling was sublime. I closed my eyes and let each muscle
of my body relax. Lying that way, alone, in that tub of hot
water, the war seemed a million miles away. A draft of cool
air hit me as the door flung open. It was the old woman
who entered, carrying a bucket. Seemingly amused by
my look of embarrassment, she walked over and poured
more steaming hot water into the tub. She laughed as I

tried to cover my nakedness. Then she sat down beside me and began washing my back with a soapy cloth. Realizing the futility of resisting, I decided to relax and be her captive.

I had little trouble choosing what to wear that evening, as my wardrobe consisted of a suit, one pair of slacks, and two shirts. I put on my suit that the landlady was kind enough to press for me. By five thirty, freshly cleaned and dressed, I was off to my date with Lucien and the Levys. I had a wonderful jaunty, jolly feeling as I walked through the streets of Novi Sad. The sun was low in the cloudless sky. The air was fresh. It was a beautiful setting that should have been cause for celebration and joy, but given the circumstances of the time, there was no place for pleasure. The mere consideration of happiness brought forth emotions of both guilt and longing in me. Reality struck. I was on the run, not knowing what I would find at the next turn.

I bought flowers—a pretty combination of azaleas and tulips—from a street vendor and headed for the Levys. The house was a two-level building that was attached to the store. On the second floor was a terrace that overlooked the street below. My knock on the door was answered a moment later by a girl whose beauty took my breath away.

"Hi," she said, smiling as she held out her hand. "You must be Lucien's friend Ernst."

I felt my face redden as I took her hand.

"And you must be Mia," I answered meekly.

Still holding my hand, Mia escorted me into the house, where Mr. Levy was standing alongside the fireplace with Lucien.

"Ernst, come on in," Lucien said, raising a glass. Seeing the flowers in my hand, he said jokingly, "For me? Ernst, you shouldn't have...."

Mr. Levy put down his drink and approached me. "Hello, Ernst, let me take those from you," he said, ignoring Lucien's levity. "Come have a seat while I fix you an aperitif." Mr. Levy turned in the direction of the kitchen. "Hanna, we have company."

Hanna appeared just as I was lowering myself into the sofa. I struggled to rise from the deep seat as Mrs. Levy entered the room.

"Oh, how lovely," she said, seeing the flowers in her husband's hand.

"My pleasure," I said, taking Mrs. Levy's outstretched hand.

We settled into seats around the coffee table. Mr. Levy handed his wife a glass then refilled all the others. It was the perfect setting and the perfect family. I couldn't help but think of my own family. I thought of the evenings in our own salon, my father reading the paper in his worn-out easy chair and my mother playing a soft melody on the piano after putting away the dinner dishes. I remembered how I would tinker with the crystal radio in search of popular music or a variety show and how often I wanted to be somewhere else, doing something adventurous, something exciting. I thought now of how I would give anything to be back in that boring world, that perfect world....

"Hello, Ernst, are you there?" I snapped out of my fog to see Mia waving a handkerchief in front of my face me. "Ernst, are you all right?"

"Why, yes, of course. The drink must have gone to my head," I said, somewhat befuddled.

"The man is starving, and so am I," Mr. Levy announced. "Why don't we eat?"

"Good idea. I'm famished," echoed Lucien.

With that, we all stood and took our places in the dining room. Mr. and Mrs. Levy took their seats at either end of the table. Mia hurried over to sit beside me. Lucien sat opposite us. Goustie served us each steaming hot broth. When she placed the bowl in front of Lucien, I noticed the two of them exchange a quick, familiar look. While tipping his head down to blow into his steamy soup, Lucien looked my way and gave me a confirmatory wink.

"I understand that you've joined up with Deutsch's group," Mr. Levy said while trying to maneuver a hot matzo ball onto his spoon. "I don't know why everyone's on the run," he said. "I take that back. Other parts of Europe are in danger, even some areas of Yugoslavia, but here in Novi Sad, all is well." Levy put down his spoon and, putting on professorial airs, said, "Novi Sad is like the calm eye in the center of a hurricane. You and Lucien would do well to remain right here where you are," Levy said as he sat back contentedly in his chair.

I didn't know what to say. Evidently, both Mr. Levy and Deutsch were blind to the political realities of the time. Granted, Novi Sad seemed peaceful, but I knew only too well that disaster could strike in a flash.

"You see," Levy said, "Novi Sad is unique. We have an unusual ethnic mix here. Our small Jewish community is intertwined in the economic fabric that is comprised primarily of the Serbs and Croats. The Serbs are quite decent and the Croats, although difficult, are, for the most part, congenial. Each group relies on the other, making for a perfect socioeconomic balance."

"OK, that's enough," Hanna said, teasing her husband. "Ernst didn't come here to listen to one of your windy speeches."

"Yes, you're right," Mr. Levy said, raising his hands in a gesture of surrender. "It's just that I'm proud of our city. It has so much to offer." Looking over to us, Levy said, "Mia, tomorrow is Sunday. Why don't you give Ernst a little tour of the town?"

"Oh, Papa," Mia said, "I'm sure Ernst has better things to do than spend the day with me."

"Why, no," I said, turning to Mia, "nothing would give me more pleasure." I felt my heart flutter as I saw the faint smile form on Mia's lips as she lowered her head modestly.

We spent the rest of the evening, talking and laughing. I ate so much that I was ready to burst. After dessert, I could barely move. I was stuffed, and it felt great. When it was time to go, I gave my thanks to the Levys.

Mia then walked me to the door. "I hope that our date is still on," she said in a soft and alluring tone.

"I'll pick you up tomorrow at ten." I took Mia's hand briefly in mine then left.

A light rain was falling on the streets of Novi Sad. The wet cobblestones looked like a sea of gems as they reflected the moonlight from the black sky above. As I hurried back to my residence, I couldn't get Mia out of my thoughts. I was euphoric. She captivated me. Once back in my room, I went straight to bed, realizing that the sooner I went to sleep, the sooner tomorrow would come, and with it, Mia.

I awoke at sunrise after a dreamless, restful sleep. I had four hours until my date with Mia. After going through my rucksack and finding that all my belongings were accounted for, I washed and dressed. I took my time grooming myself, making sure that the part in my hair was just right and each nail filed just so. I took my trousers out from under the mattress, where they spent the night being "pressed" (a trick I learned from my school days), and slipped them on. They looked like new. I put on a fresh shirt, slipped on my jacket, and entered the main room.

While engrossed by my image in the full-length mirror, I was startled by a loud clap. I spun around to see the land-lady looking at me. Her hands were clenched together under her chin, and her head was tilted to one side as she looked me over approvingly. She then took a flower from a vase on the windowsill, snipped down the stem, and placed it in my lapel. She stepped back to admire me, clapped her hands once again, and said, "Perfect!" I gave her a light kiss on the cheek and stepped out into the street.

I soon came upon a breakfast bar called "The Skyscraper." It was busy despite the early hour. It wasn't until I entered the place that I understood how it got its name—the ceiling was so low that anyone standing erect would scrape his or her head. The patrons were made up of farmers who were eating strong-smelling cheese and slices of sausage off of sheets of wax paper. Their pocketknives served as their eating utensils. Portions of bread were cut from a huge loaf. Generous glasses of dark-red wine were poured out of big unlabeled bottles. The customers were huddled together at low, wooden tables in groups of two and three, talking sotto voce, as though formulating dark and devious plans. Everyone ate in a similar manner: a bite of cheese, a slice of sausage, a piece of bread, and then the wine chaser.

My original intention that morning was to have a strong cup of coffee and a biscuit. Watching these men dine made my mouth water. *Why not give this a try?* I thought. *I could have coffee anytime.* I stepped up to the counter. On it were a variety of cheeses and meats as well as several two-liter bottles of red and white wine. I watched as a man behind the counter cut chunks of hard cheese from a large block. He looked up at me as I cleared my throat.

"Yes?" the man said, almost challengingly. His face was ruddy and unshaven. His watery and unsmiling blue eyes gazed back at me from under bushy, brown eyebrows.

In German, as well as through gestures, I told him that I wanted what everyone else was having. He grimaced as he handed me my portion. I took a seat at a table in the corner. The other patrons peered at me with suspicion as I began to eat.

"Prost," I said, raising my glass to the group of men nearby. They nodded, mumbled something, and then turned away. I took a bite of each item on the wax paper, followed by a big gulp of wine. I followed the sequence a couple more times. The wine coursed rapidly through my veins, giving me a warm and delightful feeling. When I stood, my head began to spin. I grabbed the back of my chair for support until I regained my equilibrium. I heard some of the men chuckle as I slowly navigated my way out of the bar.

Once in the street, the fresh morning air helped in clearing my head. I floated more than walked to the Levy house. When I arrived, Mia and Lucien were sitting on the front stairs waiting for me.

"Hello, Ernst, fancy meeting you here," Lucien said with a smirk.

Mia jumped to her feet. "This is going to be so much fun," she said as I approached. "Wait here one minute; I'll be right back."

"She's really taken by you. She's a wonderful girl—not my type, of course. I prefer older women," Lucien said as we watched Mia run into the house. "The Levys are quite good people. They make me feel like I'm a favorite cousin. I've been helping Mr. Levy in the store. He has told me that my being here has helped him enormously. He now has time to solicit prospective customers and have some well-deserved free time." Lucien drew me close and said quietly, "I don't know if you noticed, but I've been having a little fling with the housekeeper."

Just then, Mia returned carrying a wicker picnic basket and a blanket. "Here, this is for you," Mia said as she handed me the blanket. "And this is for you," she added, giving the basket to Lucien. Mia, taking a position between the two of us, locked her arms in both of ours and, looking to Lucien and then to me, said, "Here we are, the three musketeers, all for one and one for all, off on an exciting adventure."

We skipped off merrily as if we hadn't a care in the world.

As the three of us walked through town, I began to think of my situation. I was certainly taken by this girl, but my circumstances really weren't suited for romance. Here I was, a refugee on the run who, to date, had managed to survive by virtue of his cunning and good fortune. I could ill afford to put myself, or the Levy family, in jeopardy by having a courtship with Mia. *Then again*, I thought, *what harm could there be in the pursuit of a bit of happiness?*

We headed down the main street that led to a large portico at the northern end of town. From that vantage point one could make out the beautiful countryside below.

"That's where we're heading," Mia declared. "Beyond that group of trees is the lake. If we keep up a good pace, we should be there in less than an hour. Let's move on."

Mia looked wonderful. Her hair was pulled back in a ponytail. She was wearing a simple linen shirt and long khaki shorts. She and Lucien were both wearing ankle-high walking shoes. I made a mental note to get a similar pair for myself.

The conversation was light. We connected like old friends reunited, exchanging stories and vignettes. Mia's words, her tone, the shape of her mouth, and her smile all enthralled me. At last, we entered a windy dirt road that opened to the sandy shores of a large lake. A light breeze created a soft rippling effect on the water's surface. A half-mile off shore, a small fishing boat was bobbing lazily in place.

We unfolded the blanket in a shaded area among a grouping of pine trees. I suddenly felt the effects of the wine, the sun, and the long walk. My head was swimming, and my legs felt like rubber. I quickly sat down on the blanket.

"I'll race you two to the lake," Mia said excitedly. "On second thought...Why, Ernst, you don't look very good," she said, staring down at me.

"I'm just a little tired. Why don't you two go on, I'll just close my eyes for a few minutes."

"All right, we'll be back in a little while to check on you."

I stretched out on my back, my arms folded behind my head, and stared up at the distant blue sky.

"You steady the boat, and I'll grab her hand," the man said, his back turned to me.

I stood in the shallow water as the man hoisted Mia into the big rowboat.

"Push us off," he said, "then you jump in."

With both hands, I shoved the back end of the boat as hard as I could. At the same time, the man, holding the oar firmly in both hands, dug into the soft lake floor, catapulting the boat forward. I tried in vain to keep up. The harder I tried to run in the waist-deep water, the slower I moved. All I could see of Mia was the back of her head as the boat drifted away. A thick fog was settling on to the lake. The man turned and faced me. He had a cold, sinister smile. Icy, blue eyes looked back at me from under bushy, brown eyebrows. It was the man from the breakfast bar. He was wearing a long bloodstained apron. He laughed loudly. The fog grew thicker. I could barely make out Mia's silhouette. I watched helplessly as the boat drifted off then disappeared.

I heard a grunt. It was my own snore that awoke me. Mia was sitting beside me teary-eyed from laughing.

"That must have been some dream," she said. Mia was sitting cross-legged beside me on the blanket. "You were fast asleep the moment you closed your eyes. I didn't have the heart to wake you. Here, have some of these—they're delicious." Mia was holding a cup of raspberries. "I collected them while you were asleep."

"Where is Lucien?" I asked, looking around.

"You're not going to believe it," Mia whispered. "Goustie showed up soon after we arrived. She and Lucien are taking a walk around the lake. Did you know that Lucien and Goustie are having a secret romance?"

"Lucien hinted as much." I studied Mia's face. *My oh my is she beautiful.* I raised myself up on my elbows and watched as Mia bit into a juicy raspberry.

Her eyes closed, and her lips puckered as she swirled the pungent fruit in her mouth. "Mmm," she cooed, savoring the taste. Mia then reached over and put a raspberry to my lips.

Embarrassed, I took it between my teeth then swallowed it whole. Mia looked back at me, glowing with satisfaction. As I continued to gaze at her I wondered, *Who is this girl? I'm totally smitten, and I hardly even know her.*

I leaned over and kissed Mia full on the mouth. To my surprise, she didn't pull away. We held the kiss for a few seconds.

Then Mia jumped to her feet. "Let's go explore," she said as she ran off toward the lake.

I managed to regain my bearings then took off after her.

We walked barefoot along the rolling shoreline, tap-dancing in pace with the tide's rhythmic ebb and flow.

The joy I felt was overshadowed by a sensation of guilt, like I had no right to experience pleasure while my family was in danger. God only knew what became of my parents, Nelly, and poor little Yankl. *What was I doing? This was not the time to get entangled with this girl. What right did I have to fall in love? Where would it lead? I could be putting Mia and her family in danger.* I needed to be free to move at a moment's notice. I had to direct all my energy on survival. I had to keep a clear and level head.

"Let's eat. I'm famished," Mia said as she bolted off in the direction of the blanket. She uncovered the picnic basket and emptied out its contents. We ate cold brisket sandwiches, followed by juicy peaches and sweet, overripe plums. From the distance we heard someone calling out to us. It was Lucien waving from a boat just offshore. We ran up to the water. Lucien, Goustie, and two men were calling to us and waving from a small fishing boat. Lucien then dove off and swam to shore, while the others continued to howl with laughter.

"We met two of Goustie's friends at the cove about a mile south of here," Lucien said, all excited. "They invited us on their boat to snorkel. Come join us. The water's fine."

"Yoo hoo," Goustie said as she waved us to come along.

"Why don't you go on without me," I said. "It's getting late, and I need to get back to town."

Mia mimicked my sentiment. "Have fun," she said. "We'll meet you two back at the house later."

"Whatever you say," Lucien said. "See you later."

Mia and I waved from the shore as the boat drifted away.

We packed up and headed back to town. Walking beside Mia, I made a conscious effort to keep a proper and respectable distance. By the time we reached the Levy house, the sun was starting to set. Hanna Levy greeted us at the front door.

"Did you kids have a good time?" Mrs. Levy asked with a wide smile.

"Oh, yes, Mama, it was wonderful," Mia answered enthusiastically. "We spent the day at the lake. The weather was perfect."

"It certainly was. Mia was the perfect guide."

"Why, look at you, you're soaked," Mrs. Levy said, looking at my wet and wrinkled trousers.

"It's no big deal. As soon as I get home, I'll hang them on the line to dry."

"You'll do nothing of the sort. I'll dry them. In the meanwhile, I'll give you a pair of my husband's pants to wear. Come in before you catch your death."

I hesitated for a moment then Mia said, "You had better do as my mother says." She smiled. "It's no use arguing with Hanna Levy. She always gets her way."

"Seeing that I'm outnumbered, I'll have to give in. Thank you, Mrs. Levy." I put on a pair of Mr. Levy's pants. They were too big, but it didn't matter. I gave Mrs. Levy my wet pants and joined Mia and Mr. Levy in the living room.

Mr. Levy sat back in his armchair and said, "So, how did you like our little town? Pleasant, no?"

"It certainly is. Yet, for the life of me, I can't understand how anyone can get any work done if they breakfast on such a strong brew."

"What do you mean?" asked Mr. Levy.

"Ernst had breakfast this morning at The Skyscraper," Mia said with a laugh.

Mr. Levy took on a serious air. Then, in a quiet voice, he said, "You happened into the one place that is to be avoided. That bar is a Croatian hangout. Not that all Croats are bad, of course, but The Skyscraper is the meeting place for the more sinister politicos. The proprietor, Ante Budak is their leader." Mr. Levy leaned over and poured me some tea and then replenished his own cup. He then filled his pipe with fresh tobacco, struck a match, and puffed several times to assure a proper burn. He leaned back in his armchair, blew out a plume of blue, aromatic smoke, and said, "These Croats are always making a lot of noise about this and that. They're mostly all talk. They profess to be Nazi sympathizers. Now that the Germans are making inroads in Yugoslavia, they might well call upon the Croats to do their dirty work. One good thing is that the local government is made up predominantly of Serbs. That should be enough to quell any Croatian uprising." Mr. Levy took another puff on his pipe, glowing with pride by his erudite summation of the political situation of the day.

Mrs. Levy entered the room. "That should do it. Good as new," she said as she handed me my slacks, warm and ironed. "Go change. Dinner will be ready in just a few minutes."

"Why, thank you, but I have imposed enough. It's late, and I must be going."

"Are you sure?" Mia said. "No one cooks better than Mama."

"Yes, I'm sure," I said, rising to leave. "Thanks once again for showing me such a wonderful time."

Mia walked me to the door. "I mean it, Mia. Today was the best time that I can remember. Please also thank Lucien for me."

I took an indirect path back to my residence, following the road that circumvented a pretty duck pond. It was a beautiful setting. Walking past the small bridge that spanned the pond, I spied Goustie and Lucien kissing in close embrace. Turning to move on, I nearly bumped into the mustachioed proprietor of the Skyscraper café, Ante Budak. I noticed that he saw the two lovers as well.

"Oh, hello there," I said. "My compliments-that certainly was a tasty breakfast."

Budak shot me a cold smile. With pursed lips, he said, "Yes, yes," and continued on his way. His remark and icy glare sent a chill straight through to my bones.

I hurried to my room. Under the door was an envelope with my name on it. In it was a note from the office of Police Chief Rakovic, requesting that I be in his office first thing in the morning. I couldn't help but fear the worst.

I sat on my bed to get my bearings. *Is this the beginning of the end?* I wondered. I pictured undergoing an interrogation followed by imprisonment. *On the other hand, why wouldn't the police chief want to meet with me? After all, I was Deutsch's agent in Novi Sad, was I not? Rakovic most likely wanted to make sure that no new problems had arisen in the community. He may have gotten news from Deutsch.* My mind was in a tizzy. *Maybe this was the moment to escape. If so, where was I to go? It was Deutsch who put me in this position.* I wondered if he could really be trusted. *How was I to be sure?* Deutsch appeared to be sincere in his desire to help the poor refugees, but by the same token, he was just a stone's throw from being a refugee himself. *How naïve was he to believe that his life was not in jeopardy?* I witnessed with my own eyes what befell Vienna and Brcko. I had the premonition that these peaceful days in Novi Sad would soon come to an end, that this was the calm before the storm.

As I sat in my little room and contemplated my lot, I decided that it was best to sit tight and see how this would play out.

I slept little that night. My mind swam with visions of Mia, her family, happy-go-lucky Lucien, the surly patrons at the Skyscraper, Deutsch, and the drunken Chief Rakovic. It felt as if we were all characters in a Shakespearean tragedy and that my part had yet to be written.

Early the next morning, I headed directly for the police station. The officer behind a desk looked up lazily and pointed me in the direction of Rakovic's office.

"Come," Rakovic hollered as I knocked on the door. The room smelled of tobacco. Rakovic was staring out the window, fiddling with his cigar. "What on earth am I to do with you refugees," Rakovic said without turning around.

I didn't respond.

Rakovic picked up a paper from his desk, gave it a cursory look, and then tossed it. "We received a complaint from one of our citizens regarding the improper behavior of one of our Jewish *guests*." He stressed the last word, baring his teeth in disdain. Rakovic then sat behind his desk and motioned for me to sit as well. "There have been reports that a certain Lucien Adler was seen embracing one of our female residents." Rakovic gave me a side-glance, his eyebrows raised as though daring me to apologize for Lucien's "criminal" activity.

I looked at him square on and didn't say anything.

Rakovic then said, "This is shameful, wouldn't you agree?"

I bit my lip, trying not to react.

"Well then," Rakovic said as he cleared his throat, "I have summoned Deutsch to return to Novi Sad as soon as possible to deal with this matter. You're free to go."

The brief meeting with Rakovic left me with an odd and curious feeling. It had become clear to me that not only the Jewish refugees, but the entire Jewish population of Novi Sad was doomed. As I reflected on the events of the past two days—the Croats plotting in the breakfast bar, the cold and sinister look of Budak, and now Rakovic's ridiculous remark—my chest tightened and I sensed a cold sweat forming on my brow. These refugees, or "guests," as Rakovic called them, were like sheep awaiting their slaughter. It wasn't whether disaster would strike but when. I would await Deutsch's return before making any move.

Trying to keep a low profile, I stayed in or near my residence for the rest of the day. I distracted myself by assisting my landlady with some of the house chores. She handed me a broom, and I was off, sweeping feverishly throughout the house. While sweeping along the main corridor, I noticed a lovely mahogany cabinet with several dozen books arranged neatly on the shelves. Seeing me admiring the display, the landlady urged me to select any book that I desired. I resisted her generosity, but she insisted. I had to laugh, as the books were of little use to me since they

were all written in Serbo-Croatian. The woman pointed
to one book that was sitting high up on the top shelf. It
was a first-edition volume of American poetry that was in
near-flawless condition. I took it off the shelf and handed
it to her. Together, we walked into the main room, where
we sat, side by side, on the sofa.

The old woman opened the book. On the first page
was an inscription written in English: *To my dearest Zorisa,
with love, your brother, Boris.* The woman slowly explained
that her brother, Boris, had given her the book while
home on summer vacation. The year was 1914. Boris had
just completed his first year as a student of literature at
the University of Sarajevo. It was several weeks later, at the
outbreak of World War I, that Boris was killed in a violent
student demonstration.

The old woman looked at me with sad, teary eyes. She
told me of how much I resembled her brother and of how
shocked she was when I had first walked through the door.
I took her hands and held them in mine. Her wrinkled
face reflected a life of sorrow, each line a testament to
battles won and lost. I told her that I would enjoy reading
the book during my stay but that under no circumstances
should it ever leave her home. The woman went to the
kitchen and returned with a bowl of fruit for me to take
back to my room. She thanked me with a glowing smile
and insisted that I call her by her first name, Zorisa.

I returned to my room and placed the book on my
table. Taking a handful of grapes, I randomly opened the
book to somewhere in the middle. Before me was a poem
by Henry Wadsworth Longfellow. I sat at the open window
and began to read:

The Jewish Cemetery at Newport

How strange it seems! These Hebrews in their graves,
Close by the street of this fair seaport town,
Silent beside the never-silent waves,
At rest in all this moving up and down!

The trees are white with dust, that o'er their sleep
Wave their broad curtains in the southwind's breath,
While underneath these leafy tents they keep
The long, mysterious Exodus of Death.

And these sepulchral stones, so old and brown,
That pave with level flags their burial-place,
Seem like the tablets of the Law, thrown down
And broken by Moses at the mountain's base.

The very names recorded here are strange,
Of foreign accent, and of different climes;
Alvares and Rivera interchange
With Abraham and Jacob of old times.

Blessed be God! For he created Death!"
The mourners said, "and Death is rest and peace;"
Then added, in the certainty of faith,
"And giveth Life that nevermore shall cease."

Closed are the portals of their Synagogue,
No Psalms of David now the silence break,
No Rabbi reads the ancient Decalogue
In the grand dialect the Prophets spake.

Gone are the living, but the dead remain,
And not neglected; for a hand unseen,
Scattering its bounty, like a summer rain,
Still keeps their graves and their remembrance
green...

Moved by Longfellow's words, I paused, took a breath, and contemplated my situation. The poem, written a hundred and fifty years before, was a sad commentary on the plight of the Jew. *Was Longfellow on the mark when he wrote for the Jews that rest and peace could only be found in death? Oh God,* I cried to myself. *Was my macabre adventure just another example of what my people have been through and will forever be subjected to while on this earth? If so, when will this maze of horror, this madding journey ever come to an end?*

Sitting at the desk, my head propped in my hands, I gazed up at the sky above and wondered, *If the clouds could speak, would they one day testify to my plight or is nature just a cold, passive, and dispassionate bystander?*

While pondering these thoughts, I was suddenly brought back to earth by a knocking sound. I jumped to open the door, and standing before me was Mia. She stood facing me, her arms dangling at her sides. The expression on her face was one of sadness and longing. Without a word, I took her in my arms and held her fast. Mia's embrace was the healing salve to all my aching wounds. I cupped her face in both of my hands and drew her to me. As we kissed I could taste the salty tears running down her face.

Mia gave herself to me willingly and tenderly. As we lay listless in each other's arms, a cool breeze drifted through the open window. A light sun shower cast a soft mist in the air. Our passion transcended both time and space as our souls became one on that late summer day.

"Take me with you," Mia said, breaking the silence. She sat up and looked me square in the eye. "Time is of the essence. I know it, just as you do. My father doesn't recognize what is happening. He and everyone else are blind. Oh, Ernst, when I first met you, I was struck by the strong sense that I knew you. It seems strange, I know, but it's true."

Just as I was about to respond, Mia cut me off.

"No," she said as she wrapped the blanket over her shoulders. Her light-brown hair shimmered in the soft light; her brilliant brown eyes were intense and stunning. "It's all so clear to me," she said in a sob. "We have very little time—I can feel it."

I wanted so much to pour my heart out and tell Mia how I felt, but it wasn't possible. *How could I?* I was alone, a fugitive on the run. The entire Jewish population of Novi Sad was all in the same dire predicament. *Was it egotistical of me to think of myself and myself alone? My family had succumbed, my loved ones gone, and now Mia. How could I possibly bring her into my life? She would have been better off never meeting me, and now she is a part of me.* My head swirled. I wanted so much to declare my love out loud, but it was no use. Perhaps in another time or place, but certainly, not now. *How could I envision a life with Mia if I couldn't see beyond that very day?*

I hesitated then said, "Max Deutsch is on his way to Novi Sad. As you know, he is making the final arrangements for our exodus to Palestine." *How ridiculous—the group wouldn't stand a chance. Alone, I have barely been able to stay one step ahead of the angel of death. Imagine a group of sixty.* "My idea," I said, "is that the three of us—you, me and Lucien—go it alone. Quite possibly, with Max's help, we might find our way to safety." Why I said this I'll never know.

Mia wrapped her arms around my neck so hard that it hurt. "Yes, yes," Mia said excitedly. "We'll go together—all for one and one for all, just like the three musketeers." Mia's smile lit up the room. She seemed so precious and innocent that I wanted to cry.

What was I saying? Why on earth was I leading Mia on in this way? I knew very well that I needed to flee alone.

It was getting late. I told Mia to go home and wait for me to contact her. I wanted to stay put, as Deutsch was due to arrive at anytime. I had a horrible premonition that things were about to change, and not for the better.

I remained in my room through the following day, leaving only briefly to get some fresh air. I passed the hours either reading or simply daydreaming. While leafing through the poetry book, I became suddenly fatigued. Too lazy to walk over to my bed, I pillowed my head with my arms and took a catnap at my desk.

Not five minutes had passed when I was awakened by the sound of voices. I made out Zorisa's voice. She seemed upset. The other was a man barking orders. My door swung open, and before me stood two policemen. Zorisa was standing behind them crying.

One of the policemen walked toward me. "Ernst Mann?" he barked, more as a statement than a question.

The other one, a big, fat man, remained near the open door. I noticed that he had one hand poised on the pistol in his side-holster.

"Yes, I am Ernst Mann," I said quietly. He waved his hand in the direction of the door and said, "You will come with us." He stepped to one side, allowing me to pass. "Oh yes," he continued, "take along your personal items." I kept quiet and did as he said. I grabbed my rucksack and walked out of the room.

Zorisa was standing in the hallway crying into a hand-kerchief. She touched my arm as I walked past her.

We marched through the streets in single file. Bystanders looked at us with suspicion. Strangely enough, I wasn't the least bit concerned. I felt completely at peace with my fate.

When we entered police headquarters, my escorts pointed to the back of the room. There, engaged in con-versation, were Chief Rakovic and Max Deutsch.

Deutsch looked at me and said in a matter of fact tone, "Come with me."

I followed them into Rakovic's office. Standing alone in the middle of the room was Lucien. He gave me a quiz-zical look and shrugged his shoulders.

"I'm gone not two days and you bring shame upon us all?" Deutsch said angrily. Then, turning to Lucien, he said, "You're a guest. How dare you act in such a disgrace-ful manner?"

"May I ask to what you are referring?" I said calmly.

Deutsch pointed his finger at Lucien and, like a court prosecutor, said, "We have a witness that has testified that he saw you, Lucien Adler, kissing a local woman in public!"

Just then, I noticed none other than Ante Budak sitting crossed-legged in a chair at the other end of the room. He was smoking casually, taking in the scene, clearly amused.

I couldn't believe my ears. *Were these people crazy?* Not knowing whether to laugh or cry, I lit a cigarette and took a long, deep drag and waited to see how this was going to play out.

Deutsch then pointed his finger at me and yelled, "And you, Ernst, how could you allow this to take place after all that we have done for you? Have you no decency?"

I couldn't believe my ears. I saw red. *How dare he speak to us in such a manner? Was it to appease Rakovic or simply to feed his own stupid ego? He accuses Lucien of a crime? Since when is kissing a woman a criminal act?* I looked at Deutsch with utter disgust. I thought of the poor Jewish refugees of Novi Sad who had to suffer humiliation by the likes of such a miserable man. I wanted to scream. My heart pounded so strongly I thought it would explode.

Rakovic didn't utter a word. He had a smug look on his face, clearly enjoying the scene. I had to bite my lip, so as not to react.

While listening to Deutsch's ridiculous tirade, little did I know that the cigarette I was holding was burning a hole in my jacket. I could smell the burning wool. To everyone's amusement, I swatted wildly at the burning material, but it was of no use. It was too late. The cigarette had already burned a gaping two-inch hole, and I saw red.

What happened next occurred in a flash. Seeing the amused faces of Rakovic and Deutsch, I lost all control. The anger and frustration that was building up inside me quickly surfaced. Like a hungry grizzly bear poised to crush his cornered prey, I raised my fists and, in a furious rage, yelled, "*Jebite Se* (fuck you)!"

Deutsch and Rakovic were stunned. Their mouths agape, they both stared at me in disbelief. I lowered my arms to my sides and unclenched my fists. I was still panting, but I felt relieved.

Deutsch squinted at me angrily. He turned to Rakovic and said in a quiet voice, "Do with them as you wish, but make sure the punishment fits the crime."

Yelling as I did lifted a burden from my chest. At the time, it seemed almost worth it in spite of what was to follow. Deutsch glanced at us dismissively and left the room. A moment later, the two officers who had picked me up earlier were back.

"Cuff them and take them away," Rakovic ordered. He watched with satisfaction as the policemen snapped the cuffs behind our backs and took us to a jail cell in the rear of the building.

CHAPTER ELEVEN

Still handcuffed, the soldiers pushed us into the cell and slammed the door behind us. Aside for two small army cots, the cell was empty.

"Well done, Ernst," Lucien said with a boyish grin as we flopped awkwardly onto the cots. "You certainly have a way with words. Now what do we do?"

I looked at Lucien's fine features. He still looked like a kid. As teenagers we attended the same school but had a different circle of friends. Lucien was a remarkably good soccer player and the ladies' man. I recall seeing him after winning a match surrounded by several girls, one prettier than the next. Sports had never been my strong suit, and meeting girls never came easily. Thinking back, I had always been a bit jealous of him.

"What can we do?" I said. "We have no choice but to sit tight. No matter what, I still believe that Deutsch is on our side. In his own pompous and stupid way, I believe that he was just trying to impress Rakovic."

Lucien looked at me, unable to hide his concern. "I just hope you're right."

A guard brought us a bowl of lukewarm soup and a piece of bread. Thankfully, he removed our handcuffs. We ate in silence, finishing every last morsel. The cell was musty and damp. The only light was that which came through a window on the far side of the room. With nothing else to do, we curled up on our cots and tried to sleep.

We awoke the following morning to the sound of keys in the lock. It was Rakovic.

"Good morning, gentleman, I hope you slept well. It's time to go. Please follow me."

Rakovic led us out to a small courtyard at the back of the building. There was a horse-drawn wagon with a driver. "Climb in and sit on the floor," Rakovic ordered. Save for some hay spread on the floor, the wagon was empty. Rakovic reached in and handcuffed Lucien and me to the side-rails. He gave the cuffs a jolt to ensure that they were secure and said, "There, that ought to do it." Rakovic folded his arms across his chest and condescendingly said, "You gentlemen are about to take a little trip. I promise you it will be an adventure, an education of sorts." He then began pacing back and forth. He continued speaking to no one in particular. "You Jews believe that you're so smart. I don't know why we bother putting up with you. Yes, the money's good, that's for sure, but that won't last much longer. Your days are numbered anyway. Those *Ustasa* bastards (insurgent Croation nationalist separatist terrorist organization) are planning something good; I can feel it in my bones." Rakovic's voice dropped off. He stood in place, swaying slightly from side to side. He must have been drinking. His eyes were teary and bloodshot.

All the while, Lucien and I sat cowering on the floor of the wagon.

"You're going off on a little holiday to Tuzla," Rakovic said with a chuckle. "You'll be back in a week, that is, if the filthy Muslims don't kill you first. Who knows, they just may decide to use your heads as polo balls. Nachi will be keeping a close watch on you, won't you, Nachi?"

The driver nodded and gave Rakovic a casual salute with his index finger.

"I have all of your belongings locked in my office. They will be returned to you when, or rather, if, you make it back in one piece. Oh, one more thing—I will be keeping a watch on the Levys and especially on pretty young Mia."

Rakovic's remark sent a shiver down my spine.

With one smack of the reins, we were off. We drove through the streets of Novi Sad at a slow, but steady pace. Before long, we reached the outskirts of town and the same dusty road where I walked with Mia just two days before. As we passed the lake road, I stared with longing as the silvery-blue water flickered in and out of view through the leafy, green trees. Farmhands looked up, scratching their heads in dismay at the sight of the passing wagon with the two men shackled inside.

I asked myself how I managed to get into such a mess. I thought of lovely Mia and wondered if I would ever see her again.

After an hour or so, the wagon came to a halt. Nachi jumped off the carriage, opened his trousers, and with one hand holding his penis and the other on his hip, he relieved himself on the side of the road. He buttoned up, came to the back, unlocked our handcuffs, and smiling for the first time, let us sit up front with him.

"Just a minute," Lucien said as he jumped down from the wagon. We laughed as he undid his trousers and, mimicking Nachi, relieved himself with similar flair.

Lucien and I took our seats on either side of Nachi. He told us that he was on his way to Tuzla to spend some time with his sister who was recently married. Our going along with him had been Deutsch's idea. He was instructed to do nothing more than give us a little scare then ease up. He was aware that we weren't dangerous criminals and that the handcuffs were just for show.

"You'll still need to be careful. Tuzla is a dangerous town—full of Muslims. I'm safe since my sister married one of them. You two will need to be on your guard."

We arrived in Tuzla several hours later. Nachi was right; it was a frightful place. Dark, surly men roamed the streets. The few women we saw were covered from head to toe in burkas. We rode through the main square, passing the minaret and dome-roofed mosque. We heard the chanting of the call to prayer resonating through the alleyways. The buildings were rundown, and the streets were filled with garbage and refuse. Barefooted children ran, laughing and screaming, behind our wagon.

Nachi parked in front of a simple house with faded-blue shutters. A heavyset young woman was standing at the entrance. Noticing Nachi, she ran up to the wagon, smiling broadly. Nachi jumped down and was immediately enveloped in her open arms. As Nachi walked with her into the house, the woman looked back at us with suspicion. Noticing this, Nachi whispered something in her ear then motioned to us to remain where we were. Several minutes later, he returned carrying two large sacks. He tossed them into the wagon and climbed up into his seat. With a brisk slap of the reins, we were once again on our way.

"That was my sister," Nachi said, looking straight ahead. "She's nice, but she doesn't like strangers. The safest thing for you is to camp out in the fields."

Lucien and I shot glances at one another, shrugged our shoulders, and made no comment. We rode out of the town, and before long, we were in a beautiful, grass-filled meadow. With great care, Nachi wended his way through the foliage until we finally came to the bank of a river. We followed it for a quarter mile to where it angled off and widened. Large, jagged rocks broke through the water's surface, redirecting the stream into foaming, splashing rapids. The rushing water created a fine mist that, along with the radiating sunlight, created a colorful rainbow.

"This is as good a place as any," Nachi said, bringing the wagon to a halt. "Now help me unload those bundles from the back." Nachi stood with his hands on his hips and looked around in every direction. "This is where you will camp. In those bags you'll find everything you will need. I recommend that you don't wander too far. Sleep with one eye open; better yet, sleep in turn. If anyone catches you out here, they'll kill you without asking any questions. I'll be back one week from today at daybreak. You won't be able to reach me, so be careful."

With that, Nachi climbed back into the wagon and rode away.

"Hey, come over here and see this," called Lucien. He was sitting on a boulder staring into the river. Through the crystal clear water one could see fish swimming in all directions. Lucien stood up and took in a deep breath. He stretched out his arms and said, "You know, Ernst, this punishment of ours just might turn out to be a pleasant experience."

We emptied the bags and spread its contents on the ground. In one bag were two sleeping blankets, a frying pan, two tin cups, two spoons, a box of matches, and a ball of yarn with a fishing hook attached. In the other bag were a large, round loaf of bread, two feet in diameter, and a block of hard cheese.

Lucien and I tucked our paraphernalia away in a small alcove that was formed by some bushes and trees. The bushes were lush with berries that were free for the picking. Lucien and I decided to make the most of our little holiday. We passed the days hiking and swimming. We drank to our heart's content from the clear river water and feasted on the fish that we caught using bread as bait. Lucien was right; our punishment did, in fact, turn out to be a very pleasant experience. The days were hot and sunny, but once the sun set behind the western hills, the temperature dropped precipitously. Thank goodness for Nachi's sleeping blankets. Although they were thin and worn, they kept us from catching our death.

Early one morning, we were awakened by the whinny of horses. Nachi had returned. The week had passed in no time.

"I can see that the outing did you good," Nachi said as he stared down at us. "Come on, pack up your things. We've got to get a move on."

In no time at all, we were on our way back to Novi Sad.

"I can see by your rosy cheeks that you had quite the time. I'm sorry that I didn't join you."

"How was your visit with your sister?" I asked.

"It was good. I made some money."

Nachi told us that his brother-in-law owned a small coffee bar. On his visits to Tuzla, Nachi would work a few hours a day delivering cups of coffee and biscuits to the local merchants.

"Here, have some of this." Nachi reached back and handed me a newspaper-wrapped bundle.

As soon as I opened it, I was struck by a mouth-watering aroma—a mixture of cinnamon, honey, and pistachio. The cakes were still warm. We each took a large piece, sat back, and munched heartily as the wagon rolled through the beautiful Bosnian countryside.

CHAPTER TWELVE

As we neared the north portico of Novi Sad, the horses started to become restless. By the time we entered the city proper, they were bucking wildly. Nachi exhausted all of his strength and talents in an effort to calm the horses down and bring the wagon to a halt.

A heavy, eerie feeling filled the air. We heard the muffled sounds of voices, which gave the impression that a gathering or rally was taking place somewhere off in the distance.

We climbed down from the wagon and continued on foot. There wasn't a soul in sight. As we continued toward the city center, the sounds gradually became more distinct. Turning a corner, we were stopped dead in our tracks, as everything became brutally clear. The noise that we heard was the agonizing screams of torture.

When I was a child, my parents told me stories of the pogroms of Eastern Europe. They were murderous rampages that were carried out by the town thugs against its Jewish population. The attacks were utilized by the local government as a ploy to draw attention away from their own corruption and toward the universal scapegoat—the Jew

The world is round, and time goes full circle. As much as things change, so they, too, remain the same. Since time immemorial, man's inhumanity to man has been the theme of the cosmos. Live and let live, kill or be killed are mere clichés. Since hunting *is* a popular pastime, why should it be a surprise that man hunts man?

Theologies the world over share one thing in common: a higher power, an almighty that is in control of man's destiny. Among other things, man prays to God for mercy, health, happiness, and well-being. We pray to remain on His good side. When a loved one dies, it is often accepted as being "God's will." One aspect of the Judeo-Christian belief is that we were created in His image. If God controls our destiny, if He decides who is to live and who is to die, then it follows that man, created in God's image, should also decide who is to live and who is to die.

We peered over a low wall of an abandoned garage. Not five hundred yards from where we stood was a sight that haunts me to this very day: Hundreds of mutilated corpses were scattered throughout an open lot. It was obvious that the killing was indiscriminate. Bodies lay this way and that. Some were in heaps, piled one upon of the other. There were men and women. They included the elderly, the young, children, and even infants. On one of the mutilated bodies I could make out the torn undergarment of the orthodox Jew. I felt sick to my stomach.

We looked on with mouths agape at the beheaded, dismembered, eviscerated, and disemboweled. The ground was muddied in blood. It was a site so horrific that had I not seen it with my own eyes, I wouldn't have believed that such an atrocity was even possible.

Nachi dropped to the ground and leaned against the wall. He was breathing rapidly. He shielded his eyes with his arm and said in a low voice, "*Ustasa* bastards. I saw this day coming."

I remembered Levy telling me of the *Ustasa* and their leader, Ante Budak. "Do you really believe that the *Ustasa* did this?"

"Rakovic had suspected it all along. He believed that their leader, Ante Budak, had been planning this for months, but we didn't have solid proof. As you can see, Rakovic was right. They're vicious animals. While other species kill for survival and man for sport, these beasts torture, mutilate, and kill for pleasure." Nachi raised himself to his knees and peered over the wall. "Among these Jews are some of my brothers. I know those bastards well. Once they've gotten a taste of blood, they won't stop until they've killed each and every Serb and Muslim as well."

In my mind, I could see the thin face and the cold, blue eyes looking back at me from behind the counter of the Skyscraper. I remembered the patrons who leered at me with suspicion as I sat among them eating my breakfast. My heart stopped as Mia came to mind. I feared the worst. I then remembered my daydream at the lake, how I struggled to push the boat out to sea, out to oblivion with Mia and Budak on board. I couldn't erase Budak's murderous face from my mind.

Rising to his feet, Nachi said, "Come, let's get the hell out of here."

"No," I said, leveling my gaze squarely into his eyes. "I must get back to the police station. I can't leave Novi Sad without my papers. With any luck, they will still be somewhere in Rakovic's office."

After a moment's reflection, Nachi reluctantly agreed and said, "OK, let's go."

Nachi led us through the back streets of Novi Sad. We tried to remain unseen by darting from one doorway to the next. We could hear cries and screams echoing from a distance. After a good while, we found ourselves in the courtyard behind the police station. From our vantage point, we saw that the door to the building was ajar.

Nachi sprinted across the yard then signaled us to follow him inside. On the landing in a stairwell was the dead body of a policeman. He was lying in a pool of blood with half his head blown off. We stepped over the body and made our way to Rakovic's office. We found Rakovic sitting at his desk, staring at the ceiling. He wasn't moving. Scrutinizing him more closely, we saw the bullet hole in his forehead. Off to the side of the room was Deutsch, lying facedown on the floor. He had been shot in the back.

"Oh God, oh God," Lucien moaned as he took in the macabre sight. He rushed from the room and vomited in the hallway.

There was no time to lose. I dashed through Rakovic's office in a desperate search for my rucksack. I looked everywhere, but it was nowhere in sight. Deep inside a closet, attached to the floor, was a safe whose door had been broken open. It was empty.

I was desperate. Lucien was sitting on the floor moaning. Nachi was clearly losing his patience. Then it hit me.

Rakovic had pointed to his desk when I handed over my rucksack to him one week before. Nachi helped me push Rakovic's body off to one side, so as to get to the desk drawers. Evidently, the closet safe had contained what the killers were looking for. The desk hadn't been touched. Tucked in the lower desk drawer was my rucksack. To my delight, everything was there just as I had left it.

"I have what I need," I said to Nachi as I threw the backpack over my shoulder. I took one last look at poor Deutsch as we ran from the room. Lucien was lingering in the doorway. He was pale and gaunt. He managed to pull himself together and followed us out into the courtyard.

Like a sports coach spelling out the game plan to his players, Nachi put his hands on both my shoulders and said, "We're going back to Tuzla. We'll backtrack to the north gate. With any luck, the wagon will still be there. Come, we must hurry."

"Wait," I said as Nachi turned to leave. "You two go ahead without me. I can't leave Novi Sad without finding Mia."

Nachi stepped back and looked me over as if I were insane. He raised his arms and said, "Do as you wish. It's your head."

I grabbed his arm and said, "Nachi, please look out for Lucien."

"*Dodjavola* (damn it)," he said, squinting at me angrily. He then grabbed hold of Lucien, and the two of them hurried away.

Have I lost my mind? A massacre has just taken place, and I'm staying behind, risking my life for the sake of a girl? Retrieving

*my belongings was one thing, but this? What was I thinking?
Nachi had risked his life for me. I should go with him. He'll get
us safely back to Tuzla. No, no, I must find Mia. Oh my God,
did my daydream from the lake come true? Ante Budak was at
the helm of the boat, and poor Mia was at the stern, and silly
me, I was in the water helping Budak push the boat out to sea.
Please, God, don't let that nightmare come true. The blood on
Budak's apron was real. Shame, shame on me! We're all living
on a thread. This world is devoid of all logic and reason. The one
and only truth that I have to hold on to is Mia. No matter the
risk, I will find her and free her from this madness.*

My mind was reeling. I stood in the doorway of the police
station and tried to contain myself. I slowly and carefully
worked my way through the streets of Novi Sad. When I
finally neared Mia's neighborhood, I saw that many of the
houses were in shambles. Drunken men were shuffling
through the streets. From a distance, I could see that the
windows of the Levys' building were shattered. When I was
sure that there was no one in the vicinity, I made a mad
dash to the store. The door was open, dangling on one
hinge. Except for a few odds and ends, the store shelves
had been stripped bare. I went behind the counter and
through a hallway that led to the Levys' residence. The
house was in complete disarray. Shards of glass covered
the floor. The large curio in the dining room was lying on
its side, broken in pieces. With each step, I felt the crunch
of broken glass and china beneath my feet. As I tiptoed
toward the kitchen, I heard a low, humming sound.

The room had a dank odor. There were dark stains on
the walls. I nearly fell as I slipped on the muddied floor.

Taking a second look, I realized that the walls and floor were stained in blood!

In front of a window near the back door was a figure hunched over on a low stool. I couldn't make out who it was, as it was covered by a sheet from head to toe. Moving closer, I saw that it was Levy. He was wrapped in a prayer shawl, rocking rhythmically back and forth and reciting a prayer. It was the twenty-third psalm: "Yea though I walk in the valley of the of the shadow of death, I will fear no evil harm, for Thou art with me...."

"Mr. Levy," I said, leaning down toward him.

Levy didn't look up.

"Mr. Levy," I repeated, this time more loudly. "It's me, Ernst."

Levy then looked up at me. "The Prayer for the Dead," he whispered in a low monotone. Levy's eyes were sunken and red.

"My Hanna and my beautiful Mia are gone...at peace. We needn't worry, Ernst. They know that they will intervene for us on high...." Levy held my stare for a brief moment. His lips began to quiver then he looked down at the text and resumed his prayer.

"He has been sitting there like that for almost two days."

I turned around. It was Goustie. I hadn't noticed her enter the room.

"Goustie, my God, are you all right?" Her face was pale and drawn. She was trembling. I took her in my arms and held her tight. "Shhh, it's all right," I whispered. "Tell me, Goustie, tell me what happened."

"It all happened so fast." Goustie said, her voice quivering. "The *Ustasa*...they were like animals. I was upstairs making the beds. Mrs. Levy and Mia were in the kitchen. I heard a loud noise in the front of the house. I started down the stairs but was stopped by a man who was standing on the landing. I recognized him from town. He told me to keep my mouth shut and remain where I was or else I would be next. There were three other men running through the house. The front door had been broken in." Goustie looked over at Mr. Levy, who was still consumed in prayer. She took me by the hand and led me out to the backyard. When she was certain that Mr. Levy couldn't hear us, she said, "They ran through the house breaking everything. Then I saw Mrs. Levy run out of the kitchen. One of the men lunged at her with a knife, killing her on the spot. He saw that I was watching. I saw the whole thing. The killer, seeing that I was watching, put his finger to his lips, warning me to keep silent." Goustie began to sob. "I had no time to warn her. Poor Mia. Oh, my poor Mia. What could I do?" Goustie cupped her ears and wailed, "The screams, the screams...it was awful."

I held Goustie close as she wept on my shoulder. "Where was Mr. Levy while this was going on? How did he manage to survive?"

"He was working in the shed in the backyard. By the time he realized what was happening, it was already too late."

Tears were running down Goustie's cheeks. Her voice became shrill. "Poor little Mia. They each had her in turn.

They tortured her. By the time Mr. Levy arrived, Mia was already dead."

"They didn't hurt you," I said, more as a statement than a question.

"They are the *Ustasa*, Croatian murderers, the death squad. I am a Croat. They don't kill their own." She looked up at me as though begging forgiveness and said, "I'm sorry. I'm so, so sorry...."

"It's all right. It wasn't your fault."

Goustie wiped her eyes and continued. "When they were through, they ran out of the house laughing. I was on the stairs when Mr. Levy barged through the back door. Seeing the brutalized bodies of Hanna and Mia sent him into a whirlwind of fury. He ran back and forth, from Mia then to Hanna. He held them and caressed them while wailing in guttural sobs like a wounded animal. I wanted to scream. He then fell to his knees and tore at his own skin and ripped his clothes. I tried comforting him. He finally calmed. Looking up at me, his face blank, Mr. Levy then gave me instructions. He told me to bring him clean sheets and warm, wet towels. Tenderly, he cleansed their bodies. Mr. Levy's tears flowed as he slowly and lovingly wrapped Hanna and Mia in the white sheets in preparation for their burial. He then instructed me to remain with his Hanna and Mia until his return and to promise not to let them out of my sight. He went to the shed in the backyard to get the shovel. For the next two hours, Mr. Levy dug the graves. I helped him carry out the bodies. Hanna and Mia were buried in the garden." Goustie pointed to the other side of the yard where there was a pretty garden with several trees in bloom. Beneath them were two mounds of dark earth, the graves of Hanna and Mia lying side by side.

I went over to Levy, who was still reciting prayers in a low moan. After some coaxing, I walked him over to the kitchen table. Goustie warmed up some soup. We ate in silence. Mr. Levy barely had the strength to lift his spoon. Goustie assisted him. Like a mother with her newborn child, she fed him while periodically dabbing Mr. Levy's lips with a napkin.

The hour was late, the dangers quite real. We had to get away. While feeding Mr. Levy sips of soup, Goustie said that she would now be his caretaker.

"After all he has done for me, I can't abandon him now. I will take him back to my village. He will stay with my family and me. We will care for him now."

Goustie looked up at me and, with a sense of urgency, said, "The *Ustasa* are still wandering the streets. The Jews have been murdered, hundreds of Serbians as well. The rest have fled for their lives. There is nowhere that is safe. It is only a matter of time until the *Chetnik* (Serbian guerrilla units) forces show up and take their revenge, and that they will surely do. Ernst, you come along with us. My family will protect you."

I stood, dumbfounded. Going along with Goustie would be too dangerous. I needed to go it alone. I've managed to keep one step ahead of the angel of death as it was. As it turned out, had we not been banished to Tuzla, Lucien and I would have certainly met the same horrible fate as the rest of the poor souls of Novi Sad. That said, how could one ever manage to formulate a logical plan in a world of chaos? I looked around me, huddled with Goustie and Levy in a room reeking of death.

As I stand in this house of mourning, in this city whose streets have been turned into rivers of blood, I hear the deafening cries of suffering. On Yom Kippur we remember the destruction of the Temple of Israel. We mourn and we tremble. We kneel before our maker and pray for forgiveness. We pray that the New Year will bring with it health, happiness, and above all, life.

Not all of the Israelites had succumbed to the blades of their enemies. A handful had escaped to the hills of Safed to renew the link in the chain of their forefathers. This is my personal Yom Kippur. The gates are closing. I recall the prayers of the Day of Atonement when we pray for the gates to open. I now beseech you, oh God, open the gates, even as they are closing. The sun is low; the hour is late. Let me enter the gates at last.

I decided to return to Tuzla. *How ironic*, I thought. *I will be returning to the town to which I had been sentenced just one week before.* Ironically, the Muslim village of Tuzla now appeared to be the safest place of all. I told Goustie of our Tuzla adventure and Nachi's role in it all and of wonderful Lucien and how his light heart buoyed our spirits. Goustie's face lit up at hearing that Lucien was safe and well.

"Just one moment," Goustie said as she ran out of the room. She returned moments later with a small box that contained a fine gold chain and locket.

"Give this to Lucien," she said, handing me the box. "Tell him to be careful. Tell him that I am thinking of him." She gave me a bottle of brandy and a small package with dry fruit and stuffed it in my rucksack, tugging the buckle tight to assure that it was secure.

"On the road to Tuzla is a friend, Maxim Malkovic. Go to him. He will help you." Goustie and I turned in surprise. It was Mr. Levy speaking. He looked at us with eyes that were dazed and vacant. "Maxim lives on a farm. Go to him. You need only mention my name, and he will help you." Levy then looked downward and didn't utter another word.

"I know Maxim; he is a good man," Goustie said. "He and his wife are the caretakers of the farm. It is about ten kilometers from here." She gave me the directions then took my hands and squeezed. "You must leave right away. Please be careful. I will pray for you."

CHAPTER THIRTEEN

Rome, 1943

Save for the slow, rhythmic clacking of hoofs from horse-drawn delivery carts, the city slept. Compared to the other occupied cities of Europe, Rome was unique. Benito Mussolini, the adoptive, co-conspirator of Hitler, was, in reality, more a puppet than Hitler's staunch ally. For all his madcap ways, Mussolini tried to balance Germany's National Socialist philosophy with his country's *dolce-faniente* (happy-go-lucky) soul. As a result, the populace, despite gasoline and food rationing, lived in relative ease, Rome's Jewish population included. Intertwined at all levels of business, science, and culture, the Jews had always enjoyed a secure position in the Roman social fabric. That was all about to change.

Obersturmbannfuhrer (lieutenant colonel) Herbert Kappler, head of the Gestapo unit in Rome, reviewed *Project Judenaktion* (campaign against the Jews) one final time. It was four in the morning. Kappler had already been at his desk for an hour. Satisfied, Kappler closed his folder and looked out over the beautiful gardens of Il Pincio.

One year before, the Reich had commandeered the stately Villa Emmanuelle and gave it over to Kappler to serve as his personal residence and command post. Known for his military and political prowess, Kappler was the Führer's personal pick to run all military activities in Rome, Vatican City included.

Kappler was military through and through. After graduating top in his class from the school of military intelligence, he rose rapidly through the ranks, eventually finding his place with the Gestapo. Kappler once told a colleague he had no time to waste in frivolous matters. He lived alone and was never seen socializing with anyone— woman or man. For Kappler, the fatherland was everything. Very disciplined, Kappler never deviated from his strict routine: rise at five in the morning; perform thirty minutes of calisthenics; take a cold shower; dress; eat a breakfast consisting of one poached egg, toast, and black coffee; and finally, arrive in his office at six o'clock sharp to review the day's agenda with his personal secretary.

This day was different. Kappler had received a call from Hitler's headquarters instructing him to proceed with the "final solution" to the "Jewish problem." *Operation Judenrazzia* (raid on the Jews) was to begin: All Jews of Rome, regardless of age, sex, citizenship, or state of health were to be arrested and sent for liquidation. Kappler had less than twenty-four hours to prepare. He worked through the night, dispatching orders by phone and courier. Everything appeared to be going as planned. At midnight, the SS was to arrest the Chief Rabbi of Rome and force him to hand over the files listing the names and addresses of Rome's Jewish citizens. At five thirty in the morning, in one fell swoop, a dozen military vehicles would swarm the streets. Under the direction of SS commanders, Jews were to be brutally seized from their homes and delivered to the Collegio Militare.

Kappler rose to his feet, straightened his tunic, and then pressed a button at the side of his desk. Within seconds his personal aid was standing at attention before him.

"Bring the car around," Kappler ordered. "I want to witness my handiwork firsthand."

Kappler, however, was about to discover that his meticulous plan was not going to unfold as he had anticipated.

What Kappler would later learn was that forty-eight hours before the rampage was to take place, while he was formulating his diabolical plan of what was to be the darkest day in the history of Roman Jewry, word of the planned assault had been leaked to the German Consul of Rome, Friedrich Mollhaussen, by a secretary in Kappler's own office. Mollhaussen, in an attempt to intercede on behalf of Rome's Jews, telephoned the Reich Foreign Minister, questioning the validity and logic behind such an action. The foreign minister's response to Mollhaussen was far from conciliatory, as he believed this "Final Solution" for Rome's Jews was long overdue and urged Mollhaussen to keep his bloody nose out of affairs that didn't concern him.

Friedrich Mollhaussen was never one to make waves. He had succeeded his entire life to remain invisible. He had a nondescript appearance, looking more like a British civil servant than a German diplomat. His thin frame never seemed to fit properly in his suits, which always appeared to be half a size too small. Prior to his recent promotion to consul general, Mollhaussen had been stationed in no less than eight consulates around the globe. At age fifty-nine, he was three years away from retirement. The last thing he wanted was to jeopardize his pension, but this was different. Mollhaussen considered German culture to be head and shoulders above that of any other country. He was ashamed that his country was bullying its way through Europe. *How could a country so civilized, producing the likes of Goethe and Beethoven, reduce itself to the level of street thugs?*

If there was such a thing as the straw that breaks a camel's back, this was it. Once asked by a colleague how he managed to be so successful in advancing through the ranks of the foreign ministry, Mollhaussen answered, "It was easy; I never made a decision." The condescending words of the foreign minister triggered something in Mollhaussen. He would no longer be bullied. For once in his life he would be proactive. He would finally be making a decision. Realizing that he wouldn't get anywhere through the usual channels, Mollhaussen decided to turn to the Vatican for help. He submitted an urgent request to meet with Vatican officials posthaste. Coming from German authorities, such requests were always taken very seriously. As a result, a special session of the General Pontifical Council was set for that same day.

The General Pontifical Council is comprised of a combination of twelve bishops and cardinals, each of whom presides over one of the twelve Pontifical Council subcommittees. The subcommittees meet at regular intervals

throughout the calendar year. Issues of dire importance
that can't wait are heard by a special session of the General
Pontifical Council.

Bishop Lorenzo Giraldi's morning prayers were interrupted by a page who handed him a sealed envelope. In
it was a memo stating that the General Pontifical Council
would be meeting in special session at four o'clock in
the afternoon. No further details were given. Giraldi was
the newest member of the Pontifical Council. Having
been elevated to bishop just one year before, Giraldi was
assigned to head the Subcommittee on Interreligious
Dialogue. This would be Giraldi's first encounter with the
General Council. Not wanting to draw attention to himself, he decided that he would be more observer than par-
ticipant in this, his first meeting.

The council chamber, located on the third floor of the
Vatican's administrative wing, was an elegant room with
walls of soft teak. The rich Persian carpets that covered the
floor made for such perfect acoustics that even the softest-
spoken speech could be understood and absorbed without straining the ears. Twelve plush chairs surrounded a
large ovoid mahogany table. Each place was set with crystal glasses and the finest ceramics. Four waiters stood at
the ready to respond to the beck and call of any member.

Dispensing with any formal introduction, Cardinal
Massimo Mancini, council chairman, opened the meeting. "Gentlemen," he began, "we were asked to convene
this evening by special request of the German Consul of
Rome, Friedrich Mollhaussen. As the day is late, and if
there is no objection, I will now have Herr Mollhaussen

address the committee." The cardinal gave a cursory glance at the committee members then motioned to the secretary to fetch Mollhaussen, who was waiting in the antechamber.

Never before had Mollhaussen been in the presence of such a regal group, let alone have the occasion to address them. Mollhaussen opened his mouth to speak, but nothing came forth. The members of the committee waited patiently as Mollhaussen took a sip of water.

"Thank you for receiving me at such short notice," Mollhaussen said quietly as he stood in a pose of fawning humility. "My name is Friedrich Mollhaussen, consul general of the German Embassy of Rome." Mollhaussen stood slightly bent at the waist, his hands folded before him. "It has come to my attention, through reliable sources that the SS will be staging an assault of devastating magnitude on the Jewish population of Rome." Mollhaussen then paused in anticipation of a reaction or comment. There was none. He cleared his throat and said, "This campaign is scheduled to take place at dawn, twenty-four hours from now. The intent is the complete eradication of all Jewish elements of the city. I am turning to the Vatican to exert its influence, to use their good offices to intercede on behalf of our Jewish brethren."

Low, agitated whispers permeated the room. Bishop Luigi Santoro leaned forward in his seat and said to Cardinal Mancini, "If I may respectfully ask the consul general a question?"

Mancini nodded approvingly.

"Herr Mollhaussen, I would assume that prior to your bringing this matter before the Pontifical Council, you communicated your concerns with officials of your own government, and if that is indeed the case, I would further assume that your efforts were met with deaf ears."

Bishop Santoro's blunt comment took Mollhaussen by surprise. The room was silent. Mollhaussen stirred uncomfortably, not knowing where to put his hands. He took another sip of water then said, "My position as consul general is purely bureaucratic. All policy decisions are made at a much higher level. I nevertheless did lodge an informal protest which, as you so rightly surmised, fell on deaf ears."

Had the Reich discovered what Mollhaussen was up to, they would, no doubt, view his activities as treasonous. Having already gone this far, Mollhaussen had nothing to lose.

He scanned the faces in the room and said, "You know as well as I that once the wheels of such a campaign are set in motion, it is nearly impossible for it to change course. As members of this esteemed committee, I am turning to you all to exert your influence on my government to rethink this folly." Mollhaussen dropped his arms and let out a sigh. His emotional plea left him drained.

After a moment, Cardinal Mancini spoke. "I would like to speak on behalf of all committee members." Mancini didn't bother to look to the other members for their approbation. "Your concern for the destiny of this ethnic minority in Rome is well appreciated. We all agonize over the innocent victims of war. This is a most delicate matter. The Holy See is under a microscope. Each and every step we take is noted and assessed by the Reich. We, too, are at their mercy, that is at least for the time being. Our

primary objective is to maintain the fragile stability that
we presently enjoy."

The silence in the room was deafening. Mollhaussen
was speechless.

"Now, Herr Mollhaussen, if there is no other matter
you wish to discuss, I will close this meeting."

Mollhaussen was left paralyzed by Cardinal Mancini's
comment. He watched silently as the members of the
committee disbanded and exited the room—all members
except for one. Bishop Giraldi remained in his seat. He
was lost in thought, trying to make sense of what had just
transpired. *Of course these are most unusual times, and yes, the
Vatican is under the watchful eye of the German Reich. The world
is crumbling around us, and yes, we should put our interests first.
The Holy See is the calm eye in the center of a hurricane, yet do we
not have a historic and moral obligation to come to the defense of
our brethren? Anything less is tantamount to complicity.* Giraldi
was beside himself. He looked up to see Cardinal Mancini
leaving the room.

"Your Eminence, please wait," Giraldi said, rising out
of his chair. "Allow me to accompany you."

"Ah, Giraldi," Cardinal said, holding out his hand. "I
was pleased to see you at the meeting. Interesting, no?"

"It most certainly was," Giraldi said, his eyes cast downward, visibly perturbed.

"What is troubling you? Please tell me."

"Your Eminence," said Giraldi, carefully thinking out
what he was about to say, "if what Mollhaussen says is
true…." Giraldi's voice cracked.

Cardinal Mancini put his arm around Giraldi's shoulder as they began to walk.

"Forgive me, I'm sorry."

"Go on, my son, it's all right."

"I, too, am most concerned about the destiny of our Jewish brethren." Giraldi noticed Mancini flinch briefly. "The German government *is* a regime of terror. Jews throughout the continent are being slaughtered by the tens of thousands. We have a golden opportunity, not only to condemn these atrocities, but to intervene on behalf of these poor souls."

"My dear Lorenzo, the Holy See *must* remain neutral. Condemning these atrocities would surely have a negative influence on Catholics in German-held lands."

His voice now shaking, Giraldi then said, "But we have an historical, a biblical obligation inspired by Jesus himself. We cannot sit back idly..."

"We have *no* such obligation!" Mancini blurted out. Then in a calmer, more controlled voice he said, "My dear, misguided brother, the one and only contribution that the Jews had made on our behalf was to offer Jesus' body as the vessel for *His* precious soul, nothing more."

Giraldi was stunned by Mancini's remark. Mancini continued walking half a step ahead of Giraldi. Just beyond them, three cardinals were talking informally.

One of them, smiling broadly, said, "Wonderful meeting, Brother."

"Thank you all," Mancini said. "You all know Bishop Giraldi?"

Forcing himself, Giraldi nodded briefly to the others then excused himself. Giraldi walked slowly back to his apartment in the residential wing. He was still reeling from Cardinal Mancini's cold and callous remarks. He paced through his rooms like a caged tiger.

Something must be done, and it is incumbent upon me to act, but I can't do it alone. I will need help. Who can I turn to? Here in the Vatican there is no one whom I can trust. I will need to seek help elsewhere. The survival of Rome's Jews hangs in the balance, and there is precious little time.

Giraldi stepped out onto his small terrace that over-looked the Tiber River. Gazing across the far bank, he could see the Jewish ghetto, and through the foliage, he could just barely make out a portion of the Grand Synagogue.

Having been raised in the Veneto region of Italy, Giraldi was well versed in the history of Italy's Jewish ghettos. On his many visits to Venice, Giraldi had always experienced an unusual attraction toward the Venetian ghetto. He was somehow drawn to it. It summoned him. While strolling through the ghetto's narrow streets, he would always have the same sensation, like the feeling of coming home.

The Jewish ghetto of Rome is a seven-acre, walled quarter in the Sant'Angelo region of Trastevere. Established by Pope Paul IV in 1555, its purpose was to segregate the Jews and radically restrict their personal freedoms. Over the centuries, these restrictions were gradually lifted. While the Jewish citizens of twentieth-century Rome had come to enjoy both social and economic liberty, anti-Semitism, although quiescent, was nevertheless still quite appar-ent. In the heart of the quarter stands *Tempio Maggiore*, the Great Synagogue. It is the center of Jewish cultural activity. Until today, the majority of Roman Jewry resides in this quarter. This made Obersturmbannfuhrer Herbert Kappler's job all that much easier. To carry out his despicable deed, Kappler knew exactly where to go.

Giraldi realized that he needed to solicit the help of someone outside the Vatican, someone who he could trust implicitly, someone of the same mind. As he stepped from the terrace and back into his apartment, it suddenly dawned on him; he would ask his old schoolmate and friend from the Christian Academy of Treviso, Lucca Ricciardi, to assist him.

Like Giraldi, Lucca had been summoned to Rome by the Church. For Lucca, it was to fill the position of spiritual leader of the Church of Santa Maria in Campitelli following the death of its director, Father Visconti. The Church of Santa Maria in Campitelli is one of ten churches located in the environs of the ghetto.

Giraldi's plan was quite simple. He would have Lucca solicit the help of the neighborhood parish priests to hide as many Jews as possible within the confines of their churches. It was a radical, yet very simple plan. Giraldi realized that there was nothing to lose. The ghetto Jews were like sheep awaiting slaughter. Any number of individuals who could be saved would be considered a coup.

Thrilled to hear from his old friend, Lucca agreed to meet Giraldi one hour hence at a café in Trastevere, in walking distance from Vatican City. The evening was cool and dry. Giraldi, having arrived with a few minutes to spare, watched the attractive passersby strolling through the piazza. The carefree manner of the gentry contrasted starkly with the malignant and grim reality of the day.

Giraldi couldn't contain his merriment at the sight of Lucca racing through the square on his bicycle. "Ciao, Lucca," Giraldi said warmly as Lucca skidded to a halt beside him.

"*Come stai,* (how are you), Lorenzo?" Lucca said, taking Giraldi's outstretched hand in his. Then with a smile he added, "Or should I say, how is *His Eminence?*"

"Please sit down," Giraldi said as he maneuvered a chair close to his own. To the waiter he said, "*Due espressi, per piacere.*" Turning to his friend he said, "Thank you, Lucca, for coming on such short notice."

Seeing Giraldi's serious expression, Lucca quickly realized that this was not a social meeting. "What is it, my friend?" Lucca asked, leaning toward Giraldi.

"I am in need of your help."

"Anything, Lorenzo, you need only to ask." Lucca listened intently as Giraldi told him everything: Mollhaussen's report, Cardinal Mancini's response, and what he intended to do about it.

Neither of them commented on the position taken by the committee, or rather, that taken by Cardinal Mancini.

When Giraldi was through, Lucca sat with eyes tightly closed, both to absorb what he had heard and to organize his thoughts. Lucca then looked into Giraldi's eyes and said with a warm smile, "If we are going to be of any help, Lorenzo, we had better get a move on...."

"Grazie, Lucca. I knew that I could count on you," Giraldi said, visibly moved.

"Let me get this right," Lucca said. "We have less than twenty-four hours to hide over two thousand people from under the nose of the Gestapo. What exactly do you have in mind?"

"As head of the Subcommittee on Interreligious Dialogue, I have had the occasion to meet Chief Rabbi Simon Carpi. The two of us have a fairly good rapport. From here, I plan to go directly to the rabbi's residence to warn him. He will have to get the word out to his congregation without delay. You, my dear Lucca, will call on all nine of the parish priests of Sant'Angelo. Hopefully they will make the churches available to hide these poor souls. I expect them to cooperate, especially once you make it clear to them that the directive for this mission emanates from the Vatican itself. You will arrange to have them meet me in the sanctuary of your church at midnight tonight. I will meet you there to go over the particulars."

"Oh, Lorenzo, this will be difficult. The Germans are surely to discover what we are up to. At such short notice—"

Giraldi took Lucca's hand. "I know, Lucca," Giraldi said, cutting Lucca off in mid-sentence. "If we manage to save even a few souls, it will still be a blessing."

Giraldi looked deeply into Lucca's eyes and said, "This is what gives our life its meaning. It's not every day that one is given the opportunity to serve the Lord in this way. Now, let's go. We have much to do."

Rabbi Carpi looked up at his wife after taking the last spoonful of compote and said, "Perfect as always." He dabbed his lips with a napkin and went into his study. Late in the evening, after dinner, was the time the rabbi cherished the most. It was when he could be alone with his religious texts and immerse himself in a tract of the Talmud. He relished the challenge of unraveling a moral or legal puzzle proffered by an ancient rabbinical sage. The rabbi could study at his desk for hours. His wife, Leah, would usually come for him before it was very late to assure that he would get at least a few hours sleep, so as to be fresh for early-morning services.

That evening, the *rebbitzin* interrupted her husband for an altogether different reason. "Caro," she whispered as she opened the door to the study, "a priest is here to see you. He says it's urgent."

"Have him come in," the rabbi said as he closed the large tome on his desk.

"Forgive me for disturbing you, Rabbi," Giraldi said as he peeked in the doorway.

"Ah, Bishop Giraldi," the rabbi said as he came around from behind his desk and took Giraldi's outstretched hand. The rabbi motioned for Giraldi to take one of the chairs opposite his desk. "No disturbance at all, Father. Can I offer you something to drink?"

Giraldi kneaded his hands anxiously. "Please, Rabbi, we must talk. There is a problem. It is urgent."

"Of course, go on, please. What can I do for you?"

"I come bearing terrible news. Your people, the entire Jewish community is in grave danger. We have no time. We must act immediately."

"Calm yourself, my dear friend. You surely exaggerate. It can't be all that bad."

"I *am* calm," Giraldi blurted out.

The rabbi was visibly startled.

"Forgive me, Rabbi," Giraldi said, leaning toward the rabbi. "Please listen to me. If we don't act immediately, by the day after tomorrow there will be no Jews left. The Germans are planning to round up and deport the entire Jewish population. Of this, I am certain. My source is reliable."

The rabbi blanched and collapsed in his chair.

"Rabbi, we have to act and do so right away," Giraldi said.

The rabbi was speechless. He stared at Lorenzo in disbelief.

"My plan is to hide as many Jews as possible within the confines of the churches of Sant'Angelo. What happens after that is anyone's guess. I suggest we take one step at a time. The roundup is due to take place Saturday at dawn, little over twenty-four hours from now. Start spreading the word. Wake up the temple officials. From here, I am going to arrange a meeting with our local priests." Giraldi looked at the rabbi sympathetically and said, "I know, this is unbelievable. I swear on all that is holy that I will do everything in my power to help you."

"Thank you," whispered Carpi. "Thank you for everything."

Giraldi then hurried to take his leave. He passed the rabbi's wife who was standing outside of the study. "*Buona notte, signora,*" Giraldi said, looking at her briefly and apologetically.

"*Buona notte, Padre,*" she said as she closed the door behind him.

Sensing something awry, the *rebbitzin* entered the study.

"What was that all about?" she asked. Then seeing her husband stooped in the chair, she cried, "Simon, are you all right?" The rabbi reached out to his wife and sat her down on his lap. Rocking her like a baby, he quietly recited from the Psalms: "I am sunk in the mire of the shadowy deep where there is no place to stand; I have come into deep waters, and a whirlpool has carried me away…Save me, O God, for the waters have penetrated my soul." Looking into Leah's eyes, he said, "My darling Leah, the barbarians are at the gate. The destruction of the temple, the *Bet Hamigdash*, is near."

Giraldi ran down the stairs two at a time. He crossed to the other side of the square in the direction of the church of Santa Maria in Campitelli. Out of nowhere came the harsh sound of grinding gears. Giraldi barely managed to jump out of the way of a truck that was speeding around the corner. He watched as it stopped in front of the rabbi's apartment building. Two SS officers wearing long, black overcoats and wide-rimmed hats emerged. They were followed by four soldiers who ran ahead of them into the building.

Hearing the loud pounding on the door, the *rebbitzin* left her husband's side to see who it was. She opened the door and was immediately shoved aside by the soldiers making way for the two SS officers to enter.

"Where is your husband? Take me to him now!" Before she had time to react, there was a voice from the other room. It was the rabbi calling out to his wife, "Leah, who is there?" The soldiers pushed open the study doors. As the rabbi rose from his chair, a soldier landed him flush in the nose with the butt of his rifle. The other one restrained Mrs. Carpi as she tried to come to her husband's aid.

One of the officers looked down at Carpi and said, "You will give me the names and addresses of the Jews of your community." The rabbi, stunned by the blow, looked up at the officer with a mystified expression.

The officer repeated, "You will get me the list now, or I will kill your wife." As he said this, the soldier shoved Mrs. Carpi to the floor, his gun poised at her head.

"No, no," the rabbi cried, "I will do as you wish. Please don't hurt her." The rabbi struggled to get to his feet. His face and shirt were covered with blood. He stumbled to his desk and from the top drawer took out a large ledger and handed it to the officer. After glancing through it only briefly, he said, "*Ya, das is gut* (excellent, this is all I need)." Then to one of the soldiers he said, "Take them."

Giraldi was outside on the corner when he saw Rabbi Carpi and his wife being dragged out of the building. He cringed at the sight of them being shoved into the back of the truck. Giraldi could only watch as the truck pulled away.

He quickly walked the two blocks to the Church of Santa Maria in Campitelli. In the front pews of the sanctuary were several of the community priests speaking quietly. Lucca, seeing Giraldi enter, hurried up the aisle to meet him.

"Ciao, Lorenzo," Lucca said excitedly. "Most of them are already here. How did your meeting go with the rabbi?"

"The rabbi and his wife were just arrested by the SS. Let's do what we can There is no time." Giraldi and Lucca walked over to meet with the other priests.

"Thank you all for coming here on such short notice. I understand that Father Ricciardi has touched on the situation. Allow me to elaborate. The SS are planning an action to eliminate the entire Jewish population of Rome.

This is due to begin on Saturday morning, just one day from now. Rabbi Carpi was arrested just moments ago. We must do what we can to warn as many of these people as possible. We will open our homes and our churches. We will spread the word."

"And then?" It was Father Carlo Amati of the Church of San Gregorio. "Even if we do manage to hide some of these people, what then? What will become of them? What will become of *us* when the Germans discover that we had been complicit in this deed?"

"That, only God knows," Giraldi said passionately. "It is for us to act—and act now. What happens later…." Giraldi raised his eyes and hands to the heavens.

Father Amati let out a huff, expressing his displeasure and reluctance to go along with the plan. All the others enthusiastically agreed to participate.

Giraldi gave them all one last look and said, "Let's get to work then. The hour is late, and there is precious little time."

After the other priests dispersed, Lucca said to Giraldi, "My dear Lorenzo, maybe Father Amati was right. There is no way that we can hide these people for long. The Germans will surely get wind of what we are up to. This may prove to be just a futile attempt to postpone the inevitable."

Giraldi looked into Lucca's eyes, "And if we just sit back and do nothing, what then? Will there be any living with ourselves if we don't even try? Even one life saved is tantamount to saving the entire universe."

"Forgive me, Lorenzo, I—"

"Don't, Lucca...you needn't say anything. Go now. I will find you tomorrow. We will do what we can."

Early that next morning, Captain Manfred Keller called on Obersturmbannfuhrer Herbert Kappler and handed him the ledger that was confiscated from Rabbi Carpi's study.

"Good work, Captain," Kappler said as he leafed through the pages of the ledger. "Did you have any trouble?"

"None at all. It was as easy as taking candy from a baby."

Word of the rabbi's arrest spread through the neighborhood of Sant'Angelo like wildfire. Some of the residents left the city to stay with friends or relatives in nearby towns. Some of the elderly and infirm were brought into the confines of the neighborhood churches. There were others who were skeptical, unable to or not wanting to believe that the roundup, this action was even going to take place.

The following day, Bishop Giraldi returned to the ghetto. He used the Church of Santa Maria in Campitelli as his home base. He went from church to church to help in the evacuation. It was imperative that everyone involved maintain as low a profile as possible, for were the SS to discover that these countermeasures were being instituted, there was no doubt that they wouldn't take it lightly.

CHAPTER FOURTEEN

It was midnight, just several hours before the raid, the *Judenrazzia*, was to begin. Giraldi, along with the Jewish elders, raced nonstop from one church to the next and from home to home assisting in the evacuation. For the first time in hours, he sat down to rest in a small room in Lucca's church. Although exhausted, Giraldi didn't want to sleep. He decided to nap for just a few minutes in order to replenish his strength. The moment his eyes closed, he fell into a deep sleep that was filled with restless and violent dreams.

The sun is high, the air is arid, and the ground is parched. The procession crawls down a twisting and dusty road that extends farther than the eye can see. To either side of the road there are people talking, laughing, and gorging themselves. They pay us no mind. We plod along, determined and focused in our task. We scurry from one dark shadow to another. There is a giant boot about to crush us. I yell out, "Hurry, hurry along, you mustn't slow down. Come along, we're almost there." This, our ant colony with human faces, moves on in a single, disorderly file. We drag our feet; their mouths droop under the brutal sun. The young help the aged. The weak fall to the wayside. I holler for help, but they don't hear me. They're oblivious. They cannot hear us through their laughter and their merriment. A large man points to me and laughs. It is the contorted face of Cardinal Mancini. His mouth widens. His laugh gives way to a sudden booming voice, "Rouss, schnell...."

Giraldi was suddenly jolted awake. He was disoriented. His heart was pounding, and he was sweating profusely. *Oh my God. Lucca, the church, what time is it? I must have fallen asleep...*

"*Schnell, schnell, rouss,*" came the shouts from outside. *Could it be? Oh God, the roundup had already begun.* Giraldi jumped to his feet and ran out to the street. There were several troop carriers taking up positions in the plaza. Whistles were blowing. People were scattering, kicking and screaming in a wild frenzy as soldiers dragged them from their homes and into the waiting trucks. From all over, the local, Roman, non-Jewish residents came out and filled the streets by the hundreds. They began chanting in protest. The trucks were unable to move due to the large number of protesters. The throng kept the soldiers from entering the apartment buildings. In the melee, a good number of Jews were smuggled into the churches or right out of the neighborhood. The roundup was a failure. The soldiers were eventually ordered to leave. When the dust settled, nearly half of the Jewish residents were saved.

From his vantage point one block away, Kappler sat in the backseat of his car and watched with disgust at the scene that was unfolding before his eyes. *Scheiss! Damn*, he thought to himself. *They will pay. They all will pay.* "Driver, let's get out of here."

"We did what we could," Lucca said, standing alongside Giraldi in the doorway of the church.

They had some sense of satisfaction as the protesters remained in the streets until the last of the soldiers had gone.

"Man *is* inherently good, Lucca," Giraldi said. "Of this, I am certain."

They remained on the steps of the church until the streets cleared.

"Thank you for all of your help, Lucca."

They shook hands and embraced.

"I don't know how this is going to end, but we did what we could. I am returning to Vatican City. We will speak tomorrow."

Kappler was incensed. He instructed his driver to return immediately to his headquarters.

These people think that they can protect their neighbors. They should be happy that I didn't shoot them all. The Führer certainly wouldn't have minded. Passive resistance...bah, I spit on them all. These Jews may have dodged a bullet, but their day of reckoning has come... The time for the Final Solution has arrived. I will lull them into a sense of security then finish them off, once and for all!

Kappler summoned Captain Keller to his study to give him the details of his plan.

"It is quite simple," he said as he sat back in his cushy lounge chair. Kappler stared through the crystal snifter at the golden-brown brandy swirling within and said, "Keller, you will instruct your men to release both the rabbi and his wife. You will tell him that in order to save the Jews of Rome we are imposing a levy of fifty kilos of gold. You will specify that the entire amount must be handed over within twenty-four hours. You will lead them to believe that it will be a kind of peace offering. Upon delivery of the gold, we will go back to the ghetto in full force and finish what we started."

The rabbi and his wife were delivered back to their apartment. The rabbi was stunned to see Keller waiting for him.

Feigning warmth, Keller got right to the point. "My dear fellow," he said, forcing a smile that came out as an awkward grimace, "today's incident was most unfortunate. Upon reconsideration, my government is offering you the following arrangement: In return for fifty kilos of gold, the Reich will assure your people's safety. You will see to it that the full amount will be delivered to me within twenty-four hours." As Keller rose to leave, he turned to the rabbi and said, "The full amount, please. We don't want to be disappointed." Keller's words sent a shiver down the rabbi's spine.

The rabbi called an urgent meeting of the temple administration. Within hours, there were hundreds of people in a long queue in front of the temple.

They stood in silence, patiently waiting their turn, each holding packages of jewelry, some large, some small. They had gathered every item that they could find, from necklaces and wedding bands to the simplest trinkets. A small station was set up in the temple lobby where the items were submitted, documented, and exchanged for a written receipt. An eerie and foreboding cloud descended in the neighborhood. One sensed that this blackmail was only buying time and that the day of reckoning was near.

Upon hearing of Keller's ultimatum, Giraldi rushed to Rabbi Carpi's residence. He was led into the kitchen, where Leah was busy attending to her husband's wounds. The rabbi's face was grossly distorted by the blows that he had sustained the day before by the hands of the SS.

"Oh, my dear Rabbi," Giraldi said, "I suffer with you and assure you that I will do everything in my power to help you comply with this despicable demand."

The rabbi, his eyes sealed shut from the facial swelling, acknowledged Giraldi with a few muted words and nod of the head.

Girladi, with Lucca's help, solicited donations from the clergy of Sant'Angelo. Although the church's response was positive, it was by no means enthusiastic. Incredibly, the Jewish community managed to meet the deadline imposed by Kappler. The temple leaders documented, weighed, and packaged the last of the items. Thoroughly exhausted, both physically and emotionally, they could do nothing more than sit in silence and absorb what was taking place. Before them were the boxes of gold jewelry piled neatly on the floor.

At seven o'clock at night, a long black car pulled up at the temple. Captain Keller, along with four soldiers, entered the building and went directly to the rabbi's study.

Seeing the boxes on the floor, Keller rubbed his hands and, with a sinister smile, said, "Ah, that's what I'm looking for." He snapped his fingers, and his men got to work. When the last of the boxes was removed, Keller turned to the rabbi and said, "I hope for your sake that it is all here. *Auf wiedersehen,* (we'll be seeing you)."

When they left, one of the elders turned to the rabbi and said, "If this is our lot, so be it. We are at their mercy, but maybe, just maybe, we have bought ourselves some time."

"*Sehr gut* (very good)," *Obersturmbannfuhrer* Kappler said as he watched with pleasure as Keller's men stacked the last of the boxes of gold in his office. Then, turning to Keller, he said, "We can now finish what we started. Organize the troops, and let's get this over with, once and for all. Heil Hitler!"

"Heil Hitler!" Keller answered loudly, saluting with vigor.

When Keller was gone, Kappler opened one of the boxes, and while sifting through the shimmering gold pieces, he smiled to himself and thought, *This is the least I should get for my trouble.*

That same night, one thousand soldiers descended upon the Jewish ghetto of Sant'Angelo. Each and every one of the Jewish residents was taken from their homes at gunpoint. The first among them were Rabbi Carpi and his wife. Using loud speakers, the soldiers ordered the Roman residents to remain in their homes. One individual who countermanded that order was shot on the spot. The ghetto was under siege.

Kappler returned to Piazza Sant'Angelo as the last truck pulled away. The streets were vacant and silent. Scattered everywhere were the tattered remains of resistance, heroism, and defeat: torn and bloodied clothing, broken suitcases, baby prams, and the bodies of those who had tried to resist. From his vantage point in the backseat of his car, Kappler uncorked a bottle of champagne and toasted himself for a job well done. *I will certainly be awarded a medal for such efficient work. Who knows, the Führer may well pin it on me personally.*

Emotionally broken, Giraldi was barely able to attend to his ecumenical responsibilities. He functioned mechanically by rote. To his chagrin, life in the Holy See went on unfettered. The tragedy of Sant'Angelo was never brought up, never mentioned by a soul. It was as if it had never happened. Giraldi was in a state of emotional limbo. It was as though he was living in a vacuum. His sleep was troubled, interrupted frequently by violent and stormy dreams. Characters in his nightmares frequently had the traumatized and distorted face of Rabbi Carpi. He would pass long hours reflecting on his pre-Vatican days in Treviso and of his own little town of Possangno di Grappa whose holy tranquility and simplicity first led him to the pastoral life. He lovingly recalled his early childhood with his warm and loving Mama Angelina, to whom he so longed to return. Despite raising him single-handedly, Angelina succeeded in instilling in Giraldi a strong sense of security and confidence.

Giraldi found it difficult to rally the strength to get out of bed in the morning, let alone venture out of the

Vatican. He wanted very much to see Lucca, to talk, to
bond, to commiserate, but he found the effort of doing so
to be too great. Giraldi couldn't process the fact that the
Jewish community was no more, that from one moment
to the next it had been wiped off from the face of the
earth. He would spend hours on end on his balcony staring off at the distance to the Jewish ghetto that once was.
His thoughts drifted back to the horizons of his infancy,
far, far back to another place and time. These vaporous
thoughts, these daydreams, were the fail-safe for his tormented soul, instilling within him a temporary sense of
purity and calm.

He drifted back to years past, walking with Angelina
through the beautiful countryside. Frequently, during
their outings, Lorenzo would ask Angelina, his adoptive
mama, what had become of his actual parents. She would
take his hand in hers and swing his arm in tempo with
their pace and merrily reply that, like her own parents,
they were whisked off to heaven after a plague swept the
land and that they were happy in knowing Lorenzo was
happy. She went on to say that, each night, they would
come to him and watch over him while he slept, and when
his sleep was through, they would lovingly kiss him awake
and return to heaven on the wings of angels.

CHAPTER FIFTEEN

Trieste, 1911

The graduation ceremony was about to begin. Seeing that Angelina was nowhere in sight, Tomasso raced down the hall in the direction of her studio.

"Angelina, Angelina," he yelled loudly.

Angelina didn't hear him. As always, when engaged in an art project, Angelina would be in another world. She was working feverishly on a ceramic piece, and as a result, her creative muse was blocking out everything else.

"Angelina, don't you know what day it is?" Tomasso said as he rushed into her studio. "Everyone's waiting for you."

Angelina looked up from the pottery wheel, and seeing Tomasso, she gasped, "Oh my Lord, I didn't realize the time!" Angelina jumped up from her seat, threw off her smock, looked fleetingly in the mirror, patted her pale cheeks, and together with Tomasso, bolted from the room. Holding hands, the two of them sped down the hallway and over to the auditorium.

All heads turned in dismay as Angelina and Tomasso ran into the auditorium and skidded to a halt. Their giggling interrupted the somber graduation ceremonies that were just about to take place. Nonetheless, they made it just in the nick of time. Angelina and Tomasso were among fifteen art students who were to receive their diplomas that day.

Tomasso Cicinelli was the first person Angelina had met when she arrived at the academy two years before. As a student of art restoration, Tomasso had a discerning and critical eye and, thus, was quick to recognize and appreciate Angelina's artistic abilities. They instantly hit it off. Hardly a day went by that they weren't, if only briefly, in each other's company to review an art project or merely pass the time.

The graduation "commission" was composed of the headmaster of the academy, who was seated in the center position at a small dais. Flanking him on each side were his two assistants. A single seat in front of the dais was reserved for the graduate, behind which sat the gallery comprised of the other prospective graduates, their families, and friends.

One by one, each candidate was called up. Prior to sitting before the commission, they presented their personal librettos to the first assistant. The headmaster, after quiet deliberation with his assistants, would then ask the candidate several questions. There was nothing written. The entire examination was oral. Each graduation colloquium could last anywhere between two minutes and a half hour, after which the candidate would be given a grade. The scores ranged from the lowest grade of eighteen up to the top grade of thirty. The atmosphere was tense. The candidates fidgeted nervously as they waited for their names to be called. As they were last to enter the auditorium, Angelina and Tomasso were the last to be called. The grades awarded that day weren't stellar; most scored in the mid-twenties.

Then the assistant called out the name "Tomasso Cicinelli." Tomasso exhaled and gave Angelina a quick wink and took his place in front of the dais.

After a brief deliberation, the headmaster announced, "*Trenta* (thirty)," the top grade to be awarded so far. At hearing the high score, Tomasso's mother clapped her hands and let out a high-pitched yelp then quickly collected herself, covering her mouth from embarrassment.

As Tomasso returned to his seat, the assistant announced, "Angelina Giraldi." Tomasso squeezed Angelina's hand as she rose from her chair.

The commission reviewed Angelina's libretto and spoke to one another in hushed tones.

The headmaster then stood and said, "I am pleased to announce that today, for the first time in the history of Accademia Dell'Arte di Trieste, a student, on the day of her graduation, will be given the title of '*professoressa*.' The student to whom I am referring is Angelina Giraldi, who has graduated today with the highest honor that the accademia can bestow—summa cum laude! Should Angelina agree to stay on with us, this esteemed and honorable position is hers." The headmaster stood, faced Angelina, and applauded.

The assistants, students, and guests all followed suit.

Angelina could do little other than blush crimson and humbly accept the accolades.

"Naturally," he continued, "we will give you time to think it over. For now, please accept our heartfelt congratulations." Then, turning to all the other graduates, he said, "And congratulations to all of today's graduates. We now invite everyone to repair to the next room where refreshments are being served."

Over the next hour, the graduates, their families, and the teaching staff mingled together over tea and cakes.

"Congratulations, Angelina." It was Tomasso who was standing beside a middle-aged couple. "Allow me to introduce you to my parents."

"It is a pleasure," Angelina said, shaking their hands. "You should be proud. Without your Tomasso's guidance, I don't think that I could have made it."

"You didn't do so bad yourself, Angelina—summa cum laude *and* a position at the academy."

"I hope that I didn't embarrass you too badly, Angelina," said the headmaster, walking toward them and smiling broadly. After making small talk together with Tomasso and his parents, the headmaster excused himself, took Angelina's elbow, and escorted her away. "All of us at the academy look forward to having you with us, Angelina. I do hope that you will stay on."

"You honored me greatly with your words and your generous offer, but I must decline. My place is with the church—"

The headmaster held up his hand and, smiling warmly, said, "You need not say another word, my dear Angelina. I respect your decision. Please bear in mind that you will always have a home here with us at the academy. Two years ago, I believed that I did Bishop Franchetti a favor in awarding you the scholarship, while, in fact, the favor was all his. Feel free to stay on for a few days or longer, if you like. You can relax now, Angelina; you did well. If there is anything you desire, you need only ask."

"As much as I would like to stay, I cannot. I miss my home. My wish is to return as soon as possible to my home in Possagno."

"I will see to it that a carriage and driver be available to you. Please, Angelina, visit with us again soon. I wish you well."

Angelina arranged to leave for Possagno the following morning. From the events of the preceding day and the anticipation of returning home, Angelina hardly slept. She was too excited. To her surprise, a good number of students and faculty were outside in the courtyard the following morning for her send-off. After many embraces and well wishes, Angelina stepped toward the carriage, with Tomasso holding the door.

"You are one in a million, Angelina. I will miss you." Tomasso took Angelina's hand and kissed it. "I know that I will be seeing more of you, if not directly, then through your artwork. Never give it up, Angelina. You have been blessed with a precious gift." Tomasso helped Angelina up into her seat and closed the door behind her. "*Tante belle cose* (all the best)," he said through the window as the carriage began to pull away. "Who knows, maybe one day, with any luck, I may be called on to restore one of your magnificent pieces."

CHAPTER SIXTEEN

As the carriage made its way out of the academy grounds, the driver, Carlo, turned to Angelina and said, "Sit back, *signorina*, and enjoy the ride. We have a beautiful day ahead of us."

Angelina rested her head on the cushion and took in the exquisite countryside. She reached into her bag and removed her diploma. Written in elaborate italics was the following:

On this, the Sixteenth Day of April, in the Year of Our Lord
One Thousand Nine Hundred Eleven,
Accademia Dell'Arte di Trieste,
Presents to
Angelina Giraldi,
Il Certificato di Laurea
For Completing the Course in Advanced Art
Summa Cum Laude
Signed,
Franco Montenegro, Direttore

Angelina held the document to her breast and closed her eyes. The steady, bouncy ride lulled her toward sleep, only to be repeatedly jolted awake by a quick turn or bump in the road.

Each time, Carlo said apologetically, "*Scuzi, signorina,*" as he tried his best to navigate the rough-and-tumble road.

"*Fa niente* (think nothing of it)," Angelina would respond with a smile, truly not minding at all.

They kept up a steady pace. Under normal conditions, the trip to Possagno would take the good part of the day. The driver chose to take his time, stopping frequently along the way to take in the beautiful countryside or merely to snack and stretch his legs. Angelina's anguish that had prompted Sister Rachel to send her to the academy two years before had totally evaporated. She was now refreshed; her future was hopeful. She looked forward to returning to the church and to resume the life she loved. With her artistic talents nurtured and fortified, she was in want of nothing more. Her heart and soul were finally settled and at peace, or so she thought.

The first leg of the journey took a northern direction for several miles along the western border of Yugoslavia. The tone of the towns that they passed along the way had a touch of the Eastern European, as their populations were a mix of Italian and Slovene.

After a couple of hours, they came to the Italian town of Gorizia, located just three miles from its Yugoslavian sister town of Nova Gorica. Rather than the usual hustle and bustle normally seen on weekdays in such towns, there was none on this particular day. It was as if the town had been vacated. The few people who they did see darted here and there then would disappear out of sight. They heard window shutters being slammed closed as they passed.

Carlo had originally intended to stop in Gorizia for a little while, but given the repellent atmosphere, he decided to keep moving.

"I have a bad feeling about this place, signorina," Carlo said, his tone one of concern. "Let's go on. We'll stop at the next town."

Three miles across the border, the town of Nova Gorica was still reeling from the events of the night before. At least one quarter of the Jewish population, more than 150 souls, were attending prayers in the synagogue when it was overrun by a mob of drunken brutes. The doors were bolted shut and the building set afire. The agonizing screams of the victims being burned alive could be heard as far away as Gorizia. The horror lasted most of the night. While the synagogue was aflame, an animalistic mob continued their rampage of pillage, rape, and murder.

Jacob Senese and his young wife, Sarah, lived a modest, yet beautiful life in Nova Gorica. They had met three years before at the local school, where Jacob taught mathematics and Sarah taught music. Five years before, after receiving his teaching degree, Jacob, who was in desperate need of a job, came to Nova Gorica to fill the position of mathematics teacher.

In Nova Gorica, it was a rarity for any child to make it past eighth grade, let alone graduate from high school. Jacob decided to change all that. Starting with his very first day on the job, Jacob organized afterschool learning programs and often remained well into the evening to tutor any and all students who needed help. He even held free private sessions in his home on weekends. Many of his colleagues, some of whom barely finished high school themselves, resented Jacob's proactive style, as they considered themselves overworked as it was. When, from time to time, Jacob would solicit their participation in a new program, they would usually refuse, desiring to maintain the simple and lazy status quo. It was through Jacob's efforts, and his alone, that by his third year at the school, not only did more than 50 percent of the students graduate high school, but three students even went on to study at the university.

Meeting Sarah in his first week at the school made Jacob's decision to remain in Nova Gorica that much easier. The two soon married and lived a beautiful life together in a small apartment in the town center. Each morning, after a breakfast, they would make the half-mile stroll to the school together. On the days that Jacob wasn't tutoring the students, he and Sarah could be seen walking home together hand in hand. They lived a charming life, but there was something that was missing.

After trying for over a year, Jacob and Sarah had become resigned to the fact that they couldn't conceive a child.

Then one day in late October, Sarah began experiencing morning sickness, and lo and behold, eight months later, Jacob and Sarah's dream came true. They were blessed with a plump baby boy, whom they named Izak.

Each evening after dinner they enjoyed reading or playing music together; Sarah would play light sonatas on the piano, while Jacob, whose love for the viola greatly outweighed his artistic abilities, would struggle laughingly just to keep up. Little Izak, strapped securely in his bassinet in the center of the dining room table, would show his enjoyment by grinning widely and clapping his pudgy little hands together clumsily.

That evening, the music was suddenly interrupted by loud shouts in the yard. Startled, Izak began crying uncontrollably. The shouts were followed by screams—deafening, heart-wrenching screams. Jacob threw down his viola and ran to the window. In a flash, he took in the awful site. He watched as a madman, standing a mere twenty meters away, threw a screaming child from a terrace and onto the bayonet of a wild man standing on the street below. He also saw Maimon, the greengrocer, being dragged through the streets by a man on horseback. Poor Maimon's ankles were tethered to a rope, his bloodied deformed head bouncing in tow like a rag doll.

"Sarah!" Jacob screamed as he grabbed Izak. "Hurry, there's no time."

"What is it?" Sarah asked.

"Hurry!" Jacob yelled. He quickly wrapped Izak in a blanket, took Sarah by the hand, and ran out of the flat. Fortunately for them, their apartment was situated in the back arm of the complex, where a door exited to the garden in the rear. Holding Izak in one arm and Sarah in the other, Jacob raced out of the apartment.

They ran and ran and never looked back.

Sarah lost her footing and fell to the ground, scraping her knee. "Jacob, I can't..." Sarah called, panting. "I can't go on."

While holding Izak, Jacob grabbed Sarah's hand and pulled her to her feet. "Come along, there's no time. We have to get to the forest."

They ran nonstop through the muddied grass until they reached the rim of the forested area, a good mile away. Sarah dropped to the ground, exhausted. Jacob sat down beside her. Struggling to catch their breath, they could only stare at one another in disbelief. The muffled sounds of torture could still be heard in the distance.

"We must cross the border to Gorizia. It's our only hope."

Sarah didn't answer. She took little Izak from Jacob and cradled him in her arms. She held him close and pressed her lips against baby Izak's soft, pudgy cheeks. Sarah rocked back and forth while whispering comforting hushes into Izak's ear.

Jacob tenderly took Izak from Sarah and helped her to her feet. With his free arm, he embraced her and whispered in her ear, "Come, Sarah, come on, we can make it...."

Dazed and confused, Sarah barely managed to follow along. They hurried on for what felt like an eternity until they finally reached the road that bordered the town of Gorizia. Sarah sat with Izak while Jacob studied the surrounding area, all the while keeping Sara and Izak in view. Jacob was no more than thirty yards away when he heard the sound of shuffling pebbles. He turned and found himself face to face with a brute of a man who was wielding a sword. His eyes were bloodshot, and his bearded face had the expression of a hungry, rabid wolf.

"So, you expected to get away, did you?" the monster said with a laugh.

"Run, Sarah, get out of here!" Jacob yelled.

Two more men appeared out of nowhere, blocking Jacob's escape. The three of them had Jacob surrounded. One of them then noticed Sarah off in the distance and took off for her.

"Whatever you do," hollered Jacob in Yiddish, "save Izak!" In that instant, one of the men lunged at Jacob with his sword, stabbing him through the belly. He then turned and followed the other killer who was making his way toward Sarah.

Sarah's attempt to flee was unsuccessful. Briefly evading her killers, Sarah managed to fold the blanket over little Izak's head and place him in the nearby bushes. A moment later, the men were upon her.

CHAPTER SEVENTEEN

Angelina's carriage hurried through the town without slowing down.

Carlo turned to Angelina and said, "Monfalcone is less than one hour from here. If the signorina is agreeable, we will stop there."

"Va bene," answered Angelina. "I'll leave it up to you."

They had been on the main road for less than three minutes when Carlo brought the carriage to a sudden halt. "*O Dio mio* (oh my God)," he gasped as he jumped down to the ground.

On the roadside, lying in a puddle of blood, was Jacob's dead body. Ten meters beyond was Sarah. Angelina nearly fainted when she saw the woman's unclothed, mutilated body. She crossed herself with a shaking hand, covered her eyes, and prayed in silence.

Carlo touched her arm and said, "Please, signorina, we must get out of here."

Unable to take her eyes away, Angelina said in a low, shaking whisper, "We can't just leave them this way. We must do something."

"Please, signorina, it is unwise to remain here any longer. It isn't safe. We should leave right away."

Just then, Angelina heard a cooing, giggling sound coming from the bushes several meters away. She walked in the direction of the sound, and there in the bushes wrapped in a blanket was an infant smiling back at her. Instinctively, Angelina picked up the child and held it in her arms. She was suddenly overcome by a most peculiar sensation, unlike anything she had ever experienced before in her life. Angelina felt an instant bond, an emotional link that couldn't be defined.

"Signorina Angelina, we must go now!"

Angelina couldn't hear him. She was lost in her own world. "This was their child," Angelina said. "This orphan, this poor child…." Angelina rocked the baby in her arms and realized then that this child would forever be a part of her life. Angelina held the baby tight. "We are not leaving without this child!" she said defiantly.

"As you wish, but we must leave right away," Carlo said as he assisted Angelina back to the carriage. "We should be in Monfalcone within the hour. I am friends with an innkeeper there who will assist us in attending to this infant."

As they rode on, Angelina held the baby close to her, as though it was her very own newborn child.

One hour later, they entered the town of Monfalcone and went directly to the Pension Bella Vista. To better tend to the infant, Nino, the manager, gave Angelina a room with a private bath. He also supplied her with a clean blanket and soft cotton fabric cut from a bed sheet to use as diapers.

Two hours later, they were packed and back on their way. During the rest of the journey, the baby slept quietly and contentedly in Angelina's arms.

Late that evening, they pulled up at the entrance of the Convent of Sacro Cuore. Hearing the sound of the arriving carriage, Pepe, the caretaker, ran out to assist them.

"*Benvenuti* (welcome)," he said enthusiastically. His expression changed quickly upon seeing the infant in Angelina's arms. He, nonetheless, helped Carlo with the bags and walked the three of them inside.

Angelina turned to Pepe and said, "Please see to it that our driver, Carlo, has a bed for the night." Then to Carlo she said, "Thank you for all of your help. May God be with you." She went directly to Rachel's room.

Upon seeing Angelina in the doorway, Rachel let out a gasp and ran to embrace her. Then seeing what Angelina was holding, Rachel reacted as Pepe had just moments before. "What is this, Angelina?" Rachel said with surprise.

For the next half hour, Angelina told Rachel of the circumstances surrounding her precious little find. "I have very strong feelings toward this child," Angelina said to Rachel as she finished wrapping him in fresh clothing. "It is my hope that Sacro Cuore will adopt this child on my behalf. I will assume all responsibility in the interim. Oh, Rachel, it is beyond my comprehension. Something happened the moment I found him, the moment I touched him, something mystical, metaphysical, not of this world. He is a part of me."

"He certainly is adorable," Rachel said as she assisted Angelina in bathing the child. Rachel then took note that the infant was circumcised. She recognized that the young and innocent Angelina was oblivious to this fact. Rachel couldn't recall ever seeing Angelina so happy and at peace. For Angelina's sake, Rachel decided then and there never to divulge that secret to anyone and to keep it locked in her heart forever.

"What will you name him?" Rachel asked.

"I decided to name him Lorenzo, after my father," Angelina said as she held the baby up and stared into his eyes.

Lorenzo then giggled and flashed a broad, toothless smile that melted her heart. Angelina knew at that moment that this child would forever and always be an integral part of her life.

Angelina's appeal to the Sisters of Sacro Cuore to adopt the child was granted overwhelmingly. It was also agreed that she could raise little Lorenzo as her own. The other sisters were falling over one another to assist Angelina in rearing the child. Having Angelina back at the convent was like a breath of fresh air.

Angelina and Lorenzo were inseparable. Whether at prayer, doing chores, or working in her art studio, little Lorenzo was always at Angelina's side. For Angelina, Lorenzo was everything, her whole world, and much more. Each day she would thank the Lord for the gift that was Lorenzo. She would relive, again and again, the day that this little infant came to become an integral part of her being. *How could it be that from the seeds of misery there could bloom a flower so pure?*

Through the years, no one ever questioned or challenged the fact that Lorenzo resided with Angelina and not in the dormitory with the other children. Their special relationship was natural and unthreatening. In school, Lorenzo was cherished by the other children. He absorbed all the material like a sponge and was always quick to lend any student a hand with a difficult assignment. Lorenzo had a unique and genuine affinity for theology and all things divine. This was recognized early on by his teachers, and as a result, Lorenzo was given special research challenges in order to hone his analytical skills. In time, it became clear that Lorenzo had a higher calling.

Beginning at the age of twelve, Lorenzo would attend classes at the religious academy in Treviso, which was hailed to be one of the preeminent theological seminaries of Northern Italy, for two weeks each spring and fall. Only students of promise were given the opportunity to attend. The invitation to return was based on one criterion— academic excellence. Needless to say, Lorenzo was always the first to be invited back.

At the tender age of nineteen, the academy offered Lorenzo the position of full-time lecturer. Never had anyone so young been asked to assume such a responsible and prestigious role. Lorenzo graciously turned them down, choosing instead to remain in Possagno to take the post of assistant to his own spiritual director, Father Algieri, in the Church of Santa Maria di Speranza. Father Algieri was elderly and frail. He no longer had the strength to fulfill his pastoral duties. When Father Algieri offered him the position, Lorenzo couldn't turn him down. The Holy See was well aware of the gifted Lorenzo Giraldi, and through the years, they closely followed his progress. Rejecting the post at the academy in place of the more humble position at home only confirmed the Vatican's sentiments. In due time, Lorenzo Giraldi would be summoned to Vatican City to be groomed to one day assume a position of prestige and honor.

Within a very short period of time, Lorenzo took on the majority of the priestly duties of the church, and he thrived in doing so. It was exactly two years to the day when the elderly Father Algieri summoned Lorenzo to his study.

Lorenzo ran in, and before Algieri had a chance to say a word, Lorenzo said giddily, "Padre, we just completed our first rehearsal, and it was flawless!"

Algieri, amused by Lorenzo's enthusiasm, knew what Lorenzo was referring to, so he sat back and let Lorenzo finish. It was one of Lorenzo's pet projects, a play that he had written and was in the process of directing. It was a nativity play that had a group of Possagno's orphaned and infirmed in its main roles. Father Algieri smiled warmly and beckoned Lorenzo to be seated.

"My dear Lorenzo, I have received a very important missive. It comes from Rome, from the Vatican."

"My goodness, Father," Lorenzo said with a concerned tone, not recognizing Father Algieri's joy. "Should we be concerned?"

"No, no, not at all, my dear friend. On the contrary, today I have received the special papal directive—or should I say, request—that you, Lorenzo Giraldi, serve the Holy See in Vatican City!"

Lorenzo's jaw dropped. He was dumbfounded.

Father Algieri, smiling at Lorenzo, said, "Don't you have something to say? Are you all right?"

"Why, yes, Father, it's just that…I had no idea."

"Of course, my dear boy, it's no surprise. That is, it is no surprise to me and certainly not to those in much higher esteems. Such decisions aren't made in haste. You have been under a microscope—their microscope—for quite some time now."

"Was this your idea, Father? Tell me that it *was*, for I know that I am not deserving. My place is here, with you, in Possagno."

"Lorenzo Giraldi," Father Algieri said with a most serious expression and tone. Then, placing his hand on Lorenzo's, he said, "You have been selected for all of the right reasons. Your staying here would please me to no end, but you must move on. In fact, I won't allow you to remain. Your replacement will be arriving any day. Come now, let's toast to your noble future."

CHAPTER EIGHTEEN

I left the Levy home and quickly made my way to the road leading out of Novi Sad. My mind was reeling. Mr. Levy, Hanna, my sweet Mia—it was all too much for me to process. My feet moved in pace with my pounding heart. Walking faster and faster, I soon found myself running. The sweat ran down my brow and burned into my eyes. My legs ached. I stumbled to a halt and sat on a boulder on the roadside. I struggled to fill my lungs with air. As I finally managed to cool down, I gazed up to see a pastoral landscape that was curiously out of sync with the ugly horrors that I had only just witnessed in Novi Sad. A soft, pleasant breeze blew through the branches of the wild cedars in a nearby meadow, bending its lanky branches hither and yon, nodding to me, coaxing me to push on, assuring me that all would be well.

Filled with a fresh spirit and a new resolve, I rose to my feet and continued on my way. Following Goustie's directions, I soon came upon a ranch where the main house had the distinct chimney that was exactly as Goustie described. Taking the windy road that lead to the main house, a boy of about eight appeared from behind one of the trees.

He was struggling to free the line of his kite that was caught in a high branch of a tree. Communicating with him in very simple Serbian, I offered to lend him a hand. After several snaps of the string, the kite came free.

"Hooray," the boy cried, clapping his hands in delight.

"Why, thank you." It was the voice of a young woman who came rushing over. Taking the boy's hand, she said, "Did you thank the man for helping you?"

"No trouble at all," I said. "It was my pleasure." I introduced myself then asked her if this was the house of Maxim Malkovic.

"Yes, yes," she answered with a smile. "Maxim is my husband."

"I have regards from Mr. Levy of Novi Sad."

"Oh, that's wonderful. How is he?"

Thinking that it may be better not to mention what happened in Novi Sad just yet, I said, "Mr. Levy is fine."

Then, catching herself, she put out her hand and said, "Kristina Malkovic."

"What an adorable little boy you have, Mrs. Malkovic," I said, shaking her hand.

"He is my nephew, my sister's boy, Marko. They're staying with us. Come, let's go inside. You must be thirsty."

"Hello, everybody," Kristina said loudly as we entered the house.

Maxim, who had been in the kitchen cooking dinner, came out to greet us.

"This is Ernst, a friend of Mr. Levy."

"Levy? The saint? That's all I have to know. Any friend of Levy is certainly a friend of mine. Come on in, Ernst. I'm Maxim." Maxim wiped his hands on his apron then extended one to me. "You came just in time. Please, we're about to sit down for dinner. Ah, Magda," Maxim said, grinning widely as a pretty young woman entered the room. "Ernst, please allow me to introduce my favorite sister-in-law, Madga." Before I could say a word, Maxim said, "Let's set the table for one more; Ernst is joining us."

It was remarkable to me that I, a stranger, should be getting the red-carpet treatment.

Sensing my uneasiness, Maxim walked me over to the dinner table and said, "Just hearing Levy's name is enough of an introduction. Ernst, it makes me happy that you are here. Let's have a drink, a nice Italian *aperitivo*."

We sat at the dining room table together while Magda and Krisitna organized the place settings.

"If it weren't for Levy, we'd all be destitute. This farm was owned by my father and my uncle. As the saying goes, Levy saved the farm." Maxim took a long taste of his drink then continued. "As a result of a poor business decision, the bank was going to foreclose. My father turned to his friend, Levy, who underwrote the loan. Since then, my father passed on. My uncle has little interest in the place, so as a result, Kristina and I are...how should I say...the permanent caretakers."

A few minutes later, we were all sitting around the dinner table.

"So, how are the Levys?" Kristina asked. "And Mia, such an angel...."

I decided to tell them of the ugly events of Novi Sad. Their jaws dropped as I described what had occurred.

"My God," Magda cried, cupping her hands to her mouth as tears began to form in her eyes.

In a serious tone, Maxim said, "If we don't manage to destroy one another, the Germans will gladly do it for us," Maxim said, speaking into his glass.

Kristina reached over and put her arm around Magda.

"The big trouble is," continued Maxim, "with all the fighting between the Serbs and Croats, the Germans then come along and mix us all up. They're after the Jews, and we get caught in the crossfire. What happened to Magda was just unbelievable. Can you imagine? She was nearly mistaken for being a Jew!"

"At least Yankl is safe," Magda said. "Such a sweet boy."

Hearing this, I almost choked. I knew then that she was referring to my nephew, Yankl.

"Are you all right, Ernst?"

"Yes, thank you, the food must have gone down the wrong way." I composed myself and asked, "What, may I ask, happened to you in Sabac?"

"It happened just like that," Magda said, snapping her fingers. "We were in the clinic straightening up at the end of our shift when, all of a sudden, German soldiers entered and ordered us all outside. They grabbed poor Nelly and took her away in a truck. As they dragged her away, Nelly quickly turned to me and mouthed the word *Yankl.* As quickly as they had come, they were gone. We heard the cries of others as the truck drove off. The Germans knew who they were after. I ran back to the farm as fast as I could. Thank goodness the children were safe."

Afraid to ask, I nonetheless prodded Magda for more details. I needed to know for certain.

"This person, Nelly, of whom you speak. Why did they take her away?"

Magda looked up and, in a dreamy tone, said, "She and her husband were Jews in hiding. Nelly was such a sweet woman. She had a part-time job at our clinic. We hit it off right away. I got to know her very well. Her little boy, Yankl, was in the day nursery along with our Marko. I ran back to the nursery to collect Marko. He was playing marbles with Yankl. When I took Marko's hand and started to leave, poor little Yankl ran after us. My heart melted. I realized then that I couldn't leave him stranded. I took him by the hand and was overcome with an unusual feeling. I felt an overpowering need to help that child. I can't describe it. It was something that was not of this world. I brought him to the church. The nun who received us at the door opened her arms to him as though he were coming home."

"Why did *you* leave Sabac?" I asked.

"At first I thought that I would remain there, thinking that I would be safe—after all, I *am* Serbian. Then I heard one of the mothers say that the Germans had carted off some of our local girls as well. Being alone since my husband was called up to serve in the military, I feared the worst, so I decided that it would be safer for me and Marko to stay with Kristina and Maxim until the war is over."

My mouth became as dry as stone. I found it difficult to breath. I wanted to reach over and take a sip of water, but my hand shook violently when I merely touched the glass. I loosened my collar. "Please excuse me. I need some air," I said as I rushed out of the room. I stood on the terrace and inhaled deeply, trying to calm down.

"You all right?" It was Maxim. He put his arm over my shoulder. "For a moment there, I thought that you were going to pass out. Just a minute, I believe that I have a little something that will make you feel better." We sat down on the stoop. Maxim took a small flask from his pocket and handed it to me. "Not too much—this stuff is powerful. I made it myself."

One sip and it went right to my head. I started to cough.

Maxim took the flask from me and laughingly said, "Easy now, one sip at a time."

I took one more sip in the hope of blocking Nelly's face from my mind. *Please, God, if she is to die, let it be quick. Don't let her suffer.* I handed the flask back to Maxim.

He took a long drink then wiped his mouth on the back of his hand and said, "So, where are you headed?"

"I'm on my way to Tuzla," I said, not wanting to go into any more detail.

"What the hell do you have to do there?" Maxim said with a side-glance.

"I got stuck in Brcko when all hell broke loose. Two of my friends took off for Tuzla where a relative is giving them a place to stay."

"Tuzla is a strange place. You had better be careful." Maxim took another gulp from the flask, slapped me on the arm, and said, "Tuzla isn't that far away. You'll stay here tonight, and I'll take you there myself in the morning."

The house was grand. Maxim told me that he and his wife had been house sitting for most of the year. It was like there very own home. When his uncle would return, it would be for no more than two or three days at a time.

Maxim showed me to a lovely and spacious room on the second floor. It had a large double bed and a balcony that over looked the valley. Before leaving me, Maxim said, "You've had a long day. Settle in. Make yourself at home. You'll feel better after a good night's sleep. See you in the morning."

I stepped out onto the terrace. It was dusk. The sun seemed close enough to grab. It was like a wet, ripe plum melting in the horizon. I leaned on the railing and was mystified by the sight.

Since time immemorial, poets have described nature's beauty, which, while alluring, is, in truth, cold, dispassionate, and devoid of substance. She beckons, mocks, and draws us near, like a sultry woman of the night.

In the mist of the cool evening air, I recalled the words of William Wordsworth's poem "Ode: Intimations of Immortality from Recollections of Early Childhood:"

> *There was a time when meadow, grove, and stream,*
> *The earth, and every common sight,*
> *To me did seem*
> *Appareled in celestial light,*
> *The glory and the freshness of a dream.*
> *It is not now as it hath been of yore;—*
> *Turn whereso'er I may,*
> *By night or day,*
> *The things that I have seen I now can see no more.*
> *The rainbow comes and goes,*
> *And lovely is the Rose,*
> *The Moon doth with delight*
> *Look round her when the heavens are bare,*
> *Waters on a starry night*
> *Are beautiful and fair;*

The sunshine is a glorious birth;
But yet I know, where'er I go,
That there hath passed away a glory from the earth...

That night I slept the sleep of the dead. Upon awaking, I felt as fatigued as I had the night before. Rising from the bed felt impossible, as though I were weighted down with bricks. *What was I doing? Where was I going? Could this be a test?* Gravity seemed to transfix me to the bed. Not wanting to face the day, I rolled over one more time, trying to sleep just a little while longer. I had learned from my great adventure that to remain in one place for too long was hazardous. I needed to keep moving, to keep one step ahead of the angel of death.

In the grand scheme of things, I thought, *there must be a reason for all of this. Was it possible that I was just an actor playing a part in some vast cosmic play? And if that were the case, then who wrote the script? Who was its director?*

Rallying every ounce of my strength and willpower, I struggled to my feet and walked over to the washbasin. It was filled to the brim with cool, clear, glistening water. With both hands, I splashed myself again and again until I was soaked. Dripping wet, I stepped out onto the balcony and let the morning breeze dry my naked body. In the fluffy clouds, I could make out the forms of my loved ones drifting across the light-blue sky. There was my mama and papa in one direction, Nelly and Romy in the other, and there, in the far off distance, was little Yankl. I marveled at how the clouds' shapes changed at the whim of the morning's zephyr breeze. I had no doubt that my trials were not going to end anytime soon, yet, somehow, the sight of those nebulous forms triggered in me a fervor, a strength. I felt empowered. I would take each challenge head-on and turn suffering into a defiant rededication to survive.

Following an early-morning breakfast, Maxim and I said our good-byes and we were off to Tuzla. We drove in a simple horse-drawn wagon.

"Sit back and let's enjoy the ride," Maxim said. Then, in a strong baritone, he proceeded to sing Serbian folk songs.

Maxim told me that he had met Kristina when they were both students at the university. At the outbreak of the war, they decided to marry and, together, take on the position of caretakers of the estate, where they had been living ever since.

We were on the road for about two hours when Maxim pulled onto a side road. "We'll stop for a little while at the *kafana* (roadhouse). The horses need to drink," then, winking at me, he said, "and I think that we could use one as well. You'll like it. It's a good place."

A minute later, we pulled up to the place. Maxim secured the horses at the water trough at the back of the building. As we came around to the front door, my heart stopped when I saw a German military half-track parked outside.

"Good, they're open. Let's go in," Maxim said, putting his arm around my shoulder as we strode inside. "Good day, gents," Maxim said with a flare.

There were only a few people inside. One man was sitting by himself. A barmaid was cleaning off a table. Off to the side were three German soldiers sitting together at a table drinking. They all looked up at us briefly then resumed what they were doing.

I froze and looked straight ahead.

"What can I get you boys?" the barman asked, smiling broadly.

"Anything wet and cold would be fine," Maxim said as he, once again, wrapped his arm around my shoulder.

I wanted to get out of there—the sooner, the better. It was as though I had walked right into the lion's den.

The bartender gave us two tall glasses of *rakija* (homemade plum brandy).

"Come," Maxim said, "let's sit over there." He led the way to a table that was next to the soldiers.

I took a seat with my back to them.

Maxim raised his mug. "*Ziveli!*" he said. "To good friends!"

We clinked glasses.

I tried to act relaxed. "To good friends! *Ziveli!*" I said before taking a gulp.

After draining his glass, Maxim pounded the mug on the table and signaled to the hostess to bring another round.

Not knowing where this was going to lead, I decided that it was a good time to go to the latrine. As I was about to rise, I saw that my way was blocked by the barmaid, whose hip was rubbing against my arm. I stiffened and cleared my throat.

Seeing this, Maxim chuckled and said, "I believe my friend could use another drink." He gave her a wink then reached over and slapped me on the arm.

The waitress gave me a seductive look then walked away.

"I think she likes you, Ernst," Maxim said, grinning from ear to ear.

"Can you blame her?" I said. Out of the corner of my eye, I could sense the soldiers gawking at me. One of them muttered something that I couldn't make out. Without turning around, I got up and headed straight for the latrine.

The room was dark and had a dank, rancid odor. The central part of the floor was tiled and slanted toward a central drain. I unbuttoned my trousers and relieved myself. There was the sound of men's laughter and hands clapping coming from inside the bar. Having no other recourse, I went back inside.

In the little time that I had been gone, things had changed—and not for the better. One of the soldiers was forcibly holding the waitress down on his lap. One soldier was waving his pistol while cheering the other soldier on. The third was guarding the door. The proprietor was now sitting at my place at the table alongside Maxim.

For a moment I thought that I could evade being noticed—but no luck. The soldier at the front door motioned for me to take a seat next to Maxim. The poor girl was struggling to free herself, but the brute was holding her tight. With one hand, he tore open her blouse and grabbed at her bare breast. Then, as he reached for her skirt, the girl twisted free and quickly swung her hand around and scratched the soldier deeply across the cheek.

The soldier yelled, "*Ach, scheiss,*" as he put his hand up against his bleeding face.

Everyone froze.

I had to make a quick decision—run or stay? As I contemplated my next move, the decision was made for me. At that moment, another German officer appeared at the front door. He stood at the threshold and took in the scene that was unfolding.

"*Dumm ox* (you idiot)!" he said to the bleeding soldier.

The other two soldiers jumped to attention and gave a clumsy salute. The girl covered herself and ran behind the bar. Maxim and I didn't move.

"*Kommen schnell!* (get out)!" the officer barked. He then turned on his heels and walked out. The three soldiers gathered their belongings and scurried out after him.

Maxim and I breathed a sigh of relief.

"They're here. No place is safe anymore," Maxim said as he watched the door close behind the soldiers. Then, turning to me, he said, "Ernst, you must forgive me, but I cannot take you to Tuzla. I must return to my Kristina. For all I know, the Germans are on their way there now. I wouldn't be surprised in the least if they decided to commandeer the estate."

"Please, Maxim, there is certainly no need to explain. You have already done more than enough. I will be fine."

Relieved, Maxim then said in a hearty voice, "What do you say we have one more for the road?"

The barman, who was still sitting beside us, put his hands on both of ours and said, "Stay where you are, gentlemen. This one is on me."

The innkeeper returned to the table with a bottle of *rakija*, along with some food. We ate heartily. Maxim continued drinking, and it didn't appear to phase him in the least. Having reached my limit, I graciously abstained. When we left, Maxim drove me up to the main road and pointed to a pass about five hundred meters away that he said was a more direct route to Tuzla. He assured me that by keeping a steady pace I would get there within a couple of hours.

"Thank Kristina and Magda for me," I said as Maxim pulled away.

"Godspeed to you, Ernst. *Dovidjenja* (good-bye)!" Maxim yelled as he rode away.

"*Dovidjenja* to you, Maxim," I said, waving.

CHAPTER NINETEEN

As I walked down that country road, I was overcome with a weighty sense of insecurity. With the events in the *kafana*, things could have gone much differently. The soldiers could have easily turned on me, and that would have been the end of it. Despite my good fortune, I was down. I realized that the best formula for survival would be to continue my masquerade. *If Maxim didn't consider me to be a Jew, then why should anyone else?* I would sally forth as my new persona—Ernst Von Mann. Still, it was hard, so very hard. I began to sing in rhythm with my step. I used song as a ploy to keep my sunny side up. The melody evolved into a kind of marching song. My arms began swinging in sync with my legs. My posture straightened up in a bracing military pose. The next thing I knew, I was singing German marching songs, songs of the fatherland, songs hailing Germany. As the words came forth, it felt as though I was purging myself of a deadly poison.

SS marches, clear the streets—left right, left right
The storm troopers are ready
Out of tyranny they'll march

Their way into freedom
So, yay! All march!
To the final assault!
Just like our fathers did, left right, left right
Death shall be our comrade in battle
'cause were we are
There's the fight
And the devil grins right at us
Wua, ha, ha, ha! Left right, left right
We fight for Germany
We fight for Hitler
We'll give the enemy no chance...

I sang the "Marschiert," the marching song of the SS German military unit called the *Schutzstaffel.* Louder and louder I sang, all the while swinging my arms higher and higher. The singing filled me with enthusiasm and vigor. At one point, I began to march in a goosestep like a Nazi in a military parade. With my head held high and my back straight as an arrow, I marched down that dusty country road, singing songs like a proud German soldier who hadn't a care in the world.

I was so consumed by my act that I was oblivious to my surroundings. Without realizing it, I had marched right into the bivouac of a German military unit. The sounds of howling laughter snapped me out of my reverie. The veil lifted, and there before me were about a dozen soldiers sitting in a clearing. They were pointing at me and laughing hysterically. Two soldiers got up and continued singing the song from where I had left off. I must have been a ridiculous sight to behold. Oddly enough, I wasn't scared. Coaxed on by some mysterious instinct, I fell into my role without skipping a beat.

"Look at that idiot," one of the soldiers said, laughing uncontrollably.

I noticed that among them were the three soldiers from the *kafana*.

"What happened," one of them said, mockingly, "somebody steal your uniform?"

They slapped their knees and howled with laughter. I stood still in my tracks and assumed a dopey grin.

"Here, have some." One of the soldiers held out his canteen and motioned for me to sit down beside him.

"Thanks," I said, taking a long drink from his canteen.

"Where you from?" he asked casually.

I tried to act tough, mimicking Jerold, the "Brown Shirt" thug, from my neighborhood in Vienna. "I'm meeting friends in Tuzla. I've been hiking in the area for the past couple of weeks."

"That's where we're going. Say, that was the Waffen-SS marching song you were singing, no?"

"That's right," I said. Then, looking up, starry-eyed, I said, "Ah, the SS. That *was* my dream. Perhaps in another life—I didn't even qualify as a foot soldier." Then, pointing to my chest, I said, "Leaky heart valve."

"Too bad," said the soldier. Then, looking at me more intently, he said, "Say, didn't I just see you at the roadhouse?"

"Yeah, that's right."

"Deter Rolff," he said, extending his hand.

"Ernst," I said, shaking his hand. *What the hell,* I thought. *I may as well go all the way.* "Ernst Von Mann," I said, smiling broadly.

He seemed impressed. After a brief, contemplative pause, he said, "Why not come along with us? There's room in the truck."

What was I thinking? This could be disastrous. Then again, not accepting his offer could make him suspicious. "That would be wonderful!" I said enthusiastically. Then, remembering the bottle of brandy that Goustie gave me, I took it from by rucksack, held it high, and said, "How about this?"

Their faces lit up.

I uncorked the bottle and handed it to Deter. He took gulp after gulp until it was yanked out of his hand by another soldier. Deter laughed heartily, watching the bottle being passed from soldier to soldier.

"So, Ernst, where do you hail from?"

"From Vienna," I answered proudly.

"I have people in Vienna," Deter said. "What district?"

Without giving it a second thought, I answered, "*Der zweiten bezirk*" (the second district)." Realizing my gaff, I flinched. The second district is the Jewish quarter of Vienna. Not being from there, Deter probably wouldn't be aware of that fact, but I wasn't certain. I was caught off guard, nonetheless. I felt my face redden—enough to cause Deter to notice. *That little faux pas might have been my undoing,* I thought.

The soldiers polished off the brandy in a flash, and we all climbed into the half-track. I was the last to enter, taking a seat next to the tailgate. Deter took the seat opposite me. Our little convoy consisted of the half-track and two smaller trucks that drove ahead of us. I sat quietly in my seat, not wanting to engage in any further conversation. After a little while, I began to recognize the countryside in the outskirts of Tuzla. I imagined my next move: Upon entering the city, I would thank them for the lift, hop off the truck, and wave good-bye. Either way, I tried keeping the same German mindset that I had assumed from the start. As the truck slowed to navigate a tight turn in the road, we passed a group of civilians being marched in a ditch along the roadside. They were shackled to one another at the waist. There appeared to be men and women of all ages. As if in slow motion, I caught the eye of one old man. In that fleeting moment, I felt a connection. I somehow saw myself in that man. The truck picked up speed. Our eyes were momentarily fixed to one another until he dissolved into nothing but a mere speck in the distance.

Deter spat from the truck. "Yids," he said, with a disgusted look.

I nodded meekly in agreement, trying to hide any emotion.

The truck suddenly came to a grinding halt. There was commotion outside. We heard whistles blowing and soldiers barking out orders. I followed Deter from the truck. Before us was an open field where military vehicles were parked haphazardly. We were told that a truck from the convoy ahead of us had run over a land mine, killing one soldier and badly injuring two others. We were instructed to proceed on foot to a nearby village. We piled out of the truck and marched up to a village, a kilometer away. I had no choice but to go along. It was starting to get dark. I was hoping that in all the confusion I might be able to slip away—no luck. I was instructed to help unload the supplies from the truck and carry them up to the village. All the while I noticed Deter remaining close to my side.

Once we entered the village, things took a turn for the worse. Standing among the soldiers, I stuck out like a sore thumb dressed as I was in lederhosen.

An officer, pointing at me, asked, "*Wer ist dieser mann?* (who is that man)?" Before I could answer, he squinted and asked to see my papers.

Deter was standing nearby gloating.

The officer studied my documents intently. "Von Mann, eh?" he said with an air of curiosity. "Schooling?" he shot the word at me like an arrow. His face was now only inches from mine. He stared directly into my eyes.

"Gimnasium Nazional," I said without missing a beat.

"Home address?"

I hesitated momentarily. I was trying to come up with the name of a neutral, middle class section of the city, but it was already too late.

From behind me, a man said, "I believe it is *der zweiten bezirk*." Then to me, Deter said, "Is it not? This man is an imposter," he said, pointing at me, accusingly. "I am sure that he is a filthy Jew."

The officer snapped his fingers and yelled, "Take him away—*schnell*." Two soldiers grabbed my arms and dragged me off to a small house two hundred meters away. They shoved me inside and locked the door behind me.

The room was pitch-black. I was hit instantly by the horrid stench. That, coupled with the oppressive heat, made it nearly impossible to breathe. When my eyes finally adjusted I saw the face of misery. The room was lined with people sitting listlessly along the walls of the empty room. One or two looked up at me momentarily, only to resume their blank, lifeless poses. I stood awkwardly in place, not knowing whether to laugh or cry.

"Sit down," whispered a man next to me. "Save your strength."

I could make out the outline of an old man. I maneuvered myself beside him against a wall.

"I have heard," he whispered, "that in the camps one at least has the option of suicide. There's an electrified fence. You need only touch it and puff...."

"How long have you been here?" I asked.

"One day, two...who knows?"

There were dull moans coming from everywhere, agonizing sounds. The stench was a grotesque combination of vomit, feces, and sweat. It was unbearable.

"Where are you from?" I asked.

"Bratislava." The man's voice was shallow and weak. "We were stupid enough to believe that we would find the Holy Land. If Moses didn't make it, how could we? Aaayyeee," he moaned.

"What is it?" I asked.

"My side...where they kicked me...it's all right...all right...." His breath was weak and shallow.

This was beyond belief. What was I to do? This is unreal...no way out...relax...stay calm...oh God...the smell...it's unbearable.
Sitting with my elbows on my knees and my hands covering my face, I tried not to think at all. I remained in that position for an indeterminate amount of time then

I heard the sounds of voices outside the door. The door swung open.

Yes. They're letting us out. Take me, kill me, I don't care—anything but this.

A spotlight lit the room the moment the door opened. A mob—tens of people—came rushing toward me. They poured in like a tidal wave. There was no possible way of getting out of their way. I quickly moved off to the side. Soldiers were yelling. I realized then that these people were being shoved into the room. It was like a stampede of humanity, a mass of moving flesh. Some fell and were trampled. I tried covering my head with my arms. There wasn't room to move. There was no longer any room even to sit.

Through the chaos came the voice of the commandant. "You will all be shot at dawn, goodnight."

The door slammed shut.

The cries and screams blended into one diabolical chorus of human suffering. Like one who is sinking deeper and deeper into thick, muddy quicksand, I stretched my neck and raised my chin upward in order to lap up each and every bit of the musty air. The days of solitary confinement in the Vienna jail were a veritable holiday as compared to this. Like then, I knew that the only way to survive was to withdraw to a place deep within my soul, a place that is not of this world.

Papa, I know that you are watching from high. I beg of you, please, please don't despair. I am strong. I will get through this. Just the thought of you is your intervention.

I once more saw his figure in the misty light of the streetlamp. Once more I felt my parents' embrace as we said our last good-bye. Their blessing was the fuel that propelled me; their love was the force that sustained me.

I will never know how I made it through that night. Evidently, no matter how horrific a situation might be, one is capable of conforming to his or her surroundings. It may be that I metamorphosed into another creature, one that would relish such an environment. A rodent is delighted to wallow in a sewer and may actually feel sickened by a pleasant, pastoral setting. That night I became a rodent. The setting in which I found myself that night was so horrific and abysmal that unless I did, indeed, transmigrate into another lesser being, there was no way on earth that I could have survived.

A hum of agonizing misery permeated the room. Inch by inch, I maneuvered my way to the door. Having the door at my back rather than the skin of a wretched human being was in itself a blessing. Light began to filter into the room. The night had finally passed. The sun was rising. I knew that they would be coming for us at anytime. I knew that the end was near. There was the sound of the door latch. As the door swung open, I fell directly to the ground. Struggling to my feet, I found myself face to face with the commandant.

"Take me first. Shoot me. I am ready."

"He has spirit, this one," the commandant said. "Take him. He'll be useful."

I was handcuffed and taken to a clearing in the nearby woods where there was a huge, freshly dug hole in the ground. I watched as, one after another, the dazed, disoriented zombies stumbled about like headless chickens. Without the strength to resist, they were directed over to the grave like lame sheep and pushed in. Those that started to resist were first shot then shoved in. Soldiers, their faces covered with handkerchiefs, went into the house and cleared out the rest. The dead were piled into carts and dumped into the grave. The commandant directed the action. When it was over, only about twenty of us were spared.

Under close guard, we marched with the other soldiers back down to the trucks. Anyone too weak to walk was shot on the spot. At the bottom of the hill, soldiers were busy loading up the trucks. Pushed off to the side, we saw the remains of the truck that had been blown up by the land mine. We were lined up and given empty ammunition boxes with leather handles on either end to carry, two by two. We were then ordered into the minefield and began marching up and back. My partner and I were positioned midway along the line. He was an old man with a gray beard. He barely had the strength to stand. At first we walked slowly, fearing that each step would be our last. Shots were fired over our heads as we were ordered to pick up the pace. Within seconds, there was the sudden, ear-deafening BOOM of an exploding mine.

"Get up, get up, *schnell*," yelled the officer. The soldiers cheered and applauded. "Get up! Keep walking!"

I looked at the man on the ground beside me. There was something familiar about him. It was his eyes. This was the same man from the chain gang that I passed while riding in the truck the day before. I helped him to his feet. We each grabbed hold of either end of the ammo box and resumed walking. BOOM came another blast. We were sprayed with rocks and dirt. When I opened my eyes, there were two men lying beside us screaming in pain. Again, there came the resounding cheers from the sidelines. The soldiers took potshots at the wounded men, ending their pain, once and for all. On and on we went zigzagging the field. Again and again came the blasts, followed by screams and flying body parts. *Stand up, keep going, don't stop....*

I helped the old man to his feet. "Grab the handle," I said, coaxing the old man along. "Come on, we mustn't stop." The man hardly had the strength to stand, let alone walk. In spite of my own profound weakness, I somehow managed to pull him along with me. I moved mechanically from one end of the field to the other. My mind became numb. The explosions continued. In time, I know longer heard a thing.

Losing all sense of place and time, I didn't realize that we were now walking along with the convoy of trucks and foot soldiers. Besides the old man and me, there was no one left of our group of human mine sweepers. We were now traversing the minefield turned graveyard. How we managed to survive, I will never know. Why the Germans kept us alive, I will never know. Maybe they wanted to utilize us for some other macabre task. I was beyond hunger and thirst.

I heard the old man mumbling beside me. In a glassy-eyed daze, he repeated the same words over and over again: "The only true and pure place for mankind is the communist utopia...the communist state.... The day will surely come. When it does, we will all be free."

The darkness was settling in fast. I could now only make out his silhouette.

As we continued on, I could sense that we were now walking on a wooden gradation, each step producing a hollow sound. *It must be a bridge!* I thought. It was too dark to see anything. I strained to get some telltale sign of whether the bridge spanned water or railway. In the darkness, coupled with the noise of the convoy, there was no way of knowing for sure. I had to act. We had outlived our usefulness. It was now just a matter of time, and time was being measured in minutes, not hours. There was only one way out, and that was to jump.

There was very little time. I sensed by the slope of the ground that we were already halfway across.

"Take my hand," I whispered to the old man. "Take my hand, and we will jump off the bridge."

"Jump? Are you crazy? We may be over railway tracks. We won't survive. We might die in the fall."

"Look," I said. "It's our only chance. It's over. With any luck, we *will* die in the fall and not in the hands of these animals."

I took the old man's hand and nudged him close to the railing. It was our good fortune that the railing was only four feet high. Holding him about the waist, we straddled the railing, and before there was time to reconsider, I leaned over, and together we fell.

There was the brief sound of gunfire and then nothing.

CHAPTER TWENTY

From His heavenly mansion God beholds creation. He has no more control over man's behavior than a father has over his bickering children. Out of the depths God hears his children cry but cannot heed their plea. The angels despair as God mourns.

His child is falling. God etches the names of His children into the book of death. The angels hold the book open. God's hand aches as He signs one name after another.

His child is falling. God hesitates. He puts down his quill. The angels are bewildered. God looks up, and in teary-eyed defiance, He refuses to sign.

I am floating. Warm water caresses me. My limbs drift this way and that at the whim of an easy, flowing current. My head rests on a soft, comforting pillow of mud. I am at peace.

I was awakened by a soft, rhythmic stroking sensation on my cheeks. Inches away from me were the sensitive, loving eyes of a German shepherd who was licking my face. Believing that I was in the throes of a dream, I didn't budge, wanting the sensation to last forever. My dream ended when I saw the German soldier holding the leash. He was studying me without saying a word. Oddly enough,

I maintained a sense of calm, either because I was too weak to react or that I simply didn't care.

The soldier leaned down to me and said in crisp German, "Are you a Communist or are you a Fascist?"

"I am a Communist. I arrived from Moscow three days ago." The words came to me out of nowhere.

The soldier dropped the leash and fell to one knee.

"Here, comrade, let me help you."

He then lifted me gently to a sitting position and dragged me out of the water and onto dry land. I didn't have the strength to stand. He gave me water from his canteen. The soldier watched as I gulped down the fresh water. Looking past him, about thirty meters from where we sat, I could make out the partly submerged, lifeless body of the old man lying facedown along the shoreline.

I had responded to the soldier without hesitation. They were the words of the old man, whispered to me from his watery grave.

"We have to get you to safekeeping," he said as he struggled to get me to my feet. With my arm slung over his shoulder, we walked in the direction of a farmhouse that we saw far off in the distance. We stopped repeatedly along the way to rest. During one of those breaks, while resting in the tall grass, the soldier asked me how I managed to end up in the river. I managed to divine a tale that was so simple and plausible that I almost believed it myself.

"I was sent by the Communist Youth of Vienna to attend a members' meeting in Moscow. Before returning home, I decided to visit with friends in Serbia who were caretakers for the estate of a wealthy landowner. I was unaware that my friends were harboring a dozen Jewish refugees in the barn. The day that I arrived, a German army unit showed up at the estate. When they discovered the Jews in hiding, all hell broke loose. My friends were shot on the spot, and I was rounded up with the refugees and taken prisoner."

I then told him of the subsequent events: being packed in the schoolhouse, being marched through the mine-field, and finally, jumping off the bridge.

"You poor boy," the soldier said with pathos. "Don't you worry, I'll make certain that I get you to safekeeping."

We finally arrived at the farmhouse. It was small and in desperate need of repair. There were sheets drying on the clothesline. Pigs wallowed in a muddy pen. Chickens cooed from a half-open coop. We were received at the door by a couple in their sixties. Seeing the soldier struggle to keep me upright, the man quickly grabbed ahold of me, and together, they eased me across the threshold and onto a chair in the kitchen.

"This man needs food and shelter. You will nurse him back to health, no matter how long it takes." The soldier took some banknotes from his pocket. "Here, this should take care of it—and enough for you and your wife as well. I must return to my unit. No monkey business now; this man is my friend." Then, with a stern look, he said, "I know where to find you." The soldier turned to me and said, "Now I must go. I will try to get you identification papers. Congratulations, you're now a bona fide refugee. Be careful and good luck." Without saying another word, he turned and strutted out the door.

The farmer brought a cot from another room. He cushioned it using several blankets, and with his wife's assistance, they removed my wet clothes, covered me in a dry sheet, and gently helped me into bed. The woman sat at my side and fed me warm milk and soft-boiled eggs. After one or two tastes, I dropped down onto the pillow and was asleep in a matter of seconds. When I awoke, I heard the couple speaking in a low voice. Propping myself on my elbows, I saw them eating at the kitchen table. The woman turned to me, smiled, and in perfect German, said, "*Helf Gott*, (bless you) how are you? You must feel rested, no?"

"I'm sorry," I said, "I must have drifted off to sleep." I felt weak and very hungry.

The couple exchanged a little giggle, and the man said, "Come, let me help you."

The man helped me out of bed. Wearing the sheet like a toga, I joined the couple at the kitchen table. My appetite was ravenous. I wolfed down a plate of cucumbers, tomatoes, cheese, and yogurt, followed by a honeydew melon and coffee. It was the tastiest meal I had ever eaten. They told me that I had been sleeping for a day and a half. The woman said that her first instinct was to awaken me, and then seeing that I was sleeping so deeply, she let me sleep through.

"How is it that your German is so perfect?" I said, confused. "You speak like a native."

"That's because I am," she said proudly. "I was born in Germany in the small town of Rietberg. My family moved to Yugoslavia when I was just a young girl. My father, a Baptist minister, fell in love with this land after coming on a mission forty years ago. It was here where we remained." The woman looked at me for a long while, then, with a start, stood up and said, "Let's clean you up." She brought me to a small room abutting the kitchen and prepared my bath. Although the water was only lukewarm, it was the most marvelous sensation imaginable after what I had been through the past several days. I lay there, unmoving, and allowed the soothing water soak into my pores. I floated dreamily, not wishing to leave. When I finally got the will, I eased my way out of the tub and dried myself with towels that had been left for me. Neatly folded on a stool beside the tub were a fresh shirt and pants. Wrapped in a towel, I peeked out of the bathroom and into the kitchen.

The couple sat opposite one another chatting at the kitchen table.

"My clothes?" I said.

The man smiled and simply said, "Ruined."

"Take the clothes that my wife left on the stool. They are for you."

The woman nodded silently in agreement.

A few minutes later, I entered the kitchen wearing my "new" clothes, which were a good two sizes too big.

Noticing me standing there, the old woman put her hands to her face and, letting out a gasp, uttered, "*Helf Gott* (Oh my God) Lazo!" She walked up to me and lovingly straightened my shirt collar. After which she abruptly burst into tears and hurried out of the room.

"The clothes of our son," the man said in a monotone voice as he looked off dreamily. "He is gone." The man motioned me to wait as he left the room. He returned a moment later with a long leather belt. "Here you are, this should help," he said with a smile. The belt wrapped

around my waist one and a half times, with still some to
spare. "You'll fatten up in no time," he said as I tightened
the belt about my waist. "I left your shoes outside in the
sun. They should be dry by now. With a bit of oil polish,
they'll be as good as new. Please forgive my wife. Poor
Marisa, she has hardly gotten over our loss, and now you
appear like a phantasm. Although you are thinner and
darker, your facial features resemble those of our son,
Lazo, to a fault."

We spoke together for a while. This man, whose name
was Josep, had a quiet and humble demeanor. His strong,
rough hands and dry, wrinkled skin reflected his years of
farming under the hot sun. No doubt Josep was, in fact,
what he appeared—simple and kind. I still could not help
but second-guess his behavior. *Was it natural or merely a
reflection of instructions given to him by my rescuer, the German
soldier?*

Josep told me more of their son, Lazo. It was their
dream that one day he inherit the farm, but it was not to
be.

"Early one morning, he was struck by a high fever, and
his neck swelled rapidly. Before anyone could reach the
clinic, poor Lazo suffocated to death. The doctor called
it diphtheria. That was nearly ten years ago. With God's
help, Marisa and I have managed to keep our little farm
afloat."

After two days rest, I started to come back to life. I shad-
owed Josep. From cow shed to chicken coop to mending
fences, I kept up as best that I could. By day three, I was
actually helpful. The chore I enjoyed most was feeding the

cows. As Josep rode the hay-laden horse-drawn cart along the cow pens, I would sit high atop the pile and pitchfork hay feed down onto the heads of the cows below.

The days flew by. Rising each morning to the rooster's cry, followed by working the farm for a full ten hours felt natural. My daily chores, coupled with the hearty meals, were invigorating. The sun, the rich earth, and the pungent sweet smell of cow dung permeated my soul. I was at one with nature; I was at home.

While walking back to the house one evening, Josep told me how blessed was the day that the soldier brought me to their home. "A calm has come over Marisa, the likes of which I haven't seen since we were first married. The void made by the loss of our son has been partly filled by you."

In time, I fell right in step as part—an integral part—of the household, much like Marisa and Josep's son reincarnated.

Living on this little farm with this lovely couple made the war, death, and destruction seem like a world away. While the weeks and months sped by, living in this pastoral setting seemed to make time stand still.

Early one brisk morning in March, while loading the shed with newly cut firewood, a man seemed to appear out of nowhere. It was the soldier. His face was stern.

Without a greeting, he walked up to me and said, "You must get out of Yugoslavia right away. It's only a matter of days until our forces will be in control of all of Yugoslavia." He shook his head and, speaking more to himself than to me, lamented, "Our Fürher won't be satisfied until he takes over the world." He reached into his inner breast pocket. "Here, take these. I snatched them from a dead soldier," he said as he handed me several folded pieces of paper.

They were the identity papers of one Dietrich Struhmer. The face in the photo was of a man in his twenties. Other than us both having dark hair, we looked nothing alike.

"Thank you, comrade," I said with sincerity as I embraced him.

"There is very little time," he said. "Going northbound will be too dangerous. You will fall right into the hands of our troops that are heading this way. They're trigger-happy. If they find you, they'll shoot first and ask questions later. You can't take the chance. You should be on the next train to Split. From there it shouldn't be hard to find someone to ferry you across the Adriatic to Italy. It's the safest way."

Together, we walked back to the house. Marisa and Josep were visibly upset by the news. While Marisa was preparing us a bite to eat, Josep checked the train schedule.

"The next train for Split is at ten tomorrow morning." Looking at me, Josep said, "Marisa and I will deliver you to the station."

"Good," said the soldier. He scribbled his name and address on a piece of paper and handed it to me. "If this damn war ever comes to an end, look me up in Stuttgart. Good luck, comrade." He gulped down the tea, embraced me, and left.

Josep and I spent the evening playing checkers as Marisa kept our glasses full with hot black tea spiked with *rakija*. All too soon, the drink went to my head, and I excused myself and went to sleep. It wasn't more than two hours later when I awoke to the sounds of crickets. The air was cool and fresh. The chirping sound—the nocturnal symphony of random notes—made me think of the misdirected and random path that lay ahead.

When I awoke the following morning, the smell of freshly baked bread filled the room. I dressed and joined Josep and Marisa in the kitchen for a hearty breakfast. We ate quietly, exchanging very few words. We knew from the start that this day was coming. We had an unspoken understanding that I could never replace Lazo, yet in some ways I did. Marisa filled my large coffee cup with hot milk. As she poured, she put her free hand on my shoulder and squeezed. That was all that she did, but her message came through. As ersatz mother and son, this unspoken gesture spoke volumes. It reflected our mutual loss, our yearning, and our hope.

Josep brought the carriage around to the front of the house. As I was about to climb aboard, Marisa stepped out of the house wearing a bonnet. I helper her climb up, and moments later, the three of us were on our way. To the onlooker, we were just another family out for a ride. When we passed some German soldiers along the way, Josep touched the rim of his hat and never slowed down.

Two hours later, we pulled up at the station. My "parents" waited in the carriage while I went inside to buy the ticket. The train was on time. Walking back to the carriage, I saw before me a picture of simple, timeless beauty. Josep and his lovely wife, Marisa, were sitting quietly holding hands while awaiting my return. I held up my train ticket proudly as I walked up to the carriage to say goodbye. I reached up and took Josep's rough hand in mine. I thanked them once more for their warm hospitality.

Then Marisa handed me a small package wrapped in newspaper, smiled, and said, "A little something for your journey."

I stepped aside as the carriage pulled away. I realized right then and there that, no matter what the onslaught of evil, good will always win out as long as this earth harbored the likes of Josep and Marisa. I watched them ride off and made a silent prayer until I could see them no more.

The train ride to Split proved to be uneventful. The only "incident" occurred when an old man boarded the train an hour later. Wearing a crumpled hat and frayed jacket, he greeted me with a toothless smile, took off his hat, and settled into the seat beside me. He was wearing a garland of garlic bulbs around his neck. Each pore of the man's body emitted a stifling and overpowering odor that stopped me in my tracks. I excused myself and quickly bolted to the next car. The rest of the ride went smoothly. Two hours later, we arrived in Split.

Alighting from the train, I walked in the direction of the port. If the city were occupied, one wouldn't know it. The streets were bustling with activity. Shops were open. People were scurrying about, paying little or no attention to the German soldiers in their midst. Aside from the many machinist shops and garages situated along the port road, there were also several small restaurants. Boats of all shapes and sizes dotted the harbor. Most of them were medium-sized fishing vessels. I bought a local paper and took a seat at one of the busier outside cafés.

A waiter shuffled, wiped the table once, and said, "Do you care for something to eat or drink?"

"Thanks, just an espresso, please." Then, putting on airs of a casual Austrian, I said, "Tell me, where might I find a passenger ship that would be going to Ancona?"

"Over there," he said, pointing to a large ship called the *Apolonia*.

Two hundred meters away was an old gray ship whose hull was spattered with rust. It looked out of place among the other small fishing boats in the harbor. Stevedores were carrying baggage and crates on board, while others stood by smoking idly.

As I began to devise an exit strategy in my mind, some-one shouted in German, "Grab him!"

A man ran frantically through the café.

Behind him was a Gestapo officer who again yelled, "Get him! Don't let him get away!"

A soldier coming from the direction of the harbor intercepted the man and held him fast. "That's more like it. Now, hold him still." He then swung, landing a punch squarely on the man's jaw. The poor man fell to the ground in a heap. The officer looked down at his handiwork and, while shaking his bruised fist, spat down on the uncon-scious man and said proudly, "There, that'll teach him."

The waiter standing beside me shook his head and muttered, "Another wretched Jew trying to escape."

Watching, unmoving, while the poor man was being so brutally beaten left me feeling sick and ashamed. *How could I have just sat there doing nothing? Why didn't I make any attempt to help?* Thoughts on how I could have or how I should have behaved swirled wildly in my mind: *Had I tried to help the poor man, I quite possibly could have managed to catch the officer off guard and kill him instead. But what about the soldier? He wouldn't have stood by idly. There's no doubt that he would have shot me on the spot. Who knows? Maybe, in the final analysis, the effort would have been justified. Here I am, trying in the worst way to survive, but for what? Maybe it is egotistical of me to want to go on. Had I killed that officer, then being killed in return would have made perfect sense in keeping with the harmonious balance of nature. If only my poor brethren would take that view—kill one enemy for each one of us killed—then maybe this nightmare would finally come to an end.*

"Can I get you anything else?" the waiter asked without missing a beat.

"What's that? Oh, no thank you," I said, coming back to earth. There was no way I could remain there much longer. Danger lurked. I had to get on that boat.

"When does it sail?" I asked, looking over at the *Apolonia.*

"Around five o'clock," he said as he began to clear the table. Seeing that I still had several hours to wait, I said, "On second thought, maybe I *will* have something to eat."

From my vantage point in the café, I watched as passengers began to board the vessel. Two officials were standing at a high wooden table next to the gangplank. One of them checked the passengers' documents while the other stood by and watched.

After finishing my meal, I had another espresso and decided that it was time to make my move. I paid the waiter and walked over to the ship. Taking my place in line, I tried to get myself to relax by assuming an arrogant air. Ahead of me in line was a young family of four. I watched as the official flipped through their documents and waved them on ahead.

"Next!" he said without looking up.

"One ticket to Ancona," I said in German.

"Your papers, please."

I took my documents from my breast pocket and put them into the man's outstretched hand. I held my breath and prayed, knowing that there was no similarity at all between Dietrich Struhmer—the face pictured in the photograph—and me.

The agent glanced blankly at my papers then back at me. He stamped a page with one hard blow and said, "Pay the purser." Then, looking past me, he said, "Next!"

I bought my ticket, walked up the gangplank, and never looked back.

My cabin was located somewhere deep in the bowels of the ship. Taking one look, I knew that I wouldn't last there a minute. The cabin was tiny, damp, and windowless, and it reeked of petrol. I went back on deck. It was a balmy and beautiful evening. I found a spot along the railing and watched the goings-on in the port.

The ship wasn't due to set sail until after eight o'clock that night. The delay didn't matter to me at all; in fact, it was a godsend. Safely on board, breathing the cool air and taking in the sights was the ideal cure for my frayed nerves. As soon as the ship eased out of its berth and began making its slow crawl through the harbor and into the open sea, a heavy weight lifted from my chest. From a deck chair, I watched the port lights flicker off in the distance. I tucked myself in a blanket and passed the night on deck in a deep, relaxing, and dreamless sleep.

Early the following morning, I awoke to the sound of seagulls. The air was damp and warm. I threw off my blanket and looked over the deck railing. The water was foamy and dark blue. A school of dolphins easily kept up with the ship as it cruised steadily toward the Italian coast. I was swept with a surge of emotion in seeing the colorful port city of Ancona come into view.

What to expect, what to pray for, I hadn't a clue. Like flotsam carried at the whim of a raging sea, I knew that my journey was far from over. How this adventure would unfold was still a mystery, but one thing I knew for certain: I would not succumb; I would not despair. I had come too far to give up now. Bolstered by my father's parting prayer, I would do everything in my power to survive. In the name of my slaughtered family, no matter what my fate, I would see this thing to the bitter end.

It was almost nine o'clock in the morning when we arrived in the port of Ancona. As the passengers were organizing their belongings, there was the announcement that disembarking would be delayed temporarily due to a dockworkers' strike. One of the deckhands told us not to go far, as these strikes happen all the time and never last for more than an hour.

A young man standing beside me was struggling with the packages he was holding. "*Managgia la miseria* (damn it)!" he said as one of the packages fell to the floor. His little boy, who was trying to get his attention, pulled on his father's jacket, causing the rest of the packages to fall. "*Ma, che fai* (what are you doing)?" the man yelled at the boy. As he bent over to pick up the fallen packages, his eyeglasses then fell out of his pocket. In frustration, he screamed once more at the boy, causing him to burst into tears. The man's wife, who was holding their young daughter, put the girl down in order to comfort her little boy. As I helped pick up the packages, the girl started having a tantrum. The father picked her up, and fortunately, within a minute or two, things began to quiet down. At that moment, we all looked up at each other and began to laugh.

"*Mille grazie, signore* (thank you, sir)."

"Not at all, the pleasure was all mine," I answered in German.

The woman thanked me as well.

"Petar Kandic," he said, "and this is my lovely Italian wife, Laura."

Remembering my false papers, I introduced myself as Dietrich Struhmer. I saw then that this was the same family that had boarded the ship ahead of me in Split.

The man told me in broken German that they were on their way home to Bologna. They were on vacation in Bosnia visiting with his parents. This was the children's first opportunity to meet their paternal grandparents.

I told them briefly that I was making my way back to Vienna by way of Italy.

The children were now sitting on the floor playing while the three of us made casual conversation. Someone passing by wouldn't think this scene as being all that unusual; new friends having met on vacation were now together waiting to disembark. In reality, it was nothing of the sort. We were light-years apart. My heart melted as I beheld this beautiful family. They lived their simple and domestic life happily and painlessly. Their problems and concerns were of the everyday and of the mundane, while mine were of a fugitive on the run.

I could recall my own home years before this madness began. My teenage sister would aggravate my mother by her silly boy-crazed antics. I would tell her to talk lower while I was trying to do my homework; my father, in turn, would advise me to go to my room, as the living room was no place to study. I remembered how bored I was with that existence, how I thought that I was always missing something. I realized now how very precious that boring existence really was. I realized now that I would give anything in the world to relive that boring existence, if only for just one day.

The little boy looked up at me and smiled. I took his hand and showed him how to play the thumb-wrestling game. He was delighted. I would let him win, and he would giggle and say, "*Ancora una volta* (let's do it again)." We played nonstop until the announcement came that we were to disembark. We gathered our things as the gangplank was maneuvered into position. Two crewmembers were stationed at the head of the line to lend a hand to the passengers disembarking.

"*Avanti, prego* (right this way)," said one of them said as he unhooked the rope at the top of the stairs and ushered us by.

Trying to appear as a family member or close friend, I helped with the packages and even took the little boy's hand. As we walked down the ramp, I saw that my instincts had been correct. On the dock below there were German soldiers among the bag handlers. We walked over to the customs inspection area and took our places at the shorter of the two lines. Trying to remain composed and giving the appearance of having nothing to hide, I began joking with the little boy. We were still giggling as we stepped up to the customs agent. I nonchalantly handed him my papers. Out of the corner of my eye, I made out the two SS officers scrutinizing the activity. After only a brief glance at my papers, the agent waved us through.

"It was certainly a pleasure to make your acquaintance," I said to Petar and his family as we stepped out to the street.

"The pleasure was all ours," Petar said.

The little boy took my hand, wanting to thumb wrestle.

"*Basta, Silvio, non disturbare il signore* (don't bother the man)."

"He's not disturbing me at all," I said. "He's fine."

Petar smiled and said, "Say, our train doesn't leave for a while. Why don't you join us for a bite to eat?"

I was glad that he made the offer, as I didn't know where else to turn. "It would be my pleasure," I said.

We crossed the boulevard and settled into a café near the train station. Unlike the port of Split where soldiers wandered about casually, things were very different in Ancona. Secret Service agents were openly harassing people, making random searches, and checking identification papers. Danger loomed everywhere. No one lingered in any one place for any length of time. People scurried about with eyes cast downward like frightened mice. The sooner I got on a train out of there, the better off I would be. I took the last sip of my cappuccino and signaled to the waiter for the check.

"Take your hand out of your pocket," Petar said jovially. "You are my guest, remember?"

"Don't be silly," I said. "Please allow me." It then occurred to me that I couldn't pay even if I wanted to. All I had were dinars.

Petar laughed as I stood there holding the Yugoslavian money in my hand. "You see?" he said joyfully, "It was meant to be. Come, you can change that in the station. Let's move. We don't want to miss the train."

We crossed the street and walked through the large doors of the terminal. One look inside and I was overcome with fright. German soldiers were everywhere. I had no recourse other than to remain with Petar and his family and hope for the best.

"We're heading straight to Bologna. Are you returning directly to Vienna, or will you be making any stops along the way?"

I was so consumed with my thoughts that I wasn't even aware Petar was speaking to me. "Hello, Dietrich," Petar said jokingly, "are you there?"

"What's that?" I said, snapping out of it. "Oh, forgive me, Petar," I said, trying to force a smile. I didn't know what to do. SS agents were milling about among the soldiers. There was even one standing beside the currency exchange window.

"You can exchange your money over there," Petar said, pointing toward the *cambio*.

My mouth became parched. I didn't know where to turn.

"Dietrich, are you all right?"

I leaned in toward Petar and looked him intently in the eye then shot a quick glance over to the two SS officers who were standing nearby, hoping that he would catch on. I then let out a breath and lowered my shoulders in a gesture of surrender and whispered, "My name is Ernst Mann."

Petar held my gaze. His expression of sympathy and a quick nod of the head proved to me that he *did* catch on. Without skipping a beat, he said, "Come along, everybody, we're off to Bologna." He put his left arm over my shoulder and his right arm over his wife's, and like long lost friends, we waltzed over to the ticket counter. The board showed that our train was on schedule.

As we neared the ticket window, I handed Petar my dinars.

He pushed my hand aside and said, "You keep them. One never knows—they may still come in handy." Then he furtively pressed some lire into my palm. "I insist," he whispered. "Please don't argue."

I bought myself a third-class ticket for Milano. Petar, who would be getting off at Bologna, purchased first-class tickets for himself and his family. We walked together along the platform toward the waiting train.

"Here's where we get on," Petar said, standing before the first-class car.

I helped hoist the children up into the car then gave Laura a hand. Turning to Petar, I said, "*Grazie per tutto* (thanks for everything)."

"*Buona fortuna* (good luck), *Ernsto*," he said, shaking my hand. He then climbed on board and waved good-bye.

My car was at the far end of the train. Stepping inside was like entering another world. It was chaos. People were yelling, babies were crying, and children were running up and down the aisle. There was a man with a basket on his lap containing live chickens. I found the one vacant seat in the car.

"*Scuzi,*" I said as I maneuvered around a plump, young peasant woman in an aisle seat. She hardly paid any attention to me, as she was busy breast-feeding her baby.

A loud whistle sounded as the train began rolling slowly down the tracks. I loosened my shirt collar. The car was hot and stifling. Sweat was dripping down my face. I removed my jacket and rolled up my sleeves, but it was no use. There were no ceiling fans, and the windows were closed. I flipped the latch and opened the window all the way. I stood, unmoving, as the cool breeze hit my face. I was in heaven.

Then came the shouts: "*Chiudi la finestra. Il vento, il vento.* (Shut the window. There's a draft.)"

I had no idea what was happening.

The old woman sitting opposite me shot me an angry look and said, "*Il vento fa male* (the draft is unhealthy)."

Everyone was bothered by the draft. As soon as I shut the window, they all calmed down.

Like a schoolteacher giving a reprimanding look at a naughty student, the old woman looked at me and, shaking her head in disgust, whispered to her husband, "*Stranieri* (foreigners)!"

I laughed to myself as I recalled the words of one of my professors in the Yeshiva who, after telling a student to close the window, said, "Many people froze to death; few stank to death…."

The steady, rhythmic clang-clang of the train lulled me into a state of restful repose. Sleep was my one and only solace. I welcomed it, and I cherished it—my respite from a harsh and miserable reality.

Every half hour, for no apparent reason, the train came to a grinding halt. On each such occasion, passengers would scurry off to buy food from vendors that were camped out on the tracks. Not wishing to take any chances, I chose to remain on board. Time passed slowly. It was midnight and we still hadn't reached Bologna. At the rate we were going, we'd be lucky to arrive in Milan by sunrise.

The old woman opposite me pointed to the shelf above her. "*Per piacere* (please)," she said, looking at me.

I jumped to my feet to retrieve her bag.

"*Molto gentile*," she said, thanking me.

She took out an apple and a knife, spread a linen napkin on her lap, and went to work. With the precision of a surgeon, she wielded the knife around the sweet, red orb. I watched in dumbfounded fascination as the peel lengthened, spiraling lower and lower down toward her lap. I held my breath and prayed that the rind wouldn't snap, that it would remain in one piece. The woman worked slowly and meticulously, one hand rotating the fruit while the knife hand excised skin, and skin alone. Then, smiling from ear to ear, the woman raised the single strand proudly in the air for all to see.

Thrilled by the performance, I blurted, "Bravo, bravo."

The woman's husband and the lady next to me joined in with applause. The woman then cut the apple in four equal quarters and served us each a piece. Like children taking a play break, we sat together munching and smiling at one another as if we didn't have a care in the world. Not wanting to exclude her infant from our little picnic, the young mother delicately rubbed her infant's tender gums with her apple-moistened finger. As we all watched, our lips contorted in synchrony with the child's as the pungent nectar caused its little mouth to pucker.

That simple, impromptu act broke the social barrier and made the journey, from there on out, much more relaxed. Using bits and pieces of my broken Italian and by way of primitive hand gestures, I discovered that the young woman beside me was from the town of Recanati. Her husband was called up to serve in the military along with most of the young men of her town. She was now on her way to Milan to live with her mother until her husband's safe return.

"Oh, my poor husband," she cried. "How could they take him? He's so frail. He'll never survive."

"There, there," I said. "He will be fine. Don't you worry."

I picked up her little baby and held him up in front of my face. My heart melted as he cooed and flashed me a big toothless smile.

"I hope you're right. I do miss him so."

It was already dark when the train pulled into Piacenza, where the old couple was getting off. After assisting them with their baggage, the old woman thanked me, and before leaving, she handed me a bag containing the last few pieces of fruit. I thanked her warmly and returned to the car.

An old, disheveled man was now stretched out on their seat. He was fast asleep. I exchanged an amused glance with the young woman and took my seat beside her. Within a few minutes, we were back on our way to Milan.

The train was now rolling at a brisk pace. The young mother and child were sleeping peacefully. I quietly settled into my seat beside them and tried to sleep. I was repeatedly awakened by the train's loud whistle as it sped at full speed through the local stations along the way. Staring out the window into the dark night, the same questions would filter again and again into my mind: *Would there ever be peace? Would my trauma ever end? Would I ever be blessed with a loving wife and family?*

Realizing where I was, I quickly snapped out of it and reminded myself that there was no time for sentimentality. I would be arriving shortly in Milan. What adventures lay ahead of me there were anyone's guess. I had to be sharp and on my guard if I intended to survive.

CHAPTER TWENTY-ONE

I was jolted awake by the train screeching to a grinding halt. I peered out the window but couldn't see a thing. The night was black. A minute later, the train doors opened with a bang. Standing at either end of the car were officers of the SS. They were dressed in their typical garb: black leather coats that extended all the way to the floor, wide-brimmed black hats, and black leather gloves. They were accompanied by soldiers who were holding machine guns, poised and ready.

At the top of his voice, one of the officers yelled, "*Attenzione, documenti!*" They walked slowly and deliberately from either end of the car checking everyone's papers.

We were ordered to remain in our seats. Anxious cries and screams echoed throughout the car as people nervously rummaged through their pockets and handbags to locate their papers. I sat paralyzed in fear. With nothing to show but my dead soldier's ID, I was doomed. *Oh God, is this how it is all going to end? There must be a way out of this, there must be!*

The officers moved closer and closer toward my seat bank. Surprisingly, the woman and child beside me were still fast asleep. I furtively maneuvered my arm around the woman's shoulder. In a dreamy half-sleep, she snuggled up beside me. I carefully shifted the baby closer to me. To any onlooker, we surely appeared like a cozy, little family.

"*Achtung!*" The soldier slammed the butt of his rifle into the side of the man who was sprawled out on the seat in front of me.

The man opened his bloodshot eyes, looked momentarily at the soldier, and then slid back and resumed his snoring.

As the soldier was about to turn his attention to me, I made a silent prayer and slid my hand under the infant and, very forcefully, pinched its behind. The child's scream was deafening. So startled was the officer that he jumped back, almost losing his balance. I hugged the baby, trying to comfort it and quell its pain, but it was of no use. His crying got even louder. While rocking the child, I looked at the officer, shrugged my shoulders, and made an expression of apologetic stupidity. The ruse worked. The officer cursed, threw down his arms in disgust, and moved on.

I handed the baby over to his mother and collapsed back in my seat, emotionally drained. The woman was beside herself. She caressed and hugged her infant until his cries finally calmed to a quiet whimper. She looked at me with an expression of both curiosity and anger. I could only look back at her without saying a word.

We remained at a standstill for a very long time. Then, finally, there was the sound of spewing steam and of the steel wheels locking into gear, indicating that we were, once again, on our way. It was early morning. The sun was rising. People began collecting their bags. We would soon be arriving in Milan. I sat at the window and watched the green countryside gradually evolve into gray as trees were replaced by apartment buildings and meadows and then by city streets.

As we slowly rolled into the station, my worst fears came true. Extending the entire length of the platform, not twenty feet from the tracks, was a chain of German soldiers. Between each group of five soldiers there stood an SS agent. I remained in my seat and watched in terror as each and every one of the passengers alighting from the train was stopped and questioned by the agents. I had no choice, no recourse, but to exit the train with the other passengers. Standing on the steps between the train cars, I looked down and braced myself. My mind went blank. I saw no way out. I had no stratagem. I took one deep breath and stepped down to the platform. My feet felt like lead. With several people still ahead of me, I slowly inched my way forward toward the line of soldiers.

Standing alone and vulnerable on that station platform, my mind drifted back to my days in captivity in the Vienna jail. I saw myself peering out the little window in my cell and seeing the misty image of my father beneath the lamppost on the street below. I watched as he gazed up, not knowing if I was looking back or if I was even there at all.

"*Mascalzone, farabutto* (you son of a bitch)!" cried a man as he forced his way past the soldiers from among the crowd of onlookers. He rushed directly toward me and yelled in Italian, "*Bastardo!*" He reached out to me and pulled me close, whispering to me in German, "Follow my lead." He then pulled away and, once again, said out loud in Italian, "You son of a bitch, where have you been? I've been waiting here since yesterday!"

An SS officer turned to him and said angrily, "*Vas machst du? Vas is das?* (What's going on here?)"

In crisp, flawless German, the man said, "This is my stupid Italian cousin. I've been waiting here for him since yesterday. You leave him to me. I'll take care of him, that's for sure!" The man put his arm around my shoulder and walked me right past the guards.

The confused officer shook his head and let us pass.

CHAPTER TWENTY-TWO

We walked to the restaurant inside the terminal. The man led me to a table in the rear.

"That was a close one." He extended his hand to me. "Antonio Bertoni, *molto piacere* (pleased to make you acquaintance)."

I took his hand but was too confused to speak.

"It's all right," he said, still holding my hand. Then, in an upbeat manner, he said, "I'm famished. I suggest that we have something to eat."

"I'm sorry," I said, "but I don't understand. Why did you—"

He broke in and said, "As my train was pulling into the station, I saw the commotion at a nearby gate. German soldiers were positioning themselves on the platform. As I was walking over to see what was going on, I was suddenly overcome by a most unusual feeling. It is hard to describe. It was as though I was being summoned by a mysterious force to come to someone's aid. As it turned out, it was you whom I was summoned to assist! I stood among the crowd and watched the passengers alight from the train.

Then you appeared. As if scripted, I knew exactly what I must say and do."

"But, really," I said, "why me? There were hundreds of passengers on that train."

"When I saw you standing there between the train cars, there was something about you. I knew, beyond a shadow of doubt, that you were the one, that it was you who had to be saved. I pushed my way past the soldiers and approached you. The rest you know." Then he spread his arms and declared, "So, here you are...*cousin!*"

"I don't know what to say. Who *are* you? How can I thank you?" I said, feeling ill at ease.

Bertoni smiled and said, "I am chief counsel for Farmilan, one of Italy's largest pharmaceutical companies. In my spare time I like to dabble in creative writing—short stories, poetry, that sort of thing. I'll bet that you have some story to tell."

Before I could answer, the waiter appeared with our food.

"Ah, this looks good," Bertoni said, smacking his lips. "Let's eat."

Aside for a slight accent, Bertoni's German was flawless. While we ate, he told me a little bit about himself. He was thirty-two. After receiving a degree in jurisprudence from the University of Milan, he spent two years of postgraduate studies in Berlin. His wife, the *contessa*, and their two young daughters spend the summer in their villa in Treviso. He remains in their residence in Milan during the week and joins them for long weekends. Bertoni offered me a cigarette, took one for himself, leaned back in his chair, and after blowing a plume of smoke, said, "Now it's your turn."

I didn't know what to make of this mysterious man. He was quite charming and very well groomed. I felt that I had to take him at his word. After all, he did save my life. I told him of my upbringing in Vienna, my family, my theological studies, and my interest in chemistry and therapeutics.

Taking a long drag from his cigarette, he leaned toward me and said, "I can see that you have suffered greatly. Tell me more of what you have been through."

His engaging manner made me want to tell him everything. Like a patient lying on his or her psychiatrist's sofa, I poured my heart out. I told him of my trials, of how my family had been slaughtered, of my imprisonments, and of all of my miraculous and narrow escapes. We sat talking for more than two hours.

Bertoni then put his palms on the table with authoritative air and declared, "You'll need a place to stay. I am all alone in my big apartment. My family won't be returning to town for several weeks." Before I could respond, he said with a gleam in his eye, "That settles it. You're staying with me!"

As I was about to protest, he put his hand in the air and, with a big smile, said, "I'm sorry, but I'm afraid that you don't have any say in this matter. Come."

I sheepishly walked with him out of the restaurant and into the street.

It was a beautiful, cool morning. Bertoni suggested that we walk. His gait was smooth and confident, the kind that comes from a life of comfort, breeding, and financial security. As we walked through the city, it seemed that everyone knew him. Countless times he'd touch his hat brim, smile, and say *buon giorno* or *ciao* to the passersby.

"I can see that you're smart," he said as we strolled along. "Plus, you have an interest in chemistry. Maybe you can be of some help to me. The company that I represent is struggling with a problem. One of their most successful products, a denture powder, had to be recalled. Moisture is finding its way into the containers, turning the powder into a muddy clump! It had to be pulled from the shelves, and it is costing the company a fortune. The company chemists have been struggling to solve the problem and, so far, have been coming up empty. Do you have any ideas?"

Enjoying the challenge, I put on my thinking cap. I knew that this problem must have a simple solution. Then it hit me. *Rice in saltshakers—that was it! The rice kernels absorb the humidity, and the salt remains dry. There is certainly a "rice-like" material that would keep denture powder dry. Why, yes! The soldier's mantra: "Keep your [gun] powder dry!"*

No doubt whatever was used to keep gunpowder dry would work just as well for denture powder.

"Call your people," I said confidently. "Tell them that you have found the solution to their problem." I told my theory to Bertoni, and then I said, "A few minutes in the library, and I will know what the substance is."

"Ernesto, *tu sei fantastico* (you're unbelievable)! Let's get cleaned up, then it is off to the library we go."

Bertoni's residence was a *palazzo* (palace) in the truest sense of the word. We were met at the door by the housekeeper. After a brief introduction, she showed me to the guest room. A minute later, she returned with fresh towels.

Antonio popped his head in the door and said, "The bathroom is down there at the end of the hall. There's shaving soap and anything else that you may need." He looked me up and down and said, "We're about the same size. Try these." He tossed me a fresh shirt and slacks. "That should do fine. I'll be waiting for you in the study." He winked and smiled before walking away.

Drying off after a quick bath and shave, I marveled at my good fortune. All clean and freshly dressed, I peeked through the door of the study.

Antonio looked up at me, folded the paper he had been reading, and said, "There, that's more like it. Come in, sit down." Sensing my uneasiness, Antonio said, "I am Italian, and I am ashamed. How my government could ally with Germany is beyond my comprehension. How such a civilized nation could be so wretched and vicious is mind boggling." Tears formed in his eyes. In a trance, Bertoni quietly said, "The Jews are forever tormented and debased, while their contributions to humanity far outweigh that of any other people since the beginning of time. I have struggled with that discrepancy my entire life." After a moment of quiet contemplation, Bertoni looked up and hollered, "*Basta* (enough) of this sentimentality. Come, Ernesto, there's work to be done."

The library was only a short tram ride away. Inside, a clerk directed us to the technology section, and within minutes, I had my answer. In order to keep gunpowder dry, fine metal shavings were sprinkled into the gunpowder to absorb moisture. Now the question was how to obtain the

metal shavings. When we found the answer, Antonio and
I looked at each other, and all we could do was laugh.
The manufacturer was Fabrik Einthoven, a company in
the German town of Essen.

"Don't worry, Ernesto, we do business with Germany all
the time. The first thing tomorrow, I will arrange for a courier to go to Essen to get a sample of the stuff. We should
have it in our hands in a few days." As we walked out of the
library, Bertoni said, "It's such a lovely day. Let's take a stroll."

I hesitated. The city was crawling with surly, suspicious
types.

Bertoni, noticed my uneasiness. "Quite right," he said.
"How stupid of me. You'll do better indoors."

We took a tram back to his apartment.

Once safely inside, Bertoni said, "The housekeeper is
gone. Make yourself at home. I'll be back in a little while."
Then, from the doorway, he said, "Oh, yes, I'm sure you'll
find some fascinating books in my study. Relax. Consider
this a well-deserved vacation."

Bertoni's home was palatial. Room after room was
replete with the finest décor. The wood-paneled study was
furnished with two deep leather sofas and several large
comfortable chairs, along with strategically placed side
tables, allowing for intimate conversation. On one side
was a large fireplace, and apricot-colored curtains covered
floor-to-ceiling windows. On shelves that ran the length of
the room were hundreds of books. There were books in
every category imaginable, including many complete sets
of first-edition literature. There were volumes in Italian
and German as well as English. The books were arranged
and sequenced along the shelves in a way that pleased

the eye, yet somehow gave the impression that most were
there only for show.

While leafing through some books at random, there
was one on the top shelf that caught my eye. Unlike many
of the others that were neatly lined up in series, this book
stood alone. Its dark jacket was worn, and it was leaning
to one side. With the help of a three-stepped stool and
fully stretching on tiptoes, I just managed to nab it. It was
covered with dust, and its jacket was frayed. I blew off the
dust and settled into an easy chair next to a floor lamp.

I couldn't believe my eyes. It was an early-nineteenth-
century edition of *Chapters of Our Fathers* printed in
Hebrew! It was the same text that I had studied during
my Yeshiva days. The book's musty smell, and faded fabric, transported me back in time to my little classroom.
I recalled following along in the text as the Rabbi read
Hayyim Nahman Bialik's sad poem, aloud....

We walk the world of slaughter,
stumbling and falling in wreckage,
surrounded by the fear of death,
and eyes that gaze at us in silence,
the eyes of other martyred Jews,
of hunted, harried, persecuted souls
who never had a choice,
who've huddled all together in the corner
and press each other closer still and quake.
For here it was the sharpened axes found them
and they have come to take another look
at the stark terror of their savage death.
Their staring eyes all ask the ancient question: Why?

I was mystified. How on earth, did this book find it's way into Bertoni's library? As I flipped through the familiar tome, several loose pages fell to the floor. They were faded and of a different texture. It was a letter written in longhand in a mixture of Yiddish and Hebrew. It read as follows:

To my loving Yonatan,

   I write this letter with a very heavy heart. After a lengthy and heart-wrenching deliberation, I have decided to do what, on the surface, seems to be the unthinkable, but I am certain that it will prove to be for the best. Although the reasons for this seem obscure, they are quite clear to me. It is written that we are the people of the book.

   Through the centuries, our people have struggled and suffered indescribable torment and pain. This means that we are the conscience of all of mankind. We hold up the mirror to man's foibles and transgressions. We are the standard bearers. The entire Jewish philosophy, or religion, can be reduced and distilled into one sentence: "Live life morally, follow the commandments and pray to one Lord, our God."

   Through the centuries, whether due to individual ambition or political expediency, this simple and pure philosophy was attacked and criticized, and the concept of the Jew as scapegoat was finally born. For better or worse, that had become the destiny of the Jewish people. There hasn't been a moment anywhere on earth where that hasn't been the case.

   On Yom Kippur we lament and remember how we have suffered. We recall the ancient Roman court that decreed that the Jews could no longer teach the Torah. Rabbis who chose to ignore the decree were tortured and killed. To them, the Torah was more precious than life itself. We remember Rabbi Akiba, who chose to teach despite the decree. While being led to the executioner, and while iron combs scraped away his skin, he recited, "Hear O Israel, God is our Lord and is One," freely accepting the yolk of God's kinship...

Oh, my darling son, I have decided never, ever to allow such a fate to befall you. I am, therefore, sending you away to another place, far, far away to a new life, to a new beginning as a gentile. As I write this letter, my tears flow. What I am doing may be a sacrilege, it may be blasphemous or simply egotistical, but what I do know is that I am acting out of pure love.

On this earth, there exists a select group of individuals, thirty-six in number. It is their destiny to assume the suffering for all of mankind. You, Yonatan, are one such individual, one of the Thirty-Six, a Lamed Vav. *By sending you off, I hope to protect and free you from the heavy yolk of oppression that our people have been destined to bear since the beginning of time. Now, as Giovanni Bertoni, I hope and pray that your life will be filled with love, joy, and peace. When the day finally comes that we meet in heaven, I only hope that you will forgive me.*

Your loving father,
Moshe Bercovici
Lublin, 1850

I read the letter over and over again. *How incredible,* I thought, *Antonio's great-grandfather wrote this letter more than one hundred years ago.* Moshe Bercovici referred to the legend of the *Lamed Vav,* the thirty-six individuals who roam the earth and assume the misery of mankind and, in return, assure mankind's stability. Bercovici stated unequivocally that his young son, Yonatan, was one of the Thirty-Six, a *Lamed Vav*! As the legend goes, each of the Thirty-Six inherits his position from his father and, in turn, passes it to his first male offspring. And so it is passed on through the family line for perpetuity. *If, in fact, this is true, then the man who saved me today, Antonio Bertoni is also one of the Thirty-Six, a* Lamed Vav.

In all likelihood, Antonio never saw the letter and, thus, is unaware of his station.

I gave the letter one last look then placed it between the pages of the book. I climbed back on the stepstool and put the book back on the top shelf exactly where I found it.

"Come here and give me a hand," Antonio yelled from outside the room. He had just returned and was holding two large packages of groceries. I rushed over to help him unpack the bags in the kitchen.

As Antonio was loading the cupboards, he said jovially, "Since I'm alone at home these summer weekdays, I have been mostly eating out. Having you here has brought out the domestic in me. This should hold us for quite some time."

Antonio Bertoni treated me as if I were his long-lost friend. He sat me down at the kitchen table, poured me a large glass of wine, and had me observe as he prepared a feast. Wearing a white apron over his shirt and tie, he danced about the kitchen cooking pasta, dicing onions, slicing prosciutto, sampling wines, cutting bread…. It was like a ballet.

"To the fraternity of good men," Antonio said, raising a glass. "There's nothing better!" Then he laughed and said, "Except, of course, for *le belle donne* (beautiful women). In any event, seeing that I am with my wonderful newfound friend, we will eat and celebrate, for who knows what tomorrow will bring."

After stuffing ourselves on the delicious meal, we returned to the study.

Antonio looked around the room and said, "Impressive, no? My grandfather bought this house, and it's where our family has been living ever since. We sat opposite one another in large leather chairs. Antonio glanced upward and said dreamily, "Once, while we were hunting in the country when I was ten years old, my father said something to me that was most curious. We were walking back to our campsite after catching two fat rabbits when he said, "In this life, it is important for you to have a Jewish friend. That was all he said. It was never repeated."

As I sat in those magnificent surroundings with this interesting man, I thought of the letter that was written by Antonio's great-grandfather, Rabbi Moshe Bercovici, to his son, and I understood why, at the train station, Antonio said he was overcome by a "most unusual feeling… as if summoned by a mysterious force." It was because Antonio Bertoni (Bercovici), the *Lamed Vavnik*, had been called upon to save me.

I decided then and there that I would keep this thought to myself and never mention it to Antonio.

CHAPTER
TWENTY-THREE

It was mid-morning when I awoke. A note at my bed-side read, "I didn't want to disturb you. Make yourself at home. See you this evening. Antonio."

I passed the rest of the day mostly in the study, randomly leafing through books. I broke up the time by going outdoors to buy a newspaper or to get a cup of coffee at the corner bar. Given my precarious state, I didn't venture very far from the residence.

I must have dozed off, for I was suddenly awakened by Antonio's hearty voice.

"*Tutto fatto,*" I heard him say as he barged into the study, smiling broadly. "It's all set. A courier is already on his way to Germany to get a hold of the metal shavings for our denture powder project. Now all we must do is wait." Seeing my glassy eyes, he said, "Oh, I'm sorry, Ernesto, I see that I have startled you."

"Not at all, Antonio," I said, rubbing my eyes. "I must have dozed off."

"You certainly could use a little rest, after all." Antonio took a seat beside me. "By the way," he said, "I have something for you." He took an envelope from his breast pocket and tossed it over to me.

"What's this?" I asked.

"Open it," he said teasingly, then sat back, amused.

I couldn't believe my eyes. Inside the envelope was Italian lire. "What is this?" I asked.

"Take it. You've earned it," he said, smiling broadly. "Remember? The scientists at the firm that I represent have yet to come up with the solution to the denture powder problem. I told the company's directors that we found the solution and only need several more days to prove it. What you see is simply a monetary advance—for the courier, our efforts, and the like."

"I can't accept this," I said. "We still have to prove that it, in fact, works."

"I trust that it will, my friend, I trust that it will."

The next couple of days passed uneventfully. While Antonio was at his law office, I decided to use my free time to study Italian. With a German/Italian dictionary, newspaper, and a notebook spread on the large table in the study, I got to work. I made long lists of vocabulary words and idiomatic phrases and read them aloud, over and over, until they were chiseled into my brain. It was a wonderful pastime.

Early that Thursday afternoon, while I was studying some new phrases from the newspaper, Antonio barged into the house and hollered excitedly, "*Ecco ci qua* (here it is)!" In his hand was a small container the size of an espresso cup. He put it down on the middle of the table. It contained the metal shavings that we were after.

We looked at the object, then back at each other, and declared simultaneously, "That's it?"

Within minutes, we were at work. We put two jars of denture powder on the table. We labeled one of them No. 1 and the other No. 2. Into jar No. 1, I sprinkled in some of the splinter-like filings, replaced the lid, and then shook it vigorously. I left jar No. 2 as is. As if handling volatile explosives, we carefully carried the two jars into the bathroom. Antonio turned the bathwater to hot and let it run. We left the room, closing the door behind us. Within about ten minutes, the bathroom was like a steam bath.

Antonio said, "That should do it. What do you say, Ernesto?"

We waited another couple of minutes for good measure then entered.

The room was so steamy that we couldn't see anything. We stripped down to our underwear. Antonio felt his way over to the faucet and turned it off. Leaving the door open, the steam cleared in less than a minute. On a shelf were the two containers of denture powder. They were dripping wet. We each took a container. Mine was marked No. 2. I opened it first. Inside was nothing but a clump of thick, muddy paste. Antonio was holding container No. 1. He looked at me nervously. I gave him a nod, coaxing him on. He slowly unscrewed the cap and removed it. Inside his jar was white, fluffy powder!

Standing there dripping wet and half naked, each of us holding our container of powder, we looked quite ridiculous. We cheered and giggled like little children.

Winning the state lottery couldn't have made us happier. This little coup further cemented our newly spawned relationship.

The following day, Antonio presented the solution to the company's scientific committee. By the afternoon, a shipment of the filings was already on its way to Milan.

"Thanks to you, Ernesto, I was hailed as a hero. The people at Farmilan believe that their losses will now be only minimal. Within ten days, all pharmacies will have their shelves restocked with the new, 'stabilized' denture powder." Antonio took out a bottle of champagne. He poured two glasses. Holding his high in the air, he said, "I knew when I saw you that there was something special about you. *Auguri* (cheers)!"

We clinked glasses and drank heartily.

"I instructed Tata, the housekeeper, to prepare a nice dinner for us," Antonio said as he drained his second glass of champagne. "My brother, Andrea, will be coming over this evening. He wants to introduce me to his fiancée. This is the first time in months that he has had time off. I don't know where he found the time to meet a woman, let alone get engaged to one. Andrea is a professor of surgery at the University of Milan and first surgical attending at the famous Fatte Bene Fratelli Hospital, the university's primary teaching hospital. The present chief of surgery is getting on in years. I believe that Andrea is being groomed to take his place." Hearing the knock at the door, Antonio jumped up and said, "There, that must be them." He rushed to the door to receive them.

Andrea was a leaner version of his brother. Standing at his side was a fair and attractive young woman. I felt out of place, but my uneasiness dissipated when Antonio introduced me warmly as his close friend and colleague.

After a marvelous dinner, we went into the study. Antonio poured us glasses of *digestivo*, which is Italy's answer to port wine. We settled into the comfortable chairs and sipped our drinks. Andrea was sitting quietly, staring into space.

"You seem preoccupied, Brother," Antonio said. "Is there anything troubling you?"

"I saw Papa last week," he said quietly. "He didn't recognize me."

"I know, Andrea," Antonio said, "it's most disturbing, but such is life."

Antonio turned to me and said that their father had been institutionalized one year before after suffering a massive and debilitating stroke. As their mother had died when they were young, he and his brother essentially raised themselves.

Trying to strike a happier note, Antonio said lightly, "I sired pretty little girls. You and I, Andrea, may be the end of the Bertoni line." Then, winking at Andrea's fiancée he said, "That is, of course, unless the two of you manage to do better."

Andrea acknowledged Antonio's remark by managing to crack a weak smile. "It's not only that," Andrea said. "It's my work. It seems that with each step forward, I take one step back. With the war on, besides the routine surgeries, more and more wounded are being transferred over to us. It's those damn infections. We treat, then God heals, yet it seems that God isn't always on our side. There is an integral part of the puzzle that is missing, and I'll be damned if I know what it is."

At that moment, Tata brought the espresso.

While stirring in the sugar, Andrea said discouragingly, "My hands are scrubbed raw, the surgical field is sterile, and the postoperative infection rate is still sky-high. I don't know what more can be done."

Antonio walked over and put a supportive hand on Andrea's shoulder and said, "Don't take it to heart, my dear brother. You're doing your part—I'd say, better than anyone. You're overworked. You're exhausted. What you need is a good vacation. It's time you take a few days off and come up to the country house. The girls are dying to see you."

That night I slept very little. Something was disturbing me. I rose early and stepped into the bathroom to bathe. While brushing shaving soap on my cheeks, the events of the previous night flashed through my mind: the joyous meal in the company of such wonderful people, Antonio and his brother having been raised by nannies, the young surgeon Andrea and his strikingly attractive fiancée…. There was something else, something Andrea said that caught my attention. He was overworked and sleep-deprived, but there was something else.

I lathered my face with neat and quick concentric strokes of the brush. Gliding the razor across my face made me think of Andrea in the operating theater. *Perhaps in another time and place I, too, could have been a physician or a surgeon.* I toweled off the excess lather from my face then felt the sting of the toilet water on my cleanly shaved cheeks.

That's it! That has to be the answer!

I dressed and went into the study to formulate my thoughts. I took out a piece of paper and began writing as follows:

The night before any elective surgery is to take place, the patient's skin is shaved. Then, just prior to surgery, the surgeon scrubs his hands then cleans the surgical site with soap and water. Sterile dressings are then placed on the surgical field, and still, despite all that preparation, the infection rate still exceeds 15 percent. Such infections can range in severity anywhere from the very superficial to severe, leading to limb loss, sepsis, and even death.

"You're up early." It was Antonio standing before me in his bathrobe.

"I believe that I may have found the solution to Andrea's surgical problems."

"What do you mean?"

"Remember how Andrea lamented over the high incidence of postoperative wound infections? If my theory is correct, patients are infected *prior* to their arriving in the operating room. It matters very little if the surgeon scrubs or if a strict sterile technique is implemented."

Antonio looked at me with curious interest.

"Something occurred to me this morning when I shaved. I felt the sting after splashing lotion on my face. This was caused by the alcohol's effect on the open, microscopic tears on my skin that were caused by the razor. The hospital environment is replete with bacteria. When the patient is shaved by the orderly, the microscopic cuts in the patient's skin allow and beckon the bacteria to enter.

As a result, the patient is infected *before* he or she ever reaches the operating room. The clinical signs of that infection appear days *after* the operation is performed.

So, if we can come up with a method of removing the patient's hair without shaving to avoid irritating the skin, we may well be able to eliminate the 'post'-surgical wound infections."

"What alternative is there?" Antonio asked.

"I need to find the compound that depilates, that removes the hair without shaving, thereby leaving the skin intact. By so doing, the portal through which bacteria could enter the skin would be eliminated and, in so doing, prevent infection."

"If your theory can be validated, it would prove to be revolutionary. Just tell me what you will need. I'll get on it right away."

"First, we must tell Andrea. We could work on this project together. I will need him to get access to the hospital library and laboratory."

As chief counsel of Farmilan, Antonio Bertoni was very well connected. Later that afternoon, he handed me my new identification papers in the name of Enrico Bianchi. How he came up with that name, I'll never know. In any event, the following day I visited Andrea in his little office in the department of surgery of Fatte Bene Fratelli Hospital.

"My God, it's so simple," Andrea said after I told him my theory. "Now we must prove it."

Andrea gave me a pass to the hospital library, where I immediately got down to work.

The library had an impressive array of books, some dating back hundreds of years. Aside from general medical texts, there were books on basic science, physiology, anatomy, and the history of medicine. Medical students were sitting among physicians and researchers at the large polished-mahogany tables. I sought out books on both basic chemistry and skin physiology. Specifically, I was trying to find out how the chemical bonds in the epidermis could be broken. I approached the problem with the same methodology I used in solving the denture powder case. I asked myself the question, "In what area of science or industry does hair or skin need to be broken down?"

I sat back and pondered the problem. While letting my mind drift, I was distracted by a man who was walking through the room. With each step that he took, his shoes made an annoying squeaking sound. The funny sound, aside from causing everyone in room to chuckle, made me glance down at his feet. *That leather should be oiled,* I thought to myself. Then it occurred to me. *Of course, the shoe leather was once animal hide. The answer may be found in the steps that are used in processing the hide into leather.*

Fortunately for me, the public library was only several blocks from the hospital. With the help of the librarian, I soon found the text I was looking for. One of the ingredients used in processing and tanning cowhide is thioglycolic acid. The sentence in the text read as follows: "...this acid breaks the disulfide bond in the cortex of the hair that leads to depilation or hair removal..." *Eureka!* With any luck, I was on my way to developing a depilatory cream.

The days that followed were a blur. With Andrea's help, I was able to get a small bottle of thioglycolic acid.

I decided to mix the acid into a cold-cream base, but it wasn't as easy as I had thought. With each attempt, the acid still separated from the cream. Finally, using slow and steady mixing over a low flame, I succeeded in making a cream that remained intact and didn't separate. I rolled up my sleeve and applied a small amount of the cream on a two-inch area of the hairy part of my forearm. After about one minute I felt a tingling sensation. I waited several more minutes then wiped off the cream with a towel. My skin was red and slightly burned, yet all the hair was gone! It worked, but it burned.

I then made several more small batches of cream containing lesser concentrations of the acid. I tested each of the samples on my skin, all the while keeping detailed lab notes. My forearms were spotted with hairless patches of different shades of red. It was the 2 percent solution that worked best; the skin was left soft, smooth, and hairless. Above all, it didn't burn.

"I believe that we have a formulation that works," I said to Andrea over coffee in the hospital cafeteria. Andrea almost choked from laughter when I rolled up my sleeves and showed him my forearms.

He reached over and touched one of the hairless spots on my arm and then said, "We must sit down and plan out how to proceed. My last case is at four. I'll get in touch with Antonio. We'll meet tonight to plan our strategy."

That evening, with their pants rolled up over their knees, I applied a small amount of the depilatory cream on a hairy portion of Andrea and Antonio's legs. After waiting ten minutes, I wiped off the cream. To our delight, the skin was hairless and smooth.

"Here's the plan," Andrea said without skipping a beat. "I will set up what is called a randomized study. We will study, say, two hundred pre-surgical patients. In alternating order, patients will be directed to either the razor arm of the study or the cream depilation arm." Andrea paused momentarily and said, "Why don't we call the product 'Depilex'? Sound good to you?"

Antonio and I looked at each other and nodded.

Andrea went on. "Over the course of the ensuing weeks, we will examine the postoperative sites of each patient to determine the presence or degree of infection."

"If I'm not mistaken," I said, "we will need a comparison, a control group, against which we will compare the findings. We need to determine the infection rate that occurs after surgery that *does not* require hair removal, namely eye surgery. As we discovered in the surgical literature, the incidence of wound infections after surgery hovers around fifteen percent. The incidence of infection after eye surgery is negligible, less than one percent!"

"So, Ernesto," Andrea said, "if your theory is correct, then the incidence of postoperative infection after creaming the hair from the surgical site will be the same as that which occurs after eye surgery, namely less than one percent!"

"That's it then," Antonio said. "The two of you can put a proposal in writing, and then I will submit it to the directors of Farmilan for their approval and funding. They will jump at this opportunity. This new method of surgical preparation is revolutionary and will surely prove to be quite profitable."

The next days and weeks proved to be very exciting. Andrea and I worked out a simple and reproducible method of formulating the cream. Once Antonio hammered out an agreement with the pharmaceutical company, Andrea got together with their laboratory director to produce enough cream to carry out the study. Over the next several weeks, under the watchful eye of Andrea, the patients were randomized to be depilated by either razor or our cream, Depilex. Once that process was completed, there was nothing more to do but wait to see the results.

The hospital library was the sanctuary where I spent a good part of my time reading journals and studying up on dermatology and depilation. On several occasions, Andrea would pop in and have me join him for a quick lunch or coffee. Andrea was working exceedingly long hours. One could see it in his tired, bloodshot eyes.

"Andrea, you must slow down; you're working too hard."

"Surgery is my calling, Ernesto. When all is said and done, it is still just a technical trade like many others. To be able to contribute something new, something beneficial, will make my life worthwhile. Thanks to you, this may well be possible."

I looked into Andrea's face and saw something familiar, but I wasn't sure.

"Ernesto, if the results of our little trial are as we hope, it will truly make a difference. It will be a simple breakthrough. Isn't it that most discoveries are found right under one's nose? With this new approach in depilation, we may well alleviate suffering and even save a life or two in the process."

"Tell me, Andrea," I said, still studying his face. "Who is older—you or Antonio?"

"Funny that you ask. Actually, I am—by seven minutes. We're twins."

That explained it. The letter that I found in the study implied that the Bertonis descended from the Lamed Vav. *Antonio was moved by "some obscure force" to save me at the train station. His brother, Andrea, tormented by the suffering of mankind, could have lived out his life in the lap of luxury but, instead, chose a life of sacrifice, of healing, wearing himself to the bone trying to make a difference, a contribution, forever striving to improve.*

Is it not possible that this concept of the Lamed Vav, *the Just, might not be limited to a mere thirty-six saintly few? Couldn't it be that there is a* Lamed Vav *or the potential of one lying dormant in everyone's soul just waiting to be stirred and awakened?*

As a regular face in the hospital and being seen so frequently in the company of this well-known surgeon, it was assumed that I, too, was an important figure. As a result, I was greeted by hospital workers and staff with the title *dottore* or *professore*. I learned to acknowledge them with a simple, *buon giorno* and a nod of the head.

As the war raged on, the atmosphere in the city became bleak. People lived in constant fear. There was hardly a soul in the cafés, and the market shelves were empty, yet Antonio was somehow able to remain immune. Each Thursday he was off to his country home for his long weekend with his family. All the while, he saw to it that I had all that I needed. Tata came over regularly to straighten things up and to prepare some dishes for the entire week.

Although allied with Germany, the majority of the Italian people did not recognize that affiliation. Resistance was still strong. Along with his designs for European and eventual world conquest, Hitler never deviated from his campaign for the final solution for world Jewry. In fact, it was this very "sideshow" that galvanized his troops in the field and injected vigor in the populace of the countries under his control. They were given the carte blanche to complete the job that he started. Yet, the same could not be said for Italy and the Italian people. Here, there was a distinct difference.

Mussolini, the Italian Fascist dictator, instituted strict anti-Jewish laws to appease Hitler. He set up concentration camps throughout the country. The prisoners surely suffered, yet there was leniency. In fact, I heard of Jewish patients who, after taking ill in one such camp, were sent off to the hospital for treatment.

Although I never ventured far beyond Antonio's home or the hospital area, I witnessed time and time again the humanity and dignity of the Italian people. Many Jewish citizens were sheltered by their Christian neighbors. It is the nature, the culture, of the Italian people that sets them apart, raising Italy head and shoulders above other nations.

It was late one Monday afternoon as I was in the study reviewing some of the preliminary data of Andrea's surgical study that Antonio entered. He was huffing and agitated.

"Ernesto," he said in a somber tone, "Milan is no longer safe. You must leave as soon as possible." As I was about to respond, Antonio held up his hand, begging me to wait to let him catch his breath. He sat beside me and continued. "I met today with one of the directors of Farmilan. He is the majority shareholder of the company. He's a bastard and has strong Nazi ties. He has gotten wind of your true identity. The long and short of it is that he wants you to disappear. Because of our long-standing relationship, he said that he will give me the opportunity to handle this myself and that if I don't deal with it soon, he would, using his own words, 'deal with this matter in my own way.' Oh, my dear Ernesto, this is real. The man means business." The tortured expression on Antonio's face said it all.

I wanted to comfort *him* and quell *his* fears even though I was the one in danger, the one who needed to flee.

"You must leave Milan right away. Tomorrow, I want you on the first train to Asolo. A few miles from there, in the small hamlet of Possagno di Grappa, is the Convent of Sacro Cuore. My family has always maintained a close affiliation with that institution. A senior in their parochial hierarchy is a nun by the name of Angelina. Sister Angelina has been an integral part of Sacro Cuore her entire life. Aside from her love of religion, the bias of her mind has always been art. The church allowed her to study at the art academy, where her talents were readily recognized. She has been offered teaching positions in universities and art academies throughout Europe but has always turned them down. She has forever remained devoted to her home, the Church of Sacro Cuore. Angelina's religious purity and her artistic talents are considered by some to be the outgrowth of saintliness. I am giving you my letter of introduction. Even without it, Angelina would, no doubt, help you. It is, say, *my* insurance policy for you, further assuring your safety and well-being. What the future holds for you is anyone's guess. Times are bad and are only getting worse. Our earnings from the denture powder will carry you for quite sometime. Now, with Depilex, I expect that another hefty advance from Farmilan will be forthcoming. Try not to worry. I will be looking after you, even from afar."

We sat in momentary silence. The door opened. It was Andrea.

"*Ciao, ragazzi* (hi, boys)," Andrea said jovially. "Why the long faces? I have wonderful news." He stretched out on the sofa and declared, "We concluded our little study early. The results have been remarkable. In the first one hundred patients, there were nine infections in the razor group and none in the Depilex group." Andrea pronounced *Depilex* with a tone and expression of personal pride. Andrea continued speaking. We let him. He was euphoric. "I have already begun writing up our conclusions. Antonio, you can now tell your people at Farmilan that they can start the process of getting Depilex cleared with the health department. Given its obvious benefits and its innocuous nature, the product can be fast-tracked for approval. I can see the press release now," Andrea stood up and, spreading his arms and as though reading a theater marquee, said, "Breaking news—'Revolutionary new surgical product—stop—dramatically reduces morbidity and mortality—stop—potential in saving the lives of our citizens and battle-stricken soldiers.'"

"Andrea, please sit down. This is important." Antonio went on to tell Andrea of the news.

Andrea was stunned. He sat down and said quietly and with intensity, "Ernesto, Enrico, whoever you are—it makes little difference. No matter what your name, this project is yours, and yours alone. I am nothing more than your humble assistant. Depilex will one day soon replace the razor in the world of preoperative depilation, and you, as true as I am sitting here, will one day be recognized as its creator. I will see to that."

Early the following morning, Antonio took me to the train station. He handed me a backpack filled with some clothing as well as some other basic essentials. Together, we walked to the platform where my train was waiting.

"This is where we first met," Antonio said. "That was just weeks ago, but it's as if we've known each other a lifetime. In your bag is a letter addressed to Sister Angelina. Make certain that you give it to her personally. Ciao, Ernesto. *Ti abbraccio.*" We embraced.

As soon as I boarded, the whistle blew, and the train began to move. From my window seat, I saw Antonio standing outside on the platform. As always, he was elegantly dressed in a suit and tie. He was staring up at the cars trying to find me. The train picked up speed. I tried opening the window, but it was jammed. Seeing him there, alone on the platform, getting smaller and smaller, I was reminded of the vision of my father staring up at the windows of the Vienna jail, hoping that I could see him, without him knowing if I was there at all.

CHAPTER TWENTY-FOUR

I settled in for my four-hour train ride to Asolo. The events of the previous weeks were like a cloudy dream. I found the letter addressed to Sister Angelina in the front pocket of the backpack. I tucked it back away securely then thought of what lay ahead.

Like a seed of a dandelion, adrift in a meadow on a balmy summer day, I am being carried on the unchartered course of destiny. Like flotsam, tossed hither and yon, I am at the mercy of a wild and raging sea. Whether I succumb or safely reach a distant shore is still a mystery.

I am worn, yet hardened. I am in the hands of an unknown and mysterious force that compels me to move on. Whether logic or planning has any say in this, my macabre drama of the absurd, I will never know. But I swear to everything holy I will not despair, I will never give up, for if I do then the suffering and loss of those I hold dear will have been in vain.

It was early afternoon when we arrived in Asolo. Stepping off the train, I was instantly struck by the sweet fresh air of the Veneto. In front of the station was a man leaning casually against a small car reading a newspaper. Seeing me approach, he quickly folded his paper and humbly removed his cap.

"*Prego, signore* (right this way, sir)," he said, opening the car door invitingly.

I told him that I needed to go to the Convent of Sacro Cuore in Possagno.

"Make yourself comfortable. We should be there in no time."

We rode along a winding road that was banked by lush, green vegetation. The sky was azure blue with a spattering of fluffy white clouds. In each direction as far as the eye could see were farms and estates with miles and miles of vineyards that created a landscape of breathtaking and majestic beauty. The scene was like a page out of Aesop's Fables. Situated amid the recesses of the hills of Asolo, where they form the last undulations of the Venetian Alps, is the hamlet of Possagno.

"*Ecco,*" the driver said as he pointed to a sprawling group of stone and terra-cotta structures on a hilltop. We took the narrow vineyard road that winded its way up to the convent above. It was flanked by grapevines that drooped under the weight of its pungent, purple fruit. Workers pushing wheelbarrows gave us friendly greetings as we passed them along the way.

Minutes later, we were at the entrance of Sacro Cuore. I paid the driver and sent him on his way. I could see for miles from my vantage on the promontory point of the convent grounds. As I walked to the church entrance, the only sounds I heard were those of chirping hummingbirds and the crunch of the gravel beneath my feet. Large birch doors opened to reveal what seemed more a museum of art than a house of worship. A series of low, parallel walls were positioned in the church's large foyer, forming corridors that led all the way to the sanctuary. Displayed on these walls was an eclectic array of dozens upon dozens of magnificent paintings that included simple charcoals, soft watercolors, and rich oils. A large array of ceramics and pottery filled the thick, wooden shelves that lined the room. I wandered slowly through the large chamber, taking in one breathtaking piece of art after another.

"*Squisito, no* (exquisite, isn't it)?"

The words caught me by surprise. I spun around to find a man standing behind me intently studying one of the paintings. He was wearing a tan smock, loose slacks, and sandals. The painting that he was admiring was an oil depicting fishermen in rowboats returning to shore at sunset. The man's eyes were sparkling and intense, his facial features strong and chiseled. His posture was forward-leaning, and there was a noticeable fine tremor of his hands. At first blush, he appeared to be around forty. Looking closer, he was probably closer to fifty.

"Yes," I said, "it is most exquisite."

"Tomasso Cicinelli," he said, extending his hand to me.

After a moment's hesitation, I said, "Enrico Bianchi, *molto piacere* (my pleasure)."

"Are you visiting? I would be delighted to show you around. There isn't much doing here these days."

I got the impression that the man was lonely and looking for some company. "You could say that I am visiting," I said. "Actually, I am looking for Sister Angelina. I have greetings from a mutual friend." Hearing Angelina's name made the man's face light up. He swept his hand with a flare, sighting the paintings displayed on the walls. "This is all Angelina!" he said proudly. "I am…" he said, hesitating momentarily to find the right words, "the keeper, the curator of her works." Recognizing that my command of Italian was weak, the man spoke simply and slowly. Then, catching himself, he said, "I'm terribly sorry—please, may I offer you coffee or tea? Wine perhaps?" He took my arm and said, "Please, I insist."

We walked through a door that opened into a vast room with a marble floor and plain, whitewashed walls. In the center of the room was a long, rectangular bleached-wood table surrounded by several chairs.

"Please," he said, inviting me to sit. "I'll be right back." He returned moments later with a bottle and two glasses. "We make this here," he said proudly as he poured two generous portions.

After tasting the drink, I politely asked again of Sister Angelina.

"How stupid of me," he said. "Of course. Sister Angelina, she was called away. We're expecting her to return any day now." Sensing my dismay, Tomasso said, "Can I be of any help? Have you a place to stay?"

"Well, I don't know…"

"You needn't worry. Any friend of a friend of Angelina is certainly a friend of mine." Tomasso smiled broadly at his witticism. He slammed his empty cup on the table and said, "There, that settles it. You're my guest." As I was about to protest, Tomasso raised his hands and said, "No, no, I don't want to hear another word. Come, let me show you around."

I followed Tomasso outside.

Strolling through the grounds, his hands behind his back, Tomasso was clearly in his element. "Sacro Cuore is a wonderful place, and we owe it all to Sister Angelina," he said with pride. "Her story is a special one. At the tender age of five, Angelina was orphaned after her parents died in a plague. She was adopted by the convent and has been with Sacro Cuore ever since. As soon as Angelina could hold a pencil, her extraordinary talents became evident. The humble convent could nurture Angelina's talents only so far. The church made an appeal to a local nobleman. After learning of her gift, this man became Angelina's most zealous patron, clearing the way for her to get a scholarship at the art academy of Trieste. It was there that I first met her. We took most of our classes together. Angelina was a most exceptional student, so much so that on the day of her graduation, two years later, Angelina was asked to remain at the institution as an instructor. Thankfully for us, she chose to return to Sacro Cuore. It took no time for her name to be known throughout all of Italy."

"And you, Tomasso," I said, "you say that you studied with Angelina at the art academy. How did you end up here? Are you also a member of the cloth?"

"Oh, not at all, although that's not to say that I am not a devout Christian. Upon graduating from the academy, I continued my training in art restoration at the famous art school of Venice. Although trained in art, I never had the requisite gift, so to speak. As a result, art restoration became my true calling. Unfortunately, as you may have noticed, I was stricken by a disorder of the nervous system that caused my gait to stagger and hands to tremble. If it wasn't for Angelina, I would be destitute. It is now fifteen years that I am here, and I couldn't be happier.

"Sacro Cuore was once a poor and simple convent that served the spiritual needs of our little community. Not that we're thriving, mind you...how should I say? We are not wanting. By virtue of Angelina's art, the convent has gotten funding from private donors as well as from Rome. This allowed us to expand the property in order to make special provisions for the reception of guests, retreats, and other special purposes."

We followed a path that was lined with soft pines. There were nuns working diligently maintaining the gardens, scrubbing walls, and polishing windows.

"As you can see," Tomasso said, "we take pride in our home. Our workday is divided evenly, in periodic rotation, between the choir, maintenance, the schoolroom, and the refectory. Idleness or lack of occupation is never permitted. Sacro Cuore has never deviated from its work of Perpetual Adoration. We prescribe labor of some useful kind, the cultivation of which we consecrate to the service of God."

We continued walking to the end of the pathway. "Here we are," Tomasso said.

We were standing at the entrance of a low building with a central courtyard. It had a beautiful vine-filled trellis covering. The sunlight filtering through the vines created a warm and comforting effect. In the middle of the yard was a garden with benches. Situated at the periphery was a small chapel. Along one end were several rooms.

Stopping before one of them, Tomasso led me inside and said, "This is where we keep our guests. Make yourself at home."

The room was clean and furnished simply with only a narrow bed and small writing desk. There was a crucifix on the wall at the head of the bed.

"I will leave you. Wander the grounds. Explore. Sacro Cuore is a wonderful and relaxing place. I will come for you at four o'clock for the evening meal. Mass is at six."

It was odd, yet comforting. I had only just met this man, and he was treating me like a long-lost friend. I suppressed a slight feeling of suspicion, dropped my bag on the bed, and decided, using Tomasso's word, to explore. As I walked the serene and lovely grounds, I soon found myself back in the "art gallery" where I first met Tomasso. I studied one painting after the next. Much in the way a dramatic piece of music can bring the listener to tears, so too Angelina's artwork managed to tap into that very same emotion.

Later that afternoon, I joined Tomasso for a meal that consisted of yogurt, fruit, and thick-crusted bread that was baked on the premises. From there, we went to evening Mass. Sitting in the pew beside Tomasso, I observed him in prayer. Tomasso was the embodiment of calm and contentment. I thought of my own tortured existence, of my life in flight and in fear, and wondered how much more I could take. Sitting with the prayer book open on my lap among the congregants chanting the hymns so softly and lovingly, I thought, *Why not stay—remain here forever in this storybook place called Possagno to follow the simple monastic life in this convent on a hill, far, far from the madding world below.*

The following morning, I awoke refreshed. I quickly
dressed and stepped outside. It was mid-morning. A nun
was tending to the garden, while others were rushing to
and fro from workrooms, schoolrooms, and the refectory.
As I made my way down a walkway, I heard someone call
out my name. It was Tomasso. He was hurrying toward me.

After stopping to catch his breath, he said, "Angelina
arrived early this morning. I peeked into your room, and
seeing that you were fast asleep, I didn't want to disturb
you. I mentioned you to her. Come, I'll take you to her."

Tomasso led me to the main building. One could
sense tension as soon as we stepped inside. Nuns as well as
laypeople were huddled together in the hallway speaking
quietly. We walked to the office of the Mother Superior.
As Tomasso was about to knock on the door, it opened
in front of us. Two elder nuns exited the room, excusing
themselves as they slipped past us. Then she appeared. It
was the Mother Superior, Sister Angelina.

"*Buon giorno*, Tomasso," she said quietly. As she looked
over to me, Tomasso said, "Sister Angelina, allow me to
introduce Signore Enrico Bianchi."

"My pleasure," Angelina said, bowing modestly.

After a moment, Tomasso said, "Why don't I leave
you?"

"Thank you, my friend." Then looking at me, she said,
"Please, come in."

The room was furnished simply and efficiently. We sat
together at a small round conference table that was surrounded by four chairs.

Once seated, Angelina folded her hands and said
bluntly, "How may I help you?"

I was entranced. Angelina's face was soft, yet strong, and her warm, blue eyes were captivating. "I have greetings from Antonio Bertoni."

Until that moment, Angelina's expression was serious and businesslike. Hearing Antonio's name made her come alive. "Oh, how wonderful! How is he? The Bertoni family has always maintained a very close relationship with the Church, and with Sacro Cuore in particular. I am proud to say that Signore Antonio is also a good friend."

I reached into my pocket and took out the letter. "Antonio asked me to give you this," I said, handing her the letter. I watched as Angelina first felt the paper then studied it as though she was trying to extract something more than the written word. As she read, I watched Angelina's eyes dart from side to side as they moved through the lines. At one point, Angelina looked up from the text. She briefly held my gaze then resumed reading. When she was through, she took one last glance at the pages, folded the letter, and put it back in the envelope.

"I'm so very sorry," she said. "You needn't fear, Ernesto. I will help you in any way I can."

My mouth dropped at the sound of my true name.

"It's all right," she said, taking my hand in hers. Upon my touch, Angelina was immediately overcome with an uncanny feeling. She was catapulted thirty years back in time to when she heard the muffled cries of an infant along the forest road. She had the very same overwhelming sensation of fulfillment, of rapture, of truth, deep in the depths of her soul.

"Are you all right?" I asked, feeling the quiver in Angelina's hands.

"Yes, of course," Angelina said, blushing and confused. After composing herself, she said, "Life as we have come to know it is about to change. I have learned only yesterday that the Germans intend to commandeer Sacro Cuore. Seeing that the convent is situated on the highest point in the area, they feel that it could have some strategic importance. They intended to run us off the property. It was only after long and tedious negotiations at the highest levels that they are finally allowing us the option to remain. Those of us who decide to stay will be forced to live communally in the little chapel complex. They are expected to arrive any day. Needless to say, your remaining here will put you in grave danger." Angelina looked deeply into my eyes. There was nothing more to say.

We sat in silence as Angelina's thoughts seemed to insinuate with my own. Despite the ominous news, I somehow felt comforted and protected.

Angelina walked me outside. Turning to me, she said, "We are living in extraordinary times. There are mysterious forces at play that we cannot question, nor challenge. It was not by chance that you found your way to Antonio Bertoni, and it was not by chance that he sent you to me. Your being here reconfirms a truth that, for me, dates back thirty years. I know who you are, Ernst Mann, and I know where you are going. Don't lose faith. You are not alone." Angelina took my hands and held them tight. "Tomorrow, you will be on the first train to Rome. You will be met by an agent of the Vatican who will deliver you directly to my adoptive son, Bishop Lorenzo Giraldi."

Tomasso was at my door at seven o'clock in the morning the following morning to deliver me to the station. We made only casual small talk along the way. The reason behind why I had to leave so suddenly never came up. When we arrived at the station, my train was already there. Tomasso walked me down the platform.

"I don't know how to thank you," I said before turning to board the train. "You have been very kind."

"Don't be silly," he said. "I'm only sorry that you couldn't have remained longer. God willing, you will return one day during more peaceful times. Good luck. I will pray for you."

CHAPTER TWENTY-FIVE

Vatican City

Bishop Giraldi awoke early. He was ready to take on the tasks of the day ahead. He opened the blinds and flipped open the calendar that lay on his desk. *Could it be?* he wondered. *Nothing scheduled this morning?* He couldn't recall the last time that he wasn't overwhelmed by a full schedule. Suppressing a slight sensation of guilt, he decided to take breakfast on his terrace and examine the illuminated text that was presented to him by Cardinal Mancini. On the first page was an inscription: *To Lorenzo, my dear friend and colleague, for a job well done, as ever, Cardinal Mancini.*

When Lorenzo had received the urgent call from his mama, he could sense her anguish. With a hurried, quivering voice, she told him of the German army's intention to commandeer Sacro Cuore, and she was turning to him for help. After a series of discreet communiqués with his contact at the German Embassy, Consul General Friedrich Mollhausen, Giraldi successfully worked out an agreement, whereby the residents of Sacro Cuore were given the option of remaining onsite despite the German

presence. Cardinal Mancini, in recognition of his nego-
tiating skills, complimented Giraldi before the General
Pontificate Council and presented him with the illuminated text.

There was no doubt that receiving such an honor
before one's peers is gratifying, yet for the young Bishop,
it left a bitter taste. Staring across the Tiber, Giraldi was
reminded how, only one month prior, the Jewish residents
of the ghetto were brutally beaten and dragged through
the streets. He could hear their agonizing cries as they
were loaded into trucks, never to be heard from again.
His present victory was tainted by his inability to save the
Jewish citizens of Rome.

Giraldi had gotten his first taste of Vatican policy, pri-
orities, and politics.

While getting full Vatican backing for his efforts to
reverse the eviction orders of Sacro Cuore's residents, his
plea to protect the Jews of Rome's ghetto fell on deaf ears.

Whether or not he agreed with the decision made by
Cardinal Mancini was of little importance. Yet, perhaps
Manicini was correct. It was certainly possible that any
attempt to influence the Germans on behalf of Rome's
Jewish population would have had, as Cardinal Mancini
put it, "dire repercussions." Nonetheless, Girladi *knew* that
something could have been done. Not lifting a finger and
dispensing with the matter like just another annoying item
on the committee agenda was a crime. Now it was too late.

Lorenzo was well aware that, as the newest and youngest member of the Vatican's higher clergy, he was under
a microscope. All eyes were upon him. There was little
doubt that Giraldi's superiors had come to learn of his

role in that misadventure of trying to save Rome's Jewish population, but it was never brought up—not a word was ever mentioned. For Lorenzo, this silence was deafening, yet he needed to be cautious. Being too outspoken now and confronting the powers that be would surely backfire. He would be pegged as a maverick and, resultantly, never get anything accomplished.

Scraping the last bit of sweet coffee residue from his cup, Lorenzo thought, *One day, I hope and pray that I have the strength and the will to make this right.* As Giraldi basked on the veranda, contemplating these thoughts, there was a knock on his door.

"I'm sorry to disturb you, Father," the young page demurred. "There is a telephone call for you. I asked if I could take a message, but she said that it is of the utmost importance."

"She? Who is it? Who is calling?" Lorenzo asked.

"I'm sorry, Your Eminence. It is from Sister Angelina of the Convent of Sacro Cuore."

"I'll be right there."

How unusual, Lorenzo thought as he raced down the hallway to the telephone alcove.

I hope that all is well at Sacro Cuore. It wouldn't surprise me in the least if those bloody Germans reneged on their deal, unless…I hope that Mama is all right.

Taking the phone, Lorenzo dismissed the page and asked not to be disturbed.

"*Pronto, sono io* (it's me)," Lorenzo said. "Are you all right?"

"Yes, my dear Lorenzo, I'm fine. I'm calling regarding a matter of importance. I am directing a person to you.

He goes by the name of Enrico Bianchi. His true name is Ernesto Mann. He is in danger and in need of your protection. He had come to me by way of Antonio Bertoni. The circumstances surrounding their encounter is for another time."

"This man, Enrico—or rather, Ernesto—where is he now?"

"He boarded the morning train from Asolo and is expected to arrive in Rome later today."

"Excuse me for being so vague, Lorenzo. It is something that I cannot fully fathom. I am sure that you will be able to understand this better than me. Of one thing I am certain—this matter must be handled discretely."

"I will see to it that he is picked up and brought directly to me. Not to worry, I will ensure this man's safety."

As one of only a handful of passengers on the train, I took an empty compartment, stretched out on the seat bank, and managed to sleep the whole way. It seemed that within no time we were pulling into the terminal in Rome.

Walking from the train platform toward the main station area, I was approached by a young priest.

"Signore Enrico Bianchi?" he said. How he knew me, I had no idea. I hesitated, and he said, "*Non preoccupare* (don't worry), my name is Father Carlucci. It is my charge to deliver you to His Eminence, Bishop Giraldi."

I followed Father Carlucci out to the street, where a car with a driver was waiting.

"*Prego*," he said, opening the back door for me. He went around to the other side and sat beside me. As soon as his door closed, the car sped off.

My heart was in my mouth as we raced at lightening speed through the narrow and windy streets of old Rome. The city was lovely. At first I thought that we were taking the scenic route until I realized that the entire city was magnificent.

Within a few minutes, we crossed an old bridge that spanned the Tiber River and entered the ornate plaza of San Pietro, the anteroom of Vatican City. The car took a path around the piazza and stopped at a gate that was manned by two armed guards. The driver flashed his ID. The guard peeked inside our vehicle then lifted the gate and waved us through. The buildings scattered throughout the pristine grounds were situated among lush gardens. Poplars and fir pines bordered the lanes. The car zigzagged its way down a cobblestone road past the Stradone dei Giardini and finally came to a stop in front of an elegant two-blanched stone building in the Piazza di Santa Marta. We walked through an iron gate and up a deep, wide staircase to the first-floor landing. The entire structure was designed in soft marble. At each corner were life-sized marble sculptures. Seated behind a large desk was a priest. Seeing us enter, he came forward to greet us.

"Please," he said, "His Eminence is expecting you." The priest walked ahead of us to a door that blended into the marble wall.

Following him, I happened to noticed that the priest who had accompanied me in was no longer there.

We entered a beautiful sunlit room. The walls on either side were lined with books. The entire back wall was a window covered by sheer curtains. Staring out to the gardens below was a man wearing a long black robe with the crimson waistband of a bishop. Hearing us enter the room, the man turned. Seeing his face, I was immediately smitten. It projected a combination of warmth and cheerfulness that put me at ease.

"Please, come in," he said, walking toward me with an outstretched hand. "Lorenzo Giraldi, *molto piacere*, I am pleased to meet you."

"Enrico Bianchi," I said, "the pleasure is all mine."

Giraldi directed me inside to one of two large easy chairs that were facing one another.

"You must be starving," Giraldi said. Before I could say a word, he pressed a button on his desk, and a moment later, a priest appeared. "Would you kindly have some refreshments brought up? Thank you." Giraldi took the seat opposite me. He leaned forward and said, "You have nothing to fear, Ernst Mann. You are among friends." He held my eyes.

In that moment of silent communication, I felt as if I had come home.

We sat together for more than two hours, covering topics that ranged from Italian-German political policy to science, literature, and theology. It was uncanny how well versed and familiar Giraldi was with the sages of the Old Testament, including Rashi and Maimonedes. It was incredible how the two of us saw eye to eye on nearly everything.

We went on that way talking, eating, and drinking until hours later when a priest opened the door to ask if he was required for anything else before he left for the evening. Lorenzo and I looked up and, only then, realized the time.

He turned to me and said, "Tonight, you're my guest." Then to the aide, "Kindly show Signor Mann to the guest quarters." As he walked me out of his office, Bishop Giraldi said, "We certainly covered a lot of territory this evening. Father Teodoro will show you to your room. Tomorrow, I hope that we can continue from where we left off. Until then, *arriverderla.*"

Giraldi remained in his chambers long after Ernst had left. He couldn't recall when he had ever encountered the likes of Ernst Mann. Throughout his many years in school and in church, whether engaged in deep study or casual past time, Giraldi had crossed paths with countless students, teachers, and clergy. There had always been a barrier of spirit that, for better or worse, kept him apart. It was difficult to fathom. Now, after his brief encounter with Ernst Mann, Lorenzo felt that barrier crumble for the first time in his life. He was puzzled, and for the life of him, he couldn't understand it.

With these thoughts, Bishop Giraldi left his study and walked across the Vatican grounds to his residence. He couldn't recall if he had ever had such a vibrant and stimulating encounter with anyone. There was something that was most unusual about this Ernst Mann, something that transcended time and space, something not of this world. Giraldi was perplexed. In her phone call and letter, Mama Angelina hinted to him that she had had a similar feeling.

Giraldi passed a restless night's sleep in anticipation of the following day when he hoped he might begin piecing together this mysterious puzzle.

Father Teodoro took me along a beautiful garden path to a series of one-storey terra-cotta cottages.

"You will be most comfortable here. There are four suites in each building."

Once inside, a nun appeared out of nowhere to welcome me. "*Buona sera, signor,*" she said as she led me to one of the rooms. Father Teodoro walked me inside. The room was quaint. The lamp on the nightstand cast a warm, soft glow that filled the entire room.

"There is a nightdress for you on the bed. You may leave your clothes in the basket outside the door. They will be washed and pressed. The sister is here to see to any of your needs. *Buona notte.*"

Per his instructions, I left my clothes in the basket, slipped on the nightshirt, and crawled under the covers. As soon as my head hit the pillow, I was in a deep sleep.

After what felt like minutes, I was awakened by a knock on the door. Sitting up on my elbows, I squinted to try to make out what was happening. The door to the room opened a speck.

"The last thing you want is to miss breakfast." It was Bishop Giraldi peeking in the room. "Relax, take your time, I'll be waiting for you in the garden. The sister will show you to me."

The sound of Giraldi's voice warmed my heart. I jumped out of bed. On a nearby chair, neatly folded, were my clothes. How or when they got there, I hadn't the faintest idea.

I found Bishop Giraldi seated at a table in the garden. A waiter placed a pot of coffee on the table. Seeing me approach, Giraldi half sat up and pointed to the chair opposite.

"*Sono affamato* (I'm famished). Allow me," Giraldi said as he reached for the coffee pot and filled my cup. He topped it off with steamed milk as the waiter brought over a basket with fresh rolls and biscotti. "I hope you slept well." Then, with a wry grin, he said, "I very much enjoyed our talk last night. You know, you fascinate me, Ernst Mann. I would very much like to know more."

I felt most at ease in this man's company. There was an innocence and gentleness about him, coupled with sagacity and breeding. Strange as it seemed, I sensed that he was a part of me, a kindred spirit, and somehow, I was certain that he felt the same way.

After a second cup of coffee, Giraldi said, "My morning is clear. It would be my pleasure to spend it with you. You are now in a part of Vatican City that few people ever see. Let's walk. I'll be your guide."

We spent the morning strolling through the Vatican gardens. Our conversation continued from where we left off the night before. I marveled at Giraldi's trove of knowledge. Our dialectic brought me back to my days in the theological seminary where philosophical concepts were analyzed and hair-split to the core.

It was early afternoon when we found ourselves back at Giraldi's study.

He turned to me and said, "These are frightening times. Danger lurks everywhere. You will need safekeeping. Until that can be arranged, you will remain here, within the walls of the Vatican, as my personal guest."

Bishop Giraldi gave me a pass, giving me access to the Vatican museum galleries as well as the library. Over the next couple of days, despite his religious and administrative obligations, Giraldi would find me, and if only for a few minutes, we would pick up on topic from where we had left off on our previous chats. For me, Lorenzo Giraldi was a breath of fresh air. I felt as if I had known him all my life, and it had only been two days since we first met.

Two nights later, I was about to settle in, when I was summoned to Giraldi's study.

"Welcome, Ernesto, I'm very happy to see you. I have been occupied the entire day in closed meetings. I hope that you are well."

This magnificent man who had welcomed me with open arms moved me to the core. I saw in Giraldi the embodiment of everyone and everything that I held dear. I thought back to my journey of the past year, and in one fell swoop, all the events flashed across my mind: the last moments with my poor parents; the long year in captivity in Vienna jail; the towns of Brcko, Sabac, and Novi Sad; the dead and the dying; the peril; the minefield; the bridge; the captivity; the escape; my lovely Mia; and oh, my poor little nephew, Yankl. I was entranced.

As though reading my mind, Giraldi came over and sat me down beside me and said, "I want to hear it all—every detail."

We sat together that night for hours. I poured my heart out, telling Giraldi everything. From time to time he would stop me, asking for more details or for me to be more explicit. Girladi focused on my each and every word. I watched as his eyes softened at the mention of Sister Angelina. As I spoke of one trauma after another, I felt a weight lift from my chest. Giraldi had become my confessor and my confidant. I felt at one with this man. Reliving the torture freed me, purged me of a portion of my heartache. I knew that I could open my heart to this man and that I had nothing to hide.

As I continued to speak, it was as if Giraldi was filing away detail after detail of my story in his mind. It was when I spoke of the events with Antonio Bertoni, of how he had appeared out of nowhere to save me at the train station, that something changed. Giraldi perked up. He hung on my each and every word as if he anticipated something. I then decided to tell of the book that I had found in Bertoni's library and of the letter written by Antonio Bertoni's great-grandfather, Rabbi Moshe Bercovici, that had fallen out of it.

Giraldi suddenly flinched, overcome by a sensation that was at once both physical and spiritual.

"Is everything all right?" I asked.

"Yes, yes, of course," he said, trying to compose himself. His face was flushed. He cleared his throat and said, "It's getting late. You must be tired. We will meet again tomorrow. I'll have the page see you to your room."

Giraldi remained seated. He was stunned, unable to move. *Could this be? Is it possible?* Giraldi remembered

studying the topic in the seminary years before. He could
see the Cabalistic pages before him. In his mind, he read
the lines, written in Aramaic, describing the *Lamed Vav*,
the thirty-six Just Men who inhabit the earth and assume
all the pain, sorrow, and suffering for all of mankind, thus
assuring the integrity of all. Giraldi never imagined that
the farfetched Hebraic myth could possibly be true.

Could this man, this suffering Jew who had come to me from afar,
possibly be one of the Just? Just because Ernesto had come across
that mysterious letter in Bertoni's library doesn't really prove any-
thing. Or does it?

Giraldi slept little that night. He couldn't get the concept of the *Lamed Vav* from his mind. As blatant truths are
known to often reveal themselves in late-night solitude,
they just as readily dissipate in the warm, comforting light
of a new day.

In this way, Giraldi awoke the following morning and
quickly came to his senses, attributing his troubled sleep
to nothing more than a bad dream.

While sipping his morning espresso, Giraldi thought
of how ridiculous it was to even consider the possibility
that the myth of the *Lamed Vav* was true. *Antonio Bertoni,*
Moshe Bercovici, Ernesto...too bad that I didn't think of this far-
fetched idea in Possagno. Father Algieri and I could have used it
as a theme for one of our community skits.

Yet, there was something that still troubled him, something more. *Was it something that Ernst had mentioned during*
his lengthy tale of woe? Giraldi still wasn't quite sure.

That evening, I met with Giraldi in his study, where he spelled out his plans for me.

"The Vatican has numerous real estate holdings in the city. One in particular is a discrete residence in the city's historical center on a small street off Piazza Farnese. There is a vacant studio in the building where you will be able to stay."

Giraldi then handed me a new set of identification papers. Unlike those given to me by Antonio Bertoni, these were different, more formal looking. Although they were still in the name of Enrico Bianchi, underneath were inscribed the words *Cittadino del Vaticano* (Citizen of the Vatican).

"I assure you that, with these papers, you won't be challenged."

I put the papers in my pocket and continued to listen closely as Giraldi laid out his plan for me.

"Just one street from the Vatican is the Santo Spirito Library, which is connected to the hospital of the same name. The library has a large history of medicine section as well as a collection of biblical texts. These identification papers will give you free access to the building. I can think of no safer place for you to pass your time. There, you will be able to continue your research undisturbed." Giraldi handed me a card. "Here," he said, "this is a tram pass. It's good for all routes in Rome. I would suggest that you limit your travels to going to and from the Santo Spirito Library. Although I'm sure that you will be safe, you don't want to push your luck."

I listened half-heartedly as Giraldi spoke. It was so comfy and secure within the walls of Vatican City I could have stayed there forever.

Giraldi, reading my expression, said with a confident air, "Not to worry, Ernesto. I'm not far. I will be looking out for you. I have arranged for a car to deliver you to the apartment in the morning. Ignazio, the concierge, has been notified that you will be coming."

We sat silently. The atmosphere in the room was one of sadness and melancholy. It was the feeling of comrades in arms parting ways after having just barely survived a long and treacherous battle.

CHAPTER TWENTY-SIX

The following morning, Giraldi saw me out to where a car was waiting. As it was about to pull away, he leaned down and said to me through the open window, "We will speak again very soon. Please be careful."

In less than ten minutes, we entered Via Della Lungara, a small street off Piazza Farnese. The car came to a stop in front of No. 36, a nondescript four-story building. It was not until the large main door to the building opened and Ignazio, the concierge, appeared that the driver gave me a wave and drove off.

Ignazio was a man who appeared to be in his late-forties. His face was round and unshaven, and what little hair was on his head was thin and unkempt.

"*Buon giorno*," I said, introducing myself.

"Oh, yes, yes, I have been expecting you. I am Ignazio. Please, come right in."

He led me up a flight of stairs and unlocked the door of the flat closest to the stairwell. There was a short corridor that opened into a small, sunny room with a bed, dresser, and table. There was a large bathroom with hot and cold running water. In the entryway was a counter with a sink and a hotplate.

"This is lovely," I said.

"Here is your key. I'm around most of the day," he said flatly as he turned to leave.

"Thank you, Ignazio," I said, handing him a ten-lira note.

He stuffed it into his pocket, grunted something that I didn't understand, and then left.

Bishop Giraldi didn't have to tell me of the dangers that lurked everywhere. There was no lingering in the cafés. German soldiers were forever roaming the streets. I would venture out of the apartment at mid-morning and take the train to the Santo Spirito Library and make certain to return in the late afternoon while it was still light.

In the flat next to mine lived an elderly widow, together with her grown son who was deaf and mute. We first met while waiting for the tram. She worked as a seamstress in a fashionable dress shop in a section of town two stops away. Realizing that I would appear less conspicuous walking along with her, I timed it so that each morning I left the building when she did. Evidently, it worked, since at no time was I ever stopped or questioned.

I tried my best to be on good terms with the concierge, so from time to time, I would drop off some fresh pastries at his door. One day, on my return home from the library, Ignazio called out to me from a nearby coffee bar and asked me to join him for a beer. He told me that he was from Calabria, his wife had passed away three years prior, and his only daughter, who was married to the town postman, was struggling to make ends meet. He tried to help them as best he could, but with the war on, it was difficult. He told me that he supplemented his income by doing odd jobs—anything that paid. He then said that, from time to time, he'd rent out rooms from a nearby residence on Via Giulia that was also owned by the clergy.

"It goes to waste," Ignazio said emphatically. "The church doesn't miss it, and in any case, I'm sure that they wouldn't care."

I took Ignazio's words with a grain of salt and was happy just to be on his good side.

The Library of Santo Spirito was as formidable as Bishop Giraldi described. Its main reading room was longer than it was wide. Old and stately mahogany tables extended the length of the room. The bookcases covered the wall in two tiers. Staircases on either end of the room led to the second-level walkway that ran along the entire wall.

I spent hours on end reading through the large array of medical and biblical literature. The two librarians working on alternating shifts were always available for assistance. The primary focus of my research was to improve upon the raw depilatory preparation that I had formulated in Milan. I discovered that there are certain emollients and perfumes that could be incorporated into the cream that would make it work more effectively as well as give it a more appealing scent. As a form of relaxation, I would take one of the biblical tomes and read a page at random. It was a wonderful throwback to my years in the Yeshiva. One afternoon, while reviewing an article on chemical preservatives, the librarian sat down beside me.

"Pardon me, I hope that I'm not disturbing you."

"Not at all," I said. The man extended his hand and said, "Mauro Castelvecchio." He was about sixty and had a pleasant face and dark eyes that betrayed an underlying sadness.

I took his hand. "Enrico Bianchi, *molto piacere,*" I said, "very pleased to meet you."

"I'm fascinated by what you're reading. I have a degree in pharmacology, but that was many years ago." He glanced off dreamily then, catching himself, said, "Oh, forgive me, I'm so sorry. I shouldn't disturb you."

"Not at all, I'm happy to have someone to talk to," I said sincerely.

He leaned in toward me and whispered, "*Ich auchet bin a Yeid. Zug mir de emes, fon vor bist du?* (I, too, am a Jew. Tell me, where are you from?)"

I couldn't believe my ears. The man was speaking Yiddish!

Before I could respond, he said, "Shh, shh, there is nothing to worry about. I'll be getting off in a little while. Please join me for coffee."

We met in the coffee bar a few minutes later. The man told me that he was born and raised in Milan. His father, a nonpracticing Jew, was a professor of chemistry at the University of Milan.

"Since my mother was Christian—by definition—I am one as well, but as the saying goes, 'Smell the saffron, and you know the soup is bouillabaisse."

"And how did you determine that I am a Jew as well?"

"It was the way in which you read the Talmudic texts. You weren't merely reading the words; you were living them. It was then that I knew."

I would have enjoyed opening up to him, but I thought it best to keep my distance. Using the lateness of the hour as an excuse to leave, I thanked him and was on my way.

When I saw him the following day, I acted as though we never met. I greeted him briefly and found a seat at the far end of the room. Over the days that followed, aside from simple salutations, we didn't engage in conversation.

Several days later, Mr. Castelvecchio asked if he could speak with me in private.

"Mr. Bianchi, something has come up. I don't know where else to turn." Castelvecchio was very upset, so much so that his voice was shaking.

"Calm yourself. What is the problem?"

"Several weeks ago the Germans ravaged Rome's Jewish ghetto. Eleven hundred souls perished. A handful of people had managed to escape by hiding among neighbors and the local churches. These people are once again in danger. There is a rumor that the Germans are planning another sweep to find them. Some believe that German collaborators are involved. These people need refuge."

"But I'm also a refugee. Why come to me? What can I possibly do?"

"It's just a hunch. I saw the words *Cittadino del Vaticano* (Citizen of the Vatican) on your identification papers. I thought, maybe, just maybe, you might have some pull, some influence."

I didn't know what to think. During the course of the past several months, I had been on the run, and throughout it all, time and time again, I had the good fortune of having been saved. How this had occurred, whether it was a guardian angel or merely dumb luck, I will never know. Now, once again, through the good offices and loving heart of Bishop Giraldi, I was being protected and coddled. Now it was me who was being called on for help. Seeing the desperation in Castelvecchio's eyes, I knew then that I needed to do everything in my power to help these poor people, my brethren who had already gone through so much suffering. *But what could I possibly do?* It then occurred to me. *Why, yes, of course....* I recalled my conversation with the concierge, Ignazio. He had let on that unbeknownst to the Vatican, he would, from time to time, rent out rooms from one of their nearby residences. *Maybe I could get Ignazio to rent me some space.*

"Let me think about it, Mr. Castelvecchio. I just might have an idea. We will talk first thing tomorrow morning."

On my way back to the apartment that evening, I peeked into the coffee bar and found Ignzaio seated by himself sipping a glass of wine. After exchanging hellos, I asked him if he would be interested in renting out some rooms from the building on Via Giulia.

"What do you have in mind?" he said as he licked his lips hungrily.

"There are several people—somewhere between fifteen and twenty—who are in need of a place to stay. For how long, I'm not entirely sure."

"I see. It sounds suspicious. Let us say I can do what you ask, to be sure, it will be all your responsibility, and yours alone. I don't want to know anything about these people—not their names, nor where they come from. You must realize, Mr. Bianchi, these are very dangerous times. If these 'people' were to be discovered, I would deny any knowledge of their existence."

"Agreed. I'll get back to you tomorrow to work out the details."

As it turned out, there were seventeen people in hiding in the neighborhood of the Jewish ghetto. There was a rumor going around that the Germans were planning to weed them out. When I returned to the library and told Mr. Castelvecchio that I may have found a safe hiding place, he cried out for joy and kissed my cheek.

The next morning, Ignazio showed me the residence on Via Giulia. As soon as I saw the space, I knew that it would do just fine. The large basement apartment would easily accommodate all the people involved, and as the building was vacant, little suspicion would be drawn by having them there. The room was well ventilated, and although it was subterranean, there were several windows that ran along the upper walls that gave off some sunlight.

After we agreed on the rent, I paid Ignazio one month in advance, plus a little extra for mattresses that he supplied from the other vacant apartments in the building. Over the next several days, my secret tenants were delivered, two and three at a time, to their new refuge. Mr. Castelvecchio brought me blankets and some basic utensils that I delivered, little by little, so as not to draw too much attention to myself. The majority of the group was made up of middle-aged men and women. There was also one lovely young girl of fourteen named Valentina who had been orphaned only weeks before when her parents were killed during the siege on the ghetto.

Although these poor people were unable to leave the basement, they managed to organize some semblance of normal living. They had reading groups, played cards, and on some nights, danced to the tunes on the radio. Everyone wanted to take young Valentina under his or her wing. Two of the residents who were retired schoolteachers gave Valentina their own version of homeschooling that included homework assignments and exams.

The days and weeks passed slowly. The dark cloud of the Reich hovered over the city. Civilian roundups were commonplace. The old woman with whom I walked to the tram each morning had been hospitalized. Ignazio later said that she suffered a heart attack and that she probably would not be returning home anytime soon. As a result, I ventured out less and less.

One morning, I found a note under my door from Bishop Giraldi stating that he wanted to meet. He had arranged for a car to deliver me to Vatican City that afternoon. It had been almost one month since we had last spoken. I couldn't wait.

"You look well, my friend," Giraldi said when I arrived. "We have much to catch up on. Come in. We'll talk over lunch."

We passed the next two hours covering a myriad of topics. Although I was tempted, I couldn't bring myself to tell Giraldi of my secret tenants on Via Giulia.

"That reminds me," Giraldi said as he handed me an envelope, "this came for you."

It was addressed to me in care of Bishop Lorenzo Giraldi. Inside was several hundred lira! There was also a handwritten note that read, *Congratulations, Enrico. Here are your royalties from Depilex. Stay well. Hope to see you one day soon, Antonio.*

"Evidently, you and the Bertonis hit it off quite well," Giraldi said with a smile. Embarrassed, I didn't know what to say.

We made light talk for a little while longer, after which Giraldi walked me down to the car. "I will be contacting you very soon," Giraldi said. "Should you need me for anything at all, you will contact me, yes?"

"Yes, and thank you."

On the drive back, I shut my I eyes and could see before me the faces of those poor souls hidden in the basement. I followed my instincts not to include Giraldi in this deed. I had no doubt that Giraldi would have sanctioned it. By keeping him in the dark, I also kept him from defying church policy. I knew that the day would come that I *would* tell him, but not now. This was certainly not the time.

Now, with my pockets full of lire, rather than return to my flat, I went instead to the market and bought two large bags of treats and delicacies and brought it over to the secret residence on Via Giulia. I was received like royalty. Everyone followed me to the table and watched as I unpacked the bags. I tried to remain jovial to keep it light. From the corner of my eye, I saw that little Valentina remained by herself on the other side of the room.

"And here I have something," I proclaimed loudly, "something special that is only for Valentina." I grabbed handfuls of chocolates and candies and went over to her. "This is for you and only you. You had better grab it before someone else does," I said, smiling broadly and making a funny face, trying to get her to smile.

After a brief pause, she extended her arms and opened her hands. A smile broke through from under her teary brown eyes. I sensed that everyone was watching. I could not bring myself to make eye contact with anyone other than Valentina. Had I done so, I would have acknowledged their suffering, and that would have been too much for me to bear.

I fell back into the routine of passing each day in the Santo Spirito Library. Only now, I no longer had my neighbor to accompany me. To be less conspicuous, I waited until mid-morning, when the streets were crowded, to take the tram to Vatican City. As I would pass Mr. Castelvecchio's desk, we would exchange nods in confirmation that our secret residents were all safe and sound.

Having exhausted most of the medical texts that were of interest to me, I was now being drawn exclusively to the volumes in the biblical section. It was a throwback to my years in the Yeshiva, where each morning I would rise at four and, together with my study partner, spend hours trying to decipher the meaning behind a difficult passage proffered by one of the biblical sages of yore. I was in my own little world.

Each day I would take my place at the large table and remain there until mid-afternoon. Twice a week, I would look in on my secret residents on Via Giulia. Through my royalties, I was able to supply them with everything they needed. To remain on Ignazio's good side, I began paying him every two weeks rather than monthly. To show my appreciation, I would throw in a little gift, such as a carton of cigarettes or a bottle of brandy.

The month was October. The weather was unseasonably cool. I had been up much of the night questioning what Rambam, one of the biblical sages, had discussed in a one of his treatises that I had read the previous day. The tram rolled slowly through the streets but not fast enough. I was anxious to get to the library in the hope of finding further commentary on the subject.

I greeted Mr. Castelvecchio and made my way to my usual spot toward the back of the room. I must have searched more than an hour with no luck. The volume that I sought was nowhere to be found. As I was about to give up, one volume caught my eye. I took the book and went back to my seat. It was very old. Many of its pages were dog-eared and tattered. Sealed onto the book's outer cover was an unusual parchment-like paper covering. Upon closer examination, I noticed that there was some printed text showing through from the piece of parchment that was folded over onto the inner portion of the book cover. I tried to decipher what was written, but it was impossible, as the words were backward. It then occurred to me that I'd be able to decipher what was written by reflecting the print through a mirror.

With a small mirror that I borrowed from Mr. Castelvecchio, I was able to make out the following sentence: "...and the skin is thin and discolored in red-brown with flaky, white areas. Most commonly found on elbows and knees, these lesions can appear on any portion of the skin. More common in individuals of fair complexion... usually causing an itching sensation...it is a benign, incurable disorder...."

How incredible. The book cover was a page taken from another biblical text. The writer was describing the manifestations of a skin disease that is today referred to as psoriasis. I held the mirror with one hand, and with the other, I transcribed what I was reading. Despite the many gaps, very little of the text appeared to be missing.

This find had captured my imagination. I found the requisite dermatology texts and sat down to study. I wanted to get a general overview on skin diseases, and of psoriasis in particular. I studied for most of the afternoon. I was so consumed in thought I didn't notice that someone had sat down opposite me.

"Whatever it is that you are studying must be very interesting."

I looked up to see Bishop Giraldi. I couldn't believe my eyes.

"I've been sitting here for fifteen minutes, and you never noticed," he said, smiling warmly. "I haven't heard from you in a while, so I thought I'd come over to see if all is well."

"Indeed, everything is fine," I said, surprised. "I'm so happy to see you."

Glancing over at the book before me, Giraldi said, "What are you reading that seems so captivating?"

"It's a most unusual and incredible find. Here, let me show you."

Giraldi came around the desk and sat beside me. I showed him the text and its parchment cover with the backward text showing through.

To the onlooker, this must have been an interesting site to behold—me, Ernst Mann, the Jewish refugee, and Lorenzo Giraldi, the Vatican Bishop, huddled together side by side reading an ancient text through a little mirror.

"This is indeed a special find," Giraldi said as he examined the book from top to bottom. "What about the other side? Is there anything written on the inner back cover?"

I had gotten so involved with what I had found on the front cover that it hadn't occurred to me to look on the other side.

We opened the back cover very tentatively, much in the way children would carefully flip over a large rock in the dirt in anticipation of what lay beneath. Together, we examined the back cover from top to bottom. It was bare, without print or any written word. Then, for reasons that I never understood, I began scanning the parchment with my fingertip like a blind man reading Braille. Moments later, I felt something pass through me. It was something not of this world. It caught my breath, and then, after a brief moment, it was gone.

"Look," Giraldi said. He was staring at the page.

We were both dumbstruck as we bore witness to something undeniable.

Through an illusive vapor, a myrrh, a frankincense, several words began to appear at the bottom of the page. Just like the words on the inside front cover, they were backward. With mirror in hand, we read what had materialized: "In the extract from the skin of the pine tree lies the cure...."

Neither of us was able to utter a word. It was Giraldi who spoke first.

"Ernst, you never fail to amaze me," he said with an overtly casual air. "I can now see why you're fond of this place. It's a treasure trove of material." He quickly rose to his feet. "Don't let me disturb you any further, my friend. I can see that you are on the path to an exciting new find. Keep me posted. I'm sure that Antonio and Andrea will love to hear about it."

I could now, once again, approach each day with a new sense of purpose. Fascinated by my recent discovery, I studied everything that I could about psoriasis. From what I gathered, there was, as yet, no effective treatment for the condition, and furthermore, at no time had a preparation been made utilizing pine tar extract as an active ingredient. Using this ancient, biblical discovery as my starting point, I set off on a course to formulate a new and novel product for the treatment of this disease. I studied for hours on end, filling up one notebook after another with my research and ideas.

CHAPTER
TWENTY-SEVEN

Giraldi rushed out to the street. He couldn't believe what he had just witnessed. Wanting to corroborate his suspicions, he headed straight back to the Vatican. A few minutes later, he was standing in the imposing and stately Vatican Library. The library boasted the world's largest collection of religious texts, embracing not only Catholicism, but all other religions as well.

The vast chamber was humming with activity. Wherever one looked, one could see dozens of scholars in active study, from students of theology and parish priests to bishops and even a cardinal or two. Giraldi went directly to the library's Old Testament section. For over two hours, he perused one text after another. Finally, he found the Cabalistic text and specific passage that he was looking for: "In the legend of the *Lamed Vav*, each of the *Just* inherits his place from the closest male in his family line."

Giraldi closed the book and contemplated Ernesto's story. *Now that I have been included in this drama, and if Ernesto does, in fact, descend from the Just, then the implications of this could be enormous. It is when one of the Just is in peril that the metaphysical wheels of salvation might be set in motion. Would it not follow that the present chaos and horror of our times is partly due to the loss of a Just? Ernesto's precious father, Joseph Mann, the last in his line of the Just, tortured and murdered in the flames of these German oppressors, may well be the testimony to our present state of affairs.*

As the only son in his line, Ernst had inherited the position from his father. The next in his line would be his nephew, Yankl, the little boy who is now in hiding in Yugoslavia. Ernst spoke of his visit to Sabac, where, on his knees, he begged his sister to take her family and flee with him. They chose, nonetheless, to remain and, as a result, may have paid for that decision with their lives. What has become of them is anyone's guess.

It is now imperative that I protect Ernst Mann and do everything in my power to find his nephew and assure his safety. I pray that it isn't too late. That this child may have perished is unthinkable. The stability of mankind is dependent upon his safety and that of his uncle, Ernst Mann.

From what Giraldi could surmise, Ernst Mann, living in the residence in Rome, holding "valid" identification papers, limiting his travels to the Santo Spirito Library, wasn't in any immediate danger. The same could not be said for his only living relative, his young nephew, Yankl. By now, he may have already perished. Giraldi realized that there was much that needed to be done, and he prayed that it wasn't too late. Pacing about his study, Giraldi began to formulate his plan. Ernst appeared to be safe. Now Yankl, the next in that family line of *Lamed Vav*, had to be protected at all costs.

To determine the status of Ernst's sister, Giraldi went in person to the Vatican's Office of Foreign Affairs. He gave them what information he had regarding Nelly and Romy Schreiber. Two days later, Giraldi received the following missive: *The town of Sabac was occupied by the German army in early August. All undesirables—Jews, Gypsies and Communists—were killed. Among them were Nelly and Romy Schreiber. The destiny of the other person in question, their son Yankl, is unknown.*

Giraldi was beside himself. He paced back and forth in his study, unsure how to proceed.

The fact that there is no record of Yankl means that he might still be alive. How to find out? To whom can I turn? Remembering Cardinal Mancini's callous response to Mollhaussen's appeal to intervene on behalf of Rome's Jewish population, Giraldi knew that Mancini was the last person he could turn to, knowing only too well how he would respond. He realized that he must make his appeal to the highest authority of the Holy See, to no one other than the Pope himself.

CHAPTER
TWENTY-EIGHT

One evening in late September, after dropping off supplies at the secret residence, one of the older gentlemen, Signore Miele, asked if I would care to join the group the following week to celebrate Rosh Hashanah.

"Please come. We're starting the celebration at ten a.m. You would honor us by being here."

"Of course, it would be my pleasure."

Once again, I left them almost as soon as I had arrived, and it riddled me with guilt. The following week, I would stay. I would celebrate the holiday with them, and I would bring a special gift to little Valentina.

As God is my witness, if this horror should ever end, I will take Valentina away, far, far away, to a better place, to a better life, a life of joy and giggles and tickles, to the kind of life each and every little girl on this earth should have and should take for granted.

The time was nine o'clock in the morning on the first day of Rosh Hashanah. I had been awake since six. I felt as though I was tethered to my bed. It was as if an invisible weight were holding me down. I was overcome with an overwhelming feeling of fright and trepidation. The hands on the clock seemed frozen, moving agonizingly slow. Nine thirty, nine forty.... *What is this feeling?* I began to shiver. Curling up in a ball and pulling the cover over my head didn't do any good. Ten, ten fifteen, ten thirty.... *They're expecting me. I can't let them down. Why am I so afraid?* I finally managed to drag myself from the bed and get dressed.

I left the flat and slowly walked down Via Della Lungara, across Piazza Farnese, and over toward Via Giulia. I heard the sudden grinding of gears. From out of nowhere, a German troop carrier came barreling around the corner and came to a screeching halt in front of the secret residence. From behind a tree, not fifty meters away, I watched as a dozen soldiers stormed from the truck. An officer jumped down from the cab and was talking to someone at the entrance of the building. It was Ignazio! After their brief exchange, I saw Ignazio point in the direction of the basement entrance. With their guns at the ready, the soldiers ran into the building.

Two minutes later, I watched as all my secret residents were led out of the building at gunpoint and loaded into the truck. I watched as they were pushed and prodded, and there, walking among them, I saw little Valentina. I wanted to run to her, to sweep her up in my arms and run away. Then just as she was about to step up into the truck, she turned. Our eyes met. I extended my hand. I wanted to scream, to comfort her and tell her not to fear, but there was nothing that I could do. Trying to hold Valentina's gaze, I silently begged her to forgive me.

The officer was the last to leave the building. He walked over to Ignazio, patted him on the shoulder, and then climbed into the truck. Ignazio took out a cigarette and, while taking a long, satisfying drag, watched as the truck drove away.

What to do? Where to go? What have I done? I stood motionless, paralyzed. I was crazed. Those poor people would have been better off had they never met me. I roamed the streets for hours. I knew that I couldn't return to my residence. No doubt Ignazio had betrayed me as well. I walked aimlessly through the streets for hours. Not knowing how or why, directed by an invisible guide or by dumb chance, I found myself in the streets of the ghetto, the one place I belonged. The Jewish ghetto—the ghetto that was now devoid of Jews.

I was tired. I ached. I wanted to die. A church bell sounded. I was drawn to it, drawn to its sound. With no strength left, I sat on the steps of a church and cried.

"*Vieni. Vieni con me. Non ti preoccupi* (come with me, you needn't worry)."

I allowed the strong arms to take me, to guide me, to help me. The man wore a long black robe. He had the face of an angel. His eyes said it all; they understood.

"Oh, Father," I cried, "I have failed them. It was because of me that they all perished. I am to blame, no one else. I have deceived Bishop Giraldi. After all that he has done for me, I deceived him. What have I done?"

"Come, come, my child, you needn't worry. It will be all right." The priest brought me into the church and gave me something to eat and drink then settled me into a small room. "Don't worry. Rest here and wait for my return."

Father Ricciardi left the room to telephone Bishop Giraldi.

CHAPTER
TWENTY-NINE

To have an audience with the Pope, one must go through the proper channels. Once granted, it could be weeks until that meeting might take place. Bishop Giraldi couldn't wait. He went directly to the office of the chief of staff and stated in no uncertain terms his need to meet with the Pope posthaste. Two hours later, Giraldi received word that his request had been granted. He would have his audience the following morning at nine in the Pope's private sanctum santorum.

Giraldi was so excited over his upcoming audience with the Pope that he could barely perform his duties. Time couldn't pass quickly enough. He prepared for the meeting in the same way that he had prepared for a final colloquium or debate at the seminary years before—by studying each topic in detail and anticipating his opponent's any query or response. Throughout his many years of grueling study, Lorenzo Giraldi aced every exam and never lost a debate.

That night, Giraldi stepped out on to the little balcony of his apartment and stared across the Tiber and reflected on his spiritual Jewish brethren who were now no more. He failed in his attempt to save them. He would now do everything in his power to save Ernesto and what was left of his family.

Early the following morning, despite a long and rest-less night's sleep, Lorenzo jumped out of bed feeling at ease and refreshed. The time was six o'clock, just three hours before his scheduled meeting with Pope Pius XII.

Giraldi entered the bathroom and stood before the steamy bathroom mirror viewing his pale, boyish reflec-tion. *How incredible*, he thought, *I, of all people, am about to be face to face with Il Papa, His Holiness, Pope Pius XII.*

Lorenzo focused intently as he whipped up the shav-ing soap in a small ceramic dish. Then, with quick and efficient brush strokes, he applied the cream to his face. Lorenzo could have gotten away with shaving but once a week. His fair and delicate features belied his twenty-five years.

Giraldi recalled how the other students teased his che-rubic appearance when he first arrived at the seminary as a teenager. But the teasing was short-lived. He quickly gained their admiration and respect as his sharp, analyti-cal mind more than made up for his youthful visage. In debates, Lorenzo always left his opponents trailing far behind. The professors recognized his talents and gave him special attention, as it was evident he was destined for greater things.

After only one or two cursory passes of the blade, he snapped it closed and wiped off the remaining soap with a clean washcloth. He parted his hair to one side in a perfectly straight line then splashed toilet water on his shiny cheeks. Wincing from the sting, he looked back at his image. "*Ecco fatto* (that should do it)," he said confidently.

Through the bathroom door, he heard Sister Maria Grazia as she sang while making up his room. He waited for the door to close behind her before he reentered the room. The rich smell of brewed coffee filled the room as the little percolator completed its gurgling sonata. On the coffee table was a basket of crusty croissants. On his bed were his vestments, laid out neatly by Sister Maria. He dressed quickly and methodically, held the crucifix to his lips, walked past his uneaten breakfast, and left the room.

Giraldi walked rapidly through the Vatican's labyrinthine corridors, passing the numerous Swiss Guards who were stationed at their designated posts. It took him more than ten minutes to arrive at the papal wing. Two Swiss Guards were standing at attention at the entrance to the Pope's study. As Giraldi neared, one of the guards knocked twice on the door then opened it widely.

Expecting to find a grandiose chamber commensurate with the Pope's stature, Giraldi saw a modest, yet highly elegant sanctum sanctorum. The room's octagonal, birch-lined walls were draped in rich, flowing fabrics. The scalloped ceiling displayed breathtaking frescoes by Michelangelo himself. To one side was a large fireplace whose dancing flames filled the room with comforting warmth and soft light. Seated at a large mahogany desk, the Pope leaned forward, his hand on his brow, intently reading a document. Looking over his shoulder, Cardinal

Luigi Maglioni, secretary of state to the Vatican, stood to his side.

"Ah, Father Giraldi, please sit down," the Pope said, waving his hand toward a divan that was situated in front of his desk. "May I introduce Cardinal Maglione," he said, briefly looking at his Secretary of State. "It is my understanding that you have something of importance to discuss."

Giraldi could feel the sweat forming on his brow. "Yes, Your Holiness, it is a most delicate matter," he said hesitatingly, his voice cracking.

"Go on," said the Pope, nodding.

In a quiet whisper, Giraldi responded.

"I am concerned about the destiny of our Jewish brethren." The Pope pursed his lips and waited for Giraldi to continue.

"The German government is a diabolical regime of terror. Jews throughout Europe are in slave labor camps being slaughtered, by the tens of thousands. We have an opportunity to intervene on behalf of these poor souls."

The Pope looked at Giraldi and said, "We all agonize over this question. It is a most delicate matter. We are under a microscope. Each and every step we take is noted and assessed by the Reich. We are at their mercy, that is, at least for the time being. Our primary objective is to maintain the fragile stability that we presently enjoy."

Hardly able to contain himself, his voice shaking, Giraldi said, "But we have an historical obligation. We cannot sit back, idly...." The Pope, placing a finger to his lips, cut Giraldi off from saying another word.

The Pope folded his hands before him, forced a smile and said, "Now, Father Giraldi, if you have nothing more that you wish to discuss...?"

His heart pounding, furiously, Giraldi took a deep breath, calmed himself as best he could and said, "Yes, your Holiness. There is one more thing."

The Pope motioned for Giraldi to continue.

"I have strong reason to believe that I have one of the Thirty-Six in my midst."

Startled by the remark, the Pope looked at Giraldi and with piercing eyes asked, "What is that you say? One of the Just?"

Hardly able to meet the Pope's glance, Giraldi nodded in the affirmative.

"Are you certain of this? Is he safe?"

"I am most certain," answered Giraldi. "His name is Ernst Mann. He escaped from Vienna at the outbreak of the war. He is in safekeeping in a residence in Rome."

"Of what do you speak?" Cardinal Maglione asked, with a look of bewilderment.

The Pope, gazing across the room as if in a trance, said, "There is an ancient Hebraic legend that states that on this earth, at all times, there are thirty-six Just Men. They are called the *Lamed Vav*. They are thought to embody the pain and suffering of this earth, and as a result, they assure the delicate, moral balance for all of mankind. Each of the Thirty-Six inherits his position from his father and, in turn, passes it on to one of his male progeny. They themselves may go through life unaware, oblivious of their station. These 'Just Men,' as they are called, cross all social lines. They could be anyone—farmer, teacher, or even beggar. It still remains unclear how it is determined that one is of the Thirty-Six, one of the Just. One school of thought maintains that a Just Man can only be recognized by another, by one who himself embodies saintliness." The Pope shot a quick, brief glance over to Giraldi then continued. "For whatever reason, a Just man, or a *Lamed Vav*, who perishes before his time could throw the universe into chaos. A Jesuit school of thought considers that our own savior, Jesus Christ, may well have been a *Lamed Vav*, one of the Just."

The Pope looked up at Giraldi and said, "Tell me more of this person—Ernst Mann."

"Mann was a student of Jewish theology. At the outbreak of the war, he left his home in Vienna, made his way through Yugoslavia, and finally settled in Italy. Somehow he always managed to keep one step ahead of the Germans. His parents were captured and delivered to Auschwitz. Ernst is their only male offspring. There is, however, one surviving male in his line—his six-year-old nephew, Yankl, the son of his sister, Nelly, and her husband, Romy Schreiber. They had been in hiding in the Yugoslavian town of Sabac until it was overrun by the Nazis. Before being captured, Nelly delivered young Yankl to a neighbor for safekeeping. It is my hope that nothing has befallen this child, as our very survival might well depend on it."

The Pope, after a long and silent deliberation, responded, "Indeed, the Holy See must save this child. This is a sensitive and most delicate matter. Even if there is only the slightest possibility that this man, Ernst Mann, descends from the Just, he and his nephew *must* be protected at all costs. The future of the Church itself may hang in the balance." Holding Giraldi's glance, the Pope said, "Mind you, my dear Lorenzo, it goes without saying that we proceed with the utmost secrecy. No one outside of this room must know of what is unfolding, not even your friend, Ernst Mann."

CHAPTER THIRTY

Vatican authorities immediately began the process of locating young Yankl Schreiber. Starting their search in Sabac, Yugoslavia, they had their answer in no time. Within twenty-four hours, they received word that a child by the name of Yankl Schreiber was safely in the care of the Church of St. Michael in Sabac.

The following day, a Vatican official, Father Angelo Kovar, arrived in Sabac from the nearby town of Novi Sad. He was received by Father Jaric, the parish priest of the Church of St. Michael.

When asked about the child, Father Jaric smiled. "Yes, of course, the lad has fit in with us very well. He is a sweet boy and, despite his Jewish background, was very quick to learn the ways of the Church. In fact, he has proven to be quite studious and has excelled."

"That is good. It is important that you know that the Holy See has taken a special interest in this child. It is imperative that he remains safe."

"That, I assure you, he is. I believe that the children are at prayer in the sanctuary. Let me show you to him."

From the doorway of the sanctuary, the priests observed the children in prayer. Like little ducklings, they sat one next to the other, filling all the pews in the first three rows. They were all dressed in the same white, pleated gowns.

"That's the boy over there—second row, second seat."

They saw young Yankl kneeling in his pew, head tilted downward in prayer.

"I assure you, the boy is safe and well."

"I would like to speak with him, if I may."

A few minutes later, as the children were filing out, Father Jaric motioned to Yankl, who skipped over to the two priests.

"Greetings, Yankl, this is Father Kovar. He would like to meet you."

Father Kovar shook Yankl's little hand and said, "I am visiting Sabac and would like to know if you are happy here."

Yankl smiled and said, "Oh, yes, very. I have a lot of new friends." Yankl's eyes gleamed. He looked up at father Kovar and, with an excited smile, said, "I scored a goal yesterday."

"That's wonderful, Yankl. That's certainly wonderful," Kovar said, patting Yankl on the head. "Run along now and join the others."

Father Kovar gave a contented nod to Father Jaric as he watched little Yankl skip happily away.

"Thank you, Father Jaric. I see that the boy is in very good hands. We will be looking in on him. The Holy See is watching. Thank you again for your service."

AFTERWORD

Now that he had met with the Pope and the wheels were in motion to find little Yankl, Giraldi felt the need to reconnect with Ernesto and to assure his safety. Early the following afternoon, Giraldi walked over to the Santo Spirito library. Seeing that the reading room was empty, Giraldi asked the librarian if he knew of "Enrico's" whereabouts.

Mr. Castelvecchio, surprised to see the bishop, said, "I'm sorry, Father, I haven't seen Signor Bianchi for days."

Giraldi hurried back to the Vatican and had a car take him directly to Ernesto's residence. Seeing the bishop enter, Ignazio, who had been sitting in the inner lobby munching on an apple, jumped to his feet.

"O, *eccilenza*, (your excellency)," Ignazio said, taking Giraldi's hand and kissing it. "How might I help you?"

Sickened by Ignazio's falseness, Giraldi pulled back his hand and said, "I'm looking for Signor Enrico Bianchi. Do you know where I can find him?"

"Signor Bianchi? Indeed, a very nice man—I haven't seen him in days."

Giraldi was overcome by a terrible premonition. Ernesto wouldn't have left without informing him. Giraldi hurried back to Vatican City. There was a message from Father Ricciardi requesting that, if possible, the bishop contact him in person right away at his church, Santa Maria in Campitelli.

Bishop Giraldi went directly to find Lucca Ricciardi. Minutes later, he was at the front door of the church.

"Lucca, *che successo* (what has happened)?"

"I have a man here by the name of Ernst Mann. He is in a terrible state. He speaks of you, repeating your name over and over again."

"Please, Lucca, take me to him."

When they opened the door to Ernst's room, there was nothing but darkness. Giraldi could just make out the shadow of a man standing hunched over with his arms dangling at his sides. As his eyes adjusted to the darkness, Giraldi saw that the man was Ernesto.

"Ernesto, *sono io* (it's me), Lorenzo. *O Dio mio*, Ernesto, *che successo* (what's happened to you)?"

Staring back at him were the dark, sunken eyes of sadness—a sadness so profound that it took Lorenzo's breath.

Giraldi opened his arms and drew Ernesto close. He held him fast for fear that if he were to let go, Ernesto would fall to the floor. He coaxed Ernesto back into the room and sat him down at the small table by the window. He pulled the curtains aside and opened the windows, letting in fresh air.

Giraldi sat opposite Ernesto and took his hands in his. "It's all right, my friend. You needn't worry. I am here."

Ernesto looked up and whispered, "I have failed them, and I have deceived you." He then poured his heart out. Through his sobs and tears, Ernesto confessed everything: Ignazio and Castelvecchio, the secret residents of Via Giulia, Ignazio's betrayal, his premonition on Rosh Hashanah, and then how he watched as the "innocents" and little Valentina were carted away to their death. Ernesto's tears poured forth and ran down his cheeks.

"My dear friend, dry your eyes. You didn't fail anyone. There are forces in play that are far stronger than the two of us. What you witnessed on Via Giulia was the aftermath of a tragedy that had begun weeks before and played itself out. There is something that *you* must know. Just days before the destruction of the ghetto, I received word that the massacre was going to take place. Like you, I tried to intervene but failed. I, too, was devastated and ravaged by the thought that because of my deficiencies, the Jewish community was no more, that from one moment to the next it had been wiped from the face of the earth. Ernesto, there was no deception; you didn't fail anyone. When you were needed, you acted. What you did was sacred. What transpired was indeed a horrific tragedy. Had you not made any attempt to save those poor souls, *that* would have been the tragedy. My dear Ernesto, you had been given the opportunity to serve the Lord. You acted in good faith. It is *this* that gives your life meaning. As you have acted, so too will you be judged. I am here, and with you, I will remain, for I *am* you."

For the next two months, Ernesto remained in safe-keeping under the watchful eye of Father Lucca Ricciardi in the Church of Santa Maria in Campitelli. He lived in the very room where, on that awful night just months before, Bishop Giraldi heard the German SS storm the ghetto and exterminate the Jewish souls living within.

Ernesto never returned to the Library of Santo Spirito. He remained cloistered in the church, leaving for only minutes at a time to walk the hundred meters across the cobblestone square to say a prayer at the steps of the Grand Synagogue. Bishop Giraldi would visit weekly, and together, he and Ernesto could sit for hours over an obscure passage of scripture.

On some cool, breezy nights, with his window opened wide, Ernesto would lie in bed and, through the rustling leaves of the rich oak trees, detect the sweet sounds of the "High Holy Day Liturgy," as sung by a Cantor and choir that was no more.

"On June 4, 1944, after nearly nine months of anguish, Rome was liberated by the American Fifth Army, and the Jewish fugitives came out of their hiding places. On the following day the anti-Jewish laws were repealed, and a liberation ceremony was held in the main synagogue, attended by Jewish members of the Allied forces. The nightmare was over; but Roman Jewry had suffered a blow from which it never recovered." (Reference 3)

ROME, 1954

"Ladies and gentlemen, we are making our final approach to Fiumicino Airport, Rome. Please remain in your seats, fasten your seat belts, and place your seat backs in the upright position. Thank you and *grazie*."

Has it already been ten years? My, how time flies. I couldn't believe it. I closed my eyes and let my mind drift back in time.

As all the excitement was finally dying down in the days following the American liberation of Rome, I was approached by an agent from the State Department. Through unknown channels, my name had made its way to them, and I was offered a visa to enter The United States, no questions asked. I had planned to return to Milan to continue my dermatologic research and reconnect with Antonio and Andrea Bertoni.

"Go to America," Giraldi said when I asked his advice. "You must go. It isn't every day that one gets such a wonderful offer."

I wasn't sure, but there was something in Giraldi's tone, coupled with a gleam in his eye, that made me suspect that somehow he had something to do with it.

As it turned out, I went to America, and it proved to be a good decision. With notebooks jam-packed with patentable pharmaceutical ideas, I arrived on the shores of the United States and never looked back. I developed several pharmaceuticals that found a need and a market. I became a well-respected member of the pharmaceutical community and was often asked to lecture and present my ideas on novel approaches of combating disease.

Yet, there was much that I had left behind in Europe. A day didn't pass that I wasn't reminded of one event or another. All too often I would be startled awake by vivid nightmares that depicted one of the many horrific events: my imprisonments, my losses, my loved ones, and my shame. I knew that this was a common symptom of survivors; those riddled with guilt and shame for having simply survived.

Now, with the blessings of my new family, I was off on a two-week trip to Italy and Yugoslavia to visit with some of the many people who had so selflessly opened their hearts and risked their lives to save me.

The plane rocked back and forth as the pilot leveled the wings for touch down.

How interesting. It is the take off and landing that fills me with paralyzing fear. Imagine, I'm frightened to death, and this is nothing compared to the many bullets I dodged in my previous life. One would think that going through hell and back would immunize one to fear. The opposite is true. Horrors, loss, and humiliation actually lower the threshold to anxiety and pain; they compound an injury rather than dampen it.

I grabbed my suitcase from baggage claim and stepped out onto the street to find a cab. There was a long black car waiting at the curb with flags on its sides. People were staring at it expecting to see a dignitary or movie star appear.

As I raised my hand to hail a passing cab, someone tapped my shoulder.

"*Scuzi, ma lei e il signore Mann?*"

"Why, yes, I am Mr. Mann."

The man was dressed in the plain black suit of a chauffeur. He opened the door to the limousine, and ushered me inside. "Archbishop Giraldi is expecting you."

With no regard to the speed limit, we sped down the highway to Rome and Vatican City. As we entered the heart of the city, I could vividly remember the previous time that I had been driven to the Vatican. It was when I had first met Bishop Giraldi after arriving from Asolo, the Covent of Sacro Cuore, and Sister Angelina.

Once in the city, we drove the same route along the Tiber—past the ghetto, over the San Gregorio Bridge, and into Vatican City. The car slowed down only briefly as the guard saluted and raised the gate, allowing us to enter the grounds. We came to a stop in front of a stately and majestic building. The chauffeur jumped out and opened my door.

A young priest escorted me into the building. "Please, if you would follow me," he said graciously. He walked me inside then excused himself and closed the door behind him. The room was vast. It was decorated with simple, understated elegance. Within a few seconds, a door opened in the back of the room and Giraldi appeared.

"Ernesto!" he said out loud as he quickly walked toward me. His arms were outstretched, and he was smiling broadly.

I hesitated. I wanted to speak, but my mouth trembled. I was so overcome by emotion that nothing came out.

"Ernesto, *vieni qua* (come on over here)."

All at once, everything came back in a flash. He took me by the arm and walked me over to a comfortable sitting area.

"Come, relax. We have a lot to reminisce."

Giraldi did everything to make me feel at home and relaxed. We spent the next hour and a half covering everything. It was interesting how we spoke only of all the pleasant moments that we had shared together.

"I see that America has been good to you. You've put on weight," he said.

"And you, Bishop—or rather, Archbishop Geraldi—congratulations to you." Giraldi still had a youthful appearance despite his actual forty years. "And little Yankl—how is he? Actually, he's not so little. What is he—fourteen, fifteen?"

"He's doing quite well," I said. "And it's all thanks to you, my dear Lorenz—" I caught myself. "I mean, Archbishop Giraldi."

"Please, Ernesto, Lorenzo will do. It's just you and me, remember? No one is listening."

"Remember? How could I possibly forget? A day hasn't passed that I haven't thought of you and blessed you. And, yes, Yankl is doing quite well. The funny thing is that when your agents had found him in Sabac, he didn't want to leave at first. Don't you recall? When he was taken in by the nuns at the Church of St. Michael, he became a devoted adherent of the Church and Christianity in no time. The sisters evidently had quite an influence over him."

"Yes, I know," Giraldi said, laughing. "You know, settling him in Jerusalem was the right idea. Surrounded by both churches and synagogues, he could have had his choice...."

Ernesto shot Giraldi a glance.

"Only kidding, my dear Ernesto, Yankl is now precisely where he belongs."

"Indeed. He's a real *Sabra*, thriving and happy. His adoptive family loves him to death. I make a point of getting to Israel at least once a year to visit him. Yacov—that's his actual name—has acclimatized well. He has many friends and speaks Hebrew without an accent. After serving in the army, he wants to study to become an optician."

During those last days in Rome while I was living under the care of Father Ricciardi, Yankl, unbeknownst to me, was transported through Vatican channels to a church in Jerusalem with instructions that they see to it that he be adopted by a proper and fitting Jewish family.

"Now it's your turn, my dear Lorenzo. I can see by your countenance that you are well. Please, now, tell me, how is your mother? I intend to visit Sacro Cuore next week."

"She is well, thank you. I have told her of your coming. She sends you her regards."

"Tell me, my friend, how *did* you know that I was coming to visit? I wanted to keep it a surprise."

As Giraldi put down his glass, I noticed his subtle smile. "I have my ways, Ernesto. I have my ways."

I spent the next two days as Archbishop Giraldi's guest in the Vatican. Lorenzo treated me like a brother. We took long walks, and like we did years before, we grappled with some of the more intricate passages of scripture.

I paid a visit to the Library of Santo Spirito and found out that Mr. Castelvecchio had passed away. For the fun of it, I went back to the biblical section to find the mysterious text with the parchment cover that I studied years before. It was nowhere to be found.

Who knows? Maybe it had never been there at all.

EPILOGUE

Jerusalem, 1970

It was a hot, sunny July day in Tel Aviv. I had just graduated from high school. My parents had decided to leave New York and move to Israel. I thought that it would be the ideal time to visit Israel and spend some time with them before starting college in New England in the fall.

We were sitting on the terrace of my parents' apartment overlooking the glistening Mediterranean when my father said, "What do you say we drive up to Jerusalem and pay a visit to your cousin, Yankl?"

"Great idea."

A few minutes later we were on our way.

The road to Jerusalem from Tel Aviv courses through a landscape that is rich in biblical history. It boggles the mind to know that on those very same roads are the footprints of the biblical testament, both old and new.

During that drive, our conversation, as always, would find its way back to another time.

My father began relaying his story to me about that first winter day in New York many years ago. He would find any and every opportunity, even if it were only a few minutes, to recount an incident, a feeling, a thought, or a message from that dark and dreadful time many years ago. The tale would come to life, so much so that, in time, the characters in that drama of Santo Spirito eventually became part and parcel of my life as well.

What had made this occasion very different was the fact that one of the story's pivotal characters, Yankl, was actually here in the flesh.

I had met Yankl for the first time two weeks before. Although I couldn't speak a word of Hebrew, and Yankl spoke no English, we hit it off quite well. With my father as interpreter, we somehow managed to communicate. Even if we hadn't, I saw by the gleam in Yankl's eye that it really didn't make much of a difference. Seeing us, and being with us, would have been more than enough for Yankl, as we were his only living relatives.

Once we arrived in the city, we parked a few blocks from Yankl's shop and walked the rest of the way. One of the many fascinating characteristics of this ancient city is the mix of the world's three great religions in that one tiny area. Anywhere one looks, on a street corner or a bus stop, one could see priests, imams, and rabbis standing side by side.

As we were nearing Yankl's neighborhood, I asked my father how Yankl was doing, if he was managing to make a living.

"Watch, I'll show you." He then stopped the first person he saw who was wearing glasses and asked, "Excuse me, could you please tell me where you purchased your glasses?"

"Why, yes, the optician Yankl Schreiber."

My father then stopped the next person and then the next, asking the same question. Each time, the answer was the same.

My father turned to me and said, "As you can see, Yankl is doing quite well."

From the distance, there was a man walking toward us with a light, quick step. He was in his mid-thirties and wore black slacks and a long-sleeved white shirt.

"Look, there he is."

Yankl caught our eye and waved as we converged on the entrance of his shop, where the sign read, "Yacov Schreiber, Optician."

We kissed on the cheek and laughed as Yankl struggled to find the right key to unlock the door.

"It's so good to see you," he said. "Come in, I'll prepare some tea. There is much to catch up on."

Two Roman Catholic priests walking slowly through the neighborhood stopped when the shop came into view. They waited there for several minutes, engaging in quiet conversation.

One of them looked up. "There he is now."

They both looked on as Yankl waved and smiled at the two people who were walking toward him. They watched as they greeted one another then entered the shop.

The priests continued to watch as the shop door closed. A church bell sounded in the distance.

As the priests turned to leave, one of them said, "All is well. There is no need for concern. We can go."

ABOUT THE AUTHOR

JEFFREY SCOTT BRAUN was born in Portland, Maine, in 1952. He received his B.A. in English Literature from Tel Aviv University and went on to study medicine at the University of Rome, Italy, where, in 1982, he was awarded his M.D. degree. After completing his medical training in New York City, Jeff and his wife, Cindy, settled in Boca Raton, Florida, to begin private practice and raise their family.

REFERENCES

1. *The Messianic Idea in Judaism,* Gershom Scholem, Allen & Unwin 1971
2. *The Last of the Just (novel),* Andre' Schwartz-Bart, Atheneum House, Inc. 1960, p. 5
3. *Encyclopedia of the Holocaust,* Macmillan Publishing Company 1990, Volume 3, p.1302